SWALLOW THE DOG

WHEN JUSTICE TURNS ITS BACK

A Novel

RAY WHITE

SWALLOW THE DOG

Chapter One

Spring Plowing, Missouri, 1877

TWO DOZEN NEW FURROWS stretched across the forty acres I stood looking down. Each one as crooked as a jackleg lawyer. My own ugly work, and the awfulest work I'd ever confess to own. Wandering rows touched and parted on their way up to the northeast corner, sometimes leaving enough green to lay down for a nap. They all pinched off in a sort of triangle at a little grassy corner at the top of the hill.

Where a girl in white linen waited under the oak trees.

At the crossroads of Randalls Flats and Big Hollow.

I would have given a silver dollar and a half-dime to lay up under those trees next to that white linen picking four-leaf clovers and spinning yarns into the afternoon. Instead of choking in a bowl of dust, lashed to two lathered mules and an unruly plow – sweat draining through my eyes, and burning up in a sweet-sorghum patch in Jackson County, Missoura.

"Mind 'm mules, boy," came a warning over my left ear, the deep tones rising with waves of dust and baked particles of last year's plant stocks. But the words could have come from the next county for all I cared.

"Boy?" the voice rose again, as if my ears were plugged with the fine brown swirl lifting off the mule tracks, and drifting over this endless field of torment.

This wasn't for me. Plowing. Mule skinning. Land work. Ma even said I had a mind for big things. Great things, was her words. I guess that meant greater things than turning sod in bowls of dust in Jackson County.

"Reckon you'll be a millionaire," she had said just one week prior, smiling at me, her only son. The son of a war hero who never lived to see my face. "My sweet boy. Only thirteen, and you already got a head for commerce. Be runnin' the whole county by summer's end," she joked, stroking my hair by hearth light and hand-stitching a new cotton shirt that would likely be threadbare and ground to dirt by summer's end. "But you got to be faithful in the small things." Her slow sweet voice instructed. "That's what matters, and where you got ta come up to flush with your Pa – God rest his soul." And then her words wandered into weightier matters of chivalry and bravery and other such notions, as they were want to do whenever the subject of Pa came up, the dashing hero I would meet on that other shore when the last trump was blown and all the righteous were gathered yon.

She was probably right about the small things. But I had little idea what she actually meant. I wanted big ones. Not exactly sure what, but not this field work for sure.

"Boy… straighten 'm lines, now," the voice behind me growled. "You hearin' me? Git yer body straight and yer shoulders back. Lean back a little now… Aw Jeremiah, them mules is all over the field. Now watch that—"

My gaze snapped back to the reins. The mules flinched at the angry words and turned out of the plow lane just as I knew they would. The plowshare popped out of the soil, forcing me to lean in and get the animals pulling again. Their hooves slid into deep troughs, and then stepped up out onto hard scrabble again. Rosebud and Black Jack would not go where I pointed them. Not this Saturday.

"Alright, you got 'em now. Keep 'm straight."

"Yessir," I managed, but soon lost the fight to the distractions of squawking crows, and prairie dogs, and chivalry and bravery, and adventures beyond Randalls Flats and Big Hollow, and the bright afternoon under a copse of oak trees next to that white linen dress, where tall grass bent in the wind, and honeysuckle fell into my mouth, and a pretty little face laughed and teased above me. What was a pair of sweaty plow mules to all that?

Just then, up yonder hill two horsemen raced up the lane and dissolved behind a brown haze.

Where were they off to in such a fuss? I knew practically every horse in Jackson County on account of Grandpa and me tramping every black acre of it. There weren't nearly two able horses in this whole county fat enough to sport riders. That is, that hadn't been skinned, dressed, and eaten. I'm sure of that. And I'm sure if a raw-boned hound had loped through this very morning, it too would have been skinned, dressed, and eaten.

But I never et dog.

Nope, never seen them riders. Going west, I reckon. Colorado Territory? California? Maybe the gold fields. Riches for the taking, I heard. They ain't workin' no forty acres.

"Aw, boy," the voice moaned. "I flat give up. Are you even listening?"

Grandpas don't know much about riches for the taking. And out west, and chivalry and bravery. Not no grandpas in Randalls Flats, anyways. And not much about white linen skirts up under oak trees at the end of a twenty-rod furrow. Cuz they spend their nights wearing out rocking stools and smoking white clay pipes and such. And polishing old three-band muskets and tending war wounds what don't heal. They never had no adventure, so they don't know such things. Practically don't know nothin', I guess. 'Cept plowing.

But my grandpa can drive a mule team like none else in Jackson County. That's why they hire him. He knows mule flesh. Like Rosebud and Black Jack. They're a matched pair, two-year-old's, raised by him and not nobody else. "Not no Union-bred Kentucky mules," Grandpa always bragged. Or Kansas, where they don't know mules from millstones. Rosebud and Black Jack was good Missoura stock. Best in the world. Never separated and never hitched out to no other teams. But Grandpa rarely has a lick of patience when I'm behind them. He drives me harder than the livestock.

But I got plans. Millionaire plans. Like Ma said.

I squinted for the two horsemen in the distant hollow. Sure tearing out of this territory in a hurry. Going west, I guess–

CRACK, came a leather belt across my new shirt.

Grandpa's leather belt curled around my chest and bit into my empty stomach like a gray rattler's fangs. An echo rang off the big oaks. The strike sucked the last breath from my lungs and loosened my uncommitted grip on the reins. I barely held footing on the black clods. The animals lurched, snapping leather from my grasp.

CRACK. The belt landed again. This time hard.

My eyes fastened on the work ahead. I got my footing, grabbed the reins with a will and snapped the mules into line.

It didn't hurt bad.

Grandpa's don't whoop like real Pa's. I guess they ain't got the virility. But still, it's enough to make a body straighten up and plow right. Just glad it wasn't a hiding I'd feel the next day, or the buckle. Grandpa's big brass CSA buckle could lay a bruise on for a week, so I rarely provoked him to the point of that. He ain't mean like some. But Grandpa says, "A man what spares the rod hates his own son." I guess that meant he loved me.

And I loved him too.

"Jeremiah," Grandpa hollered. "Where is your mind at, boy? First, you're gawking up at them oak trees, and then–"

"I'm workin' this here field, ain't I? You ain't got to whoop me like that."

Grandpa cocked back for another lash, but thought better of it. "I got to tell you, boy. This field's dang near ruined. We got to pull a drag over it and start over. Can't leave it like this. It's ruint, and we won't get paid. And I won't tolerate backtalk, neither."

"Ruuuint?" I cried, forgetting the warning. "We've been at this since the chickens was fed. We can't start over. I got to get up to–"

The two horsemen reappeared along the ridgeline at the oak trees, drawing my notice again. There was a little woodlot off to the west, and a clear patch betwixt that and the oak trees where wagons pulled in for loads of seasoned oak and maple – wood I split with wedge and maul for two bits a load. The men had trotted up onto that grassy knob and

4

looked down at us. Were they there for a load? One nudged the other and pointed. But I said nothing. I guess if I had the choice of gawking at a coupl'a old horsemen or that little white dress, there wasn't much to decide. But I wasn't about to linger at neither, not with Grandpa so hot. I didn't want another spell with that big black belt, especially if it included the use of a brass buckle. Best get to the task at hand.

"Well, we can't run a cultivator over this ground now." Grandpa groaned. He hadn't seen the men, and grew even more indignant over the field's poor condition, stomping around, spitting and swearing oaths. "Look at dem bare spots." He pointed to a dozen spots where the plow had run wide, mostly where the oak trees had come into view and I had lost concentration.

"It's only two dollars," I said, but a shirking guilt smote me all the same.

"Well, it's the only two dollars we'll live on this week. And it's the Cantrell name on the job. We can't leave a field in this condition. You know that. What'll folks say? Now watch me." Grandpa grabbed the reins and laid a strap over his shoulder. "Hup, up. Gee. Rosebud, Black Jack. Gee! I swear. Gee now, or by the Living God you will know my–"

The animals snapped into line like a steam engine on rails. They didn't kick and sit down, or bray loudly as they had all morning. They went right to work down that field. Or Grandpa would have turned the air blue with a string of vigorous oaths and threats.

That's how he talks to mules… and boys that don't mind.

A compliant No. 10 plowshare dived under the sod on a perfect line for the far end of the field – as if it too feared the big black belt. In less than a minute, Grandpa returned on his second pass. His work could not be improved by machine, if such a contraption were ever invented.

"Haw. Rosebud, Haw!" He circled and commenced a second row. "Haw now!" After returning from the far side, he stopped and said, "Let dem animals do the work, son. Not you. Yer bobbing and weaving like a cork in the river. Now git Blackjack into that furrow and don't let him out until you reach that far side. That trench will keep ya straight. Same thing on the way back."

"Gee… Haw!" Grandpa spit. "You know the language, now use it."

Grandpa had such a strong eye on the team that he hadn't noticed a third horseman at the top of the hill. Or that the white linen dress had disappeared over the other side into Big Hollow. Maybe Grandpa had scared her off with that big black belt and all his hollering. Had she witnessed the strapping? Would she wait for me? Or did she despise me now, now that I'd been beaten like a greasy dog?

"Grandpa, you make it look so easy. I can't do it like you."

"You just got to fix hard on it 'til it comes natural. Like fork and spoon. Hand to mouth, like sorghum syrup and hoecake."

I guess he was right, on account of he'd plowed his whole life. 'Cept when he went off to war against the vandal hordes of the Northern Tyrant, whoever they were.

Hey, that reminded me of something.

"Grandpa, what are those fourteen notches on your musket? Them ones under the lock plate?"

Grandpa dropped the reins. His knees dipped and he stumbled back. I thought he'd taken ill. That is, until he turned back with an angry stare and a black strap. "Them's not what you think!" His face drained and twisted. Maybe he was sick.

"Sorry, Grandpa. I unscrewed the lock plate to—"

"They ain't for you to be askin' about. Now stay clear of what don't concern you." He turned away to take up the reins again. But I saw his face. Wrong thing to ask.

It was the same look when he weeps over his big black Bible. I saw him a fortnight prior in his old rocking stool. I asked him why he sits there with that old Book. Mosttimes he don't even read it. He just said, "repentin' of my misdeeds" and went back to rocking and smoking out on the front porch with that old three-bander and Bible under the maple tree.

"Now, what was I saying?" Grandpa asked. "Oh, yes… Now, Jeremiah, you got to concentrate on your livestock. A mule's a skittish beast. He's got twice the wits of your average horse but… now, you take Rosebud here. You so much as strike a Lucifer next to her and she'll jump off a cliff. And Black Jack don't cotton to no whipping and yanking, and… and they know when you ain't paying attention to yer—"

Just then, he turned and noticed the horsemen.

A fourth man joined the other three from the west; they all began trotting down the unplowed section toward us. A cloud of dust and last year's plant stocks kicked up and covered the horses to their withers, but the sky was bright blue, clear enough to see them well. I still didn't know them. Not even the tall one leading the gang. He set spurs awful bad, and spared no rein. It made me wonder if he cared anything for the animal under him. Grandpa never mistreated an animal, so I noticed things like that.

Grandpa handed the reins over.

The four men were still fifty yards off as Grandpa peered into the distance, squaring his shoulders toward them. A sudden breath escaped his lips.

"Them notches ain't what you…" he said, trailing off.

The lead man jerked his pony at the last minute and the animal dug its hooves into the crusty ground, sliding to a stop just yards from us. The two-year-old's flinched and brayed at the sudden commotion – sharp painful brays like shafts of straw down your ear drums. They kicked and dragged the plow twenty feet before deciding there was little to fear from the approaching men. Grandpa was right about their spookish nature.

The riders surrounded Grandpa as layers of fine powder filtered down. The lead man lifted a hand.

"Looking for a man named Hiram Cantrell," he announced. He was rough-hewn, not like the others who were geared up in blue federal duds, a color all Missoura had learned to hate. Instead, he had brown leather and chaps for distance. And bloody rowels, just like I thought. The mounts were well-bred and well-fed, not like any in the area. Fifteen or sixteen hands. Powerful and fast.

"That'd be me," Grandpa said, extending a calloused hand. "Hiram Cantrell. What can I do fer you all boys?" The man's nervous horse wheeled, thwarting his attempts to complete the handshake. Ought to go lighter on them hooks, I thought.

"Folks said we'd find you up on this field." Then he nodded out over the crooked rows and quipped, "Got a playful pair of animals."

Grandpa shook his head.

"Got a few questions for ya, Mister Cantrell. If you got the time."

"Yessir, but not much." Grandpa looked up the field, and then into the burning yellow sun, still aiming for its peak.

"The Pulaski Six mean anything to you?" The man's horse settled down, but still snorted and stamped as the man threw out more questions than Grandpa had answers to. "Ever ride with Forrest? Nathan Bedford Forrest?"

Grandpa's brow wrinkled as he raked a calloused hand through dusty hair. "Nosir. I know the crew you're calling out, but I never rode with them Klan boys. Weren't they mostly down in Tennessee and Arkansas way?"

The man seemed not to hear. "Folks say you made a brave name for yourself. Night rides, I heard. Terrorizing darkies and riling up citizens against them."

Grandpa rolled his eyes. "I see you got a badge, there, Mister. What's yer name?"

"Daniel P. Upham, U.S. Marshal for the Western District Court. I'm rounding up the last of them freebooters for Judge Parker down in Fort Smith. Heard you might be one to talk to."

Grandpa snorted. "Keep talkin', Mr. Upham. I'll brang out a picnic spread and a minstrel show. Ain't you a little wide of your territory, up here in Missoura? And Jackson County at that?" Grandpa flicked his hand and turned his back on the Marshal. I guess he didn't think much of the night-riding claim.

"Bring 'em mules up, son," Grandpa said. "We got a field to clear." He stretched out his hand to take the reins and proceed with his lesson on proper plow handling. A lesson I had little interest in continuing. This was more exciting. But the morning hours had been wasted, and I knew Grandpa wanted to finish a hog slaughtering we had started earlier. And he had no patience with bluebellies, carpetbaggers, and scalawags. All the same class in his mind – the scourge of the whole South. The boll weevil had greater moral temperament. And you could negotiate with it.

"Don't even think of laying a hand on that hog leg," the marshal warned, edging in. "Yeah… I seen it strapped to that plow handle."

Grandpa didn't even listen; he just went for the plow.

A second rider clucked his horse forward. He aimed the whirling tip of his whip across Grandpa's outstretched arm. Just as the whip wrapped thrice, the man reined back, yanking Grandpa off his balance. Tufts of dirt exploded as Grandpa stumbled to the horse's feet. But Grandpa dug in a heel and yanked right back, pulling the man off his horse and into the dust beside him.

Grandpa spun around the man, wrapped the whip around his neck and cinched up like you would a calf's legs on branding day. Grandpa's knife was at the man's forehead, and hair in his grasp. The man thrashed wildly, which only earned him three more tugs on the cinched-up whip around his throat. He finally slapped dirt.

Never seen nothing like that. Not even from an Injun.

And never from no grandpa!

"You want to tussle with me, you little crop-eared Yankee?" Grandpa said, tugging the noose again. The man slapped dirt again, and Grandpa let off.

"Corporal, stow that flea-flicker!" the marshal shouted. "And get control of that mount." Grandpa released the man's neck but not his stare.

"Yessir." The corporal coiled the whip and stowed it in his saddle bag. He favored his reddening neck, mounted again, and set eyes on the pommel ahead.

"Now, Mr. Cantrell," the marshal said calmly, like he was the King of Texas. "I aim to get my man. And I heard tell you done a little riding against the dark communities down south. Now ain't that so? If you will oblige me, I'd like to know exactly where you done that riding."

Grandpa brushed off. "You Yankees got no better entertainment than to harass the citizenry? I already done told you."

"Not to my satisfaction. Seems you mule skinners are as stubborn as your animals."

"I've been right here in this county for the best of ten years,"

Grandpa said. "Everyone knows me. Just ask. Yes, I rode with some fellers after the war, in '67 and '68, but that was—"

He paused and sucked breath.

"Was what?"

Grandpa gritted. "Bidnez..."

"What type of business?" the marshal probed.

"Had dealings with the Freedman's Bureau, but that's done with, and I've settled up here in Jackson County. Got a little hundred-and-sixty acre spread, passed down from my great granddaddy. I never rode with no night gangs in Tennessee. Now, is that all?"

The four riders studied each other.

The marshal sniffed. "Freedman's Bureau in '68, huh? Must have been there during the militia wars. How about Wilson's Creek? August '61?"

"Yeah, I saw the elephant. Who didn't?" Grandpa threw back his hands.

"Ever been to Little Rock or Lawrence?"

"Yes, of course. Now is that all? I got a field to clear."

"Could be him," one of the riders said. The others nodded.

"You a private soldier back then. In the Rebel Confederacy?" Upham asked.

Grandpa growled, "I was a sergeant. Quantrill's Raiders. Bill sent me on jobs from time to time. Sharpshooting, mostly. Surprise attacks and such."

"A Raider, then? Happen to know a Colonel Raines down in Woodruff County, Arkansas?"

"He was my regimental commander for a time."

Looks shot across the circle of riders. Knowing looks. "That's him," the corporal said, releasing himself from the pommel. "Raider... Quantrill... Raines."

"That supposed to mean something?" Grandpa asked, squinting against a hard sun. He was getting hot, and not just from the thick air and menacing sun. "There were ten-thousand raiders in the western border counties. Picked off Yanks like turtles on a swamp log." Grandpa nodded at the corporal's chest. "Them shiny brass buttons made fine targets at five-hundred yards."

"Don't get smart with me, secesh," the marshal said. "I've had practically enough o' you Southern traitors."

Another rider circled. "Let's give him the cure for secession: a box of lead pills." He drummed his sidearm, staring down at Grandpa.

"I could be home in Little Rock if it weren't for this detail," said the marshal, edging in again. "Or running the family business in Massachusetts. Half the fire-eating bushwhackers down here are fighting to bring the slave trade back. Night rides and terrorism. I'd rather be a dead man than a Negro on one of them big plantations."

"Never owned no slaves," Grandpa said, nodding to me and the mules. "Just a daughter, grandson, and a few younguns on that little hundred-and-sixty. And you can call me anything but a gentleman or a coward." He bowed up to spit. "The slave trade ain't no concern o' mine."

"Then why'd ya fight, secesh? Could have joined the Missouri Home Guard or the 21st, and fought for the Union."

"Cuz you was down here." He glared at the marshal with a hand on his hip. "Northern aggression."

The corporal regained his courage and slammed the butt of his carbine into Grandpa's back. The blow fell like a sack of feed on a granary floor. "Awful brave with them words, secesh."

Grandpa went down again with the riders howling in delight.

"Get up Grandpa!" I yelled, tugging at the mules and fixing to pull that soldier right off his horse like Grandpa did. "Get up and lick 'im." Grandpa just snorted and waved me off.

The corporal stared down from the horse. "Swallow the dog, secesh," he demanded, growing braver as his words spilled out. "You take the oath of loyalty right now, rebel."

"Swallow the dog... Humph. I won't give you the entertainment," Grandpa said. "I took that oath twenty times since the war. Done with that." He staggered to his feet. "That oath don't make me no more loyal than before the war. And I don't need no pardon from the likes of you."

The corporal touched his forehead for blood.

"You do a little scalping during the war, bushwhacker?" The corporal threw down his Bowie knife. "Bad hombre, wuz ya? Got some federal scalps?"

Grandpa didn't answer. He just clenched his teeth and kicked the knife.

The men circled. "Come on, secesh… Get started on me," one of the federals taunted, nodding at the knife and tugging at his forelocks. "You know Judge Isaac Parker down in Fort Smith? He's the Hanging Judge. Want to go see him? Now swallow the dog, rebel. Or get started with that skinning knife."

The fourth man finally dismounted and retrieved the knife. "I think he's had enough," the man finally said, leaving his pony to help Grandpa. "We're not savages." The man dusted Grandpa's shoulders and apologized. He uncorked his canteen.

While he tended to Grandpa two more men appeared at the top of the hill on a cabriolet buggy. They talked and nodded down on the scene below.

Marshal Upham trotted around the other three and faced Grandpa again.

"The man I'm looking for shot United States General Smith in the head in Little Rock, and General Thomas at Bald Knob, Arkansas – also in the head, a full two years after the war was over. Right behind the ear, from five-hundred yards," the marshal said. "Know anything about that, secesh? You're a sharpshooter, right? That's two generals in two months. Both in the head by the same man. And both after the hostilities had already ended."

Grandpa wiped his lips and glared at the corporal. "At the risk of another round with your chained monkey, Marshal, I think you got your facts mixed up. The hostilities were not ended in '65. Not by a good deal."

"Suppose you enlighten me, Mister Cantrell. We all thought General Lee surrendered."

"Arkansas, right? Little Rock and Bald Knob? I hate to inform you, Marshal, but the hostilities still ain't ended in them parts. Not down there, they ain't." Grandpa sniffed. "Ain't nobody surrendered down there. Not how you got ex-rebels penned up like hogs for slaughter."

Upham threw up his hands and turned to the ridgeline. "Colonel!"

he shouted up the hill to the two men in the cabriolet – with some rough reckoning about thirty-rods off. "Colonel… May be him…"

One of the men on the hill waved, flicked his pony and started out toward us.

Grandpa pointed straight at Upham. "I don't know who you think you got, but I ain't your man. Now you can trot right back down to Little Rock, Sonny, before you regret your actions up here."

This time the rifle butt landed squarely on the back of Grandpa's head. His scalp split and a splash of blood furrowed the dust.

Grandpa went down.

"Grandpa!" I yelled, throwing down the leather reins. He lay in the center of the riders. "Get up, Grandpa. Get up." I shook his shoulders and yanked his shirt. "Get up."

No movement.

"You killed him!" I screamed, ready to buck that corporal off. The three mounted men just laughed so I lunged into the corporal's horse until it stumbled into a deep furrow. A second later I would have wrestled the horse's neck like a steer.

The corporal reined fiercely until he wheeled and faced me again. "He ain't dead, boy. Now attend to your livestock." I stood there panting, but set my jaw and returned to Grandpa who still wasn't moving. At least he was breathing.

The colonel and his man appeared at the edge of the circle atop their buggy. They grimaced at the crumpled body. My efforts to wake Grandpa had failed, and blood flowed freely from his open scalp. I pulled off my new shirt and wrapped his wound.

"I believe that's him," the marshal whispered. "He was in Lawrence, Kansas with Quantrill's Raiders. Got a scar under his right eye and a bullet wound in his left hand. See that?"

"Yessir, I do," the colonel said. "Well, if he was a Quantrill man, then he's plenty good at killing. Better get him in leg irons before he comes to his senses. He ain't going to be too awful jubilant about where he's headed."

"How 'bout the boy?"

"Get that mangy whelp some rations. From the looks of them

ribs, he ain't et in a week. I've seen more meat on a coyote dog. Is everyone in this county starving? A crow flying over this territory would have to carry its own rations. And for all we did for them. So much for Lincoln's reconstruction."

"But what if he—"

"Oh, that kid won't remember a dern thing. Just get that man into custody. I guess the jig's on now. You've got my authority to take him in. Let General Blunt know I gave the go-ahead, but you deal with him from here on out. I don't want to know a thing about it. I swear, Upham… you are one mad individual. Are you ever going to give up this antagonistic fight and let these people to themselves? They can do without your bayonet rule."

Upham shrugged.

The buggy driver came around from the back of his wagon with a large black box which he erected on three wobbly legs. It stood three feet off the ground. He pointed the contraption at Grandpa but said nothing. I stepped up to tackle the man. But after fussing under a black curtain for some time, he emerged and headed for the front of the box. He removed a black cover from a long brass barrel, peered into his pocket bob for ten seconds, and then returned the cap to its place.

Silence.

Had the weapon failed to discharge? I heard no percussion snap. No fizzled powder. Not a sound from the strange machine. But if he had shot Grandpa with it, I'm not sure what I would have done. Probably lashed him to the back of them mules and dragged him a mile.

The man seemed happy with the failed machine, and returned the entire rig to the cabriolet. He walked around front, took up the reins and sat quietly on the black leather seat.

The colonel boarded and signaled the quiet driver who whipped the horse into motion. "Lord, deliver me from this rebel territory and its demons."

Chapter Two

Hot streaks of sunlight tormented my sleepy eyes, draining sweat and tears down my cheeks.

Under the big maple tree next to the porch, a thousand blowflies buzzed around a hog Grandpa and me killed the day before. It hung from an iron chain, twisting slowly in the dead heat. A black pool of blood had collected under it and three layers of flies fed on its soft skin, laying a million maggot eggs under the surface. I'd probably get the belt for not finishing that job.

Ma and Uncle Olin sat arguing on the porch not twelve feet from the twisting hog. Ma pounded her fist, and Uncle Olin's fighting blood was up too. He was saying, "Northern Hessians and hirelings. I'll strangle every one of 'em. I'll gut 'em. I swear I will. Sister, why don't you just quit and move down to Randalls Flats with us?"

Uncle Olin kicked a stray cat off the porch. "Don't pay them a red cent. Not a bald blinking cent. How much do you owe anyways?"

That made Ma cover her eyes and sob.

A half-dozen folks stood around, trying to comfort her. One of them was the county sheriff, in his big black slouch hat and rat-eaten overalls. His evident love for drippy fatback attracted the vermin, which fed on his trousers by night. Cousin Buford paced back and forth on the porch dragging his left foot and swaying from side to side, arguing with himself. Out in the front dooryard a dozen kids raced around a rusty corn grinder and chaff cutter shrieking at the top of their lungs. A half-dozen barking dogs chased them. Boys were shooting crows off the lightning rods of the barn, and the whole commotion made my head ache. The screen door banged behind me and I stopped to clear my face. The air was so hot.

And it wasn't a dream. Grandpa was gone.

"Oh, son!" Ma breathed out a long sigh. The others parted to let her speak. "You're up!"

"Practically snored the danged shingles off," Uncle Olin said, grinning. He had lost another tooth which reduced his smile to a gob of black gums, decayed stumps, and oozing tobacco juice. I guess he'd never taken to the bitter taste of tooth powder. Not like Ma, who insisted I use it even when the can was empty. "Figured you'd just snooze the chores away?" Uncle Olin teased, wiping his lower lip of the overflow. "Your granddaddy gone and all?"

"Oh, shut up, Olin," Ma said, raising her hand. "The boy needed sleep. It was a bad day yesterday. You know that." Uncle Olin cowered and swallowed black juice. He turned an eye at Ma who reached out to me. "Come over here, son. Let me clean your face. You're all smeared up. Must have cried yourself to sleep yesterday."

"Bawled like a five-legged calf is how I heard it," Uncle Olin added with a laugh, which earned him another glare from Ma and the threat of her backhand.

Ma no longer let me sit on her lap on account of her tired heart but I still wanted to. But I guess real men don't coddle up in their mama's lap skirts. So the porch floor was fine with me. She spat on the corner of her dress and wiped my cheeks and ears. The old folks watched.

"Where's Grandpa?" I moaned.

Heads fell.

"We wuz hoping you'd tell us. Ain't nobody stopped by since you trudged in yesterday. Leastwise, nobody what knows nothing."

"So, where is he?"

"I wasn't able to get a handful of words out of you. Just, 'They took him. They took him.' was about all. And you never said where."

16

"Well, I didn't know where. That bluebelly soldier just threw down a sack of hardtack and kicked me in the shoulder from his horse. I just seen 'em ride over the hill toward Randalls Flats. That's all."

The sheriff looked at Ma and Uncle Olin from under his floppy hat. "That'd be south, I reckon." He removed his hat and twisted it into a knot, still trying to console Ma or maybe just trying to get closer. Sheriff Cletus sometimes pined for ma, but I never exactly knew why.

I added, "They had Grandpa in the back of a cabriolet buggy. He was shackled up and knocked out. Did I tell you that?"

"Some," Ma said, stroking my hair. "You said some but I didn't push you. You was bad off last night. Real bad off."

"Where's Rosebud and Black Jack?"

"Down in the barn. I curried them down and bedded them," Uncle Olin said. "They was all lathered up yesterday. Must'a worked a little."

I could see the wandering furrows in my mind. "Well, what are we going to do about Grandpa? Is somebody looking?"

Ma grimaced. "Not sure. But right now, you and Olin are going to dress that hog before she turns to mush."

"Ma!" I jumped to my feet before her. "No! I want to find Grandpa right now. This morning. They must a taken him some—"

Uncle Olin's eyebrow snapped up. "Morning? You done slept the morning away, boy," he muttered, shrinking back, shy of Ma's backhand. And he clearly didn't cotton to the task of hog-slaughtering in this awful heat. He shifted an earthen jug to his lips and frowned at Cousin Buford who still seemed unaware of the conversation.

Buford just shuffled back and forth, mumbling. "Could be south. Mm-yep. Sherriff Cletus says could be south."

"I'm sorry, Jeremiah. But we got to get that hog in. That's our winter provisions. I want you and Olin to cut it up right now. We'll figure out what to do about Grandpa."

Uncle Olin swallowed hard and cringed but said nothing.

"Salt it down and get it into that pork barrel," she said. "It'll only take an hour. Now, git." Ma stared at Uncle Olin until he wagged his head and threw up his hands.

"Awright, boy," Uncle Olin said, heading for the steps with Buford in tow. "We're in a bad row of stumps now. Them bluebottles is made a home in that sow belly. How you reckon we root 'em out?"

I wiped thick sweat from my eyes on our way to the old maple, and stared at the swarm of hungry insects crawling over hog flesh, louder than a beehive. Layers of carrion flies covered the swinging carcass and we could not brush them all off. They just kept coming – thousands of them.

I wheeled around and around. "We could burn 'em off?" I offered, after fighting to clear the swarm with a burlap sack. "Or scald the hide. That might do it. But they'd probably just come right back. Grandpa'd know what to do."

Uncle Olin didn't look anxious to tackle the job; he just wanted to jabber.

"We et a fair quantity pork during the war, you know," Uncle Olin tip-toed around the hog with a big grin and a sloppy chaw. "Every Sunday night, we'd forage up and down the road. A pistol would appear in a knothole and little piggy would fall down." Uncle Olin slapped a knee and staggered around the dooryard cackling.

"Okay," I said. "But what about this one."

"You know…" Uncle Olin stopped to think. "We could just leave 'em be. Salt 'em down with the rest o' the meat. Maggots ain't got no taste, ya know. Leastwise, no different than pork belly. We et plenty of maggots and worms in corn pones made up fer the Army boys." I just looked at him like he was still joking, but he went on. "Some a the boys cracked up the hard corn bread into their coffee and skimmed off the maggots and weevils when it boiled. But I just et 'em. They ain't got no taste atall. 'Specially after dark."

"Naw…" I said. "It's an idea… but Ma wouldn't have it."

Uncle Olin shrugged, allowing his eyes to wander the barnyard for another solution.

"Whitewash!" he announced, as if he'd had another stroke of genius. "When flies get thick in the barn, I just whitewarsh over 'em. A thick layer of that covers anything. And then we could scrape 'm off later. After a nip of the jug." He brandished a Bowie knife and grinned.

Sometimes, Uncle Olin's reasoning made my eyes cross.

"Okay, here's what we'll do," I said. "Get a big oilcloth from the shed. We'll lay her down on a bed of salt. And then scrape off the flies and roll it over quick. It won't take long to scrape it clean. Flies won't swarm on salted flesh."

"Jay, you are one bright lad. I don't know where you get it from. Off your Pa, the brightest lieutenant of the Rebel Confederacy? Reckon off him?" He set his jaw and headed for the shed to fetch the tarpaulin.

Cousin Buford followed hard after, tracking right through the hog's blood and entrails. He only wore one boot, and it was half off.

And he carried a rusty iron wheel everywhere he went.

For what earthly reason, no one had yet cyphered out.

"I know yer heart aches, Jeremiah," Ma said, coming down off the porch. The others stayed, still arguing over Grandpa. "But you finish up, and then we'll sort your granddaddy out." She primed the red iron pump with a few hard strokes and handed me a cup of cool water. "He can't be far. It's only been a day. Maybe the sheriff can track him. Or somebody's got to know."

"Ma," I said. "That federal marshal said something about hanging Grandpa. On account of night rides and terrorism." Ma spooked, lifting her hand to her cheek. The sheriff stopped jabbering and peered down from the porch.

"Hanging? That'd be Judge Parker," Uncle Olin said, ambling up with the oilcloth we had nailed to the barn wall a month prior to cure in the sun. The linseed and lampblack had hardened to a stiff glaze just like Grandpa liked it – practically bulletproof to .22's and birdshot. Uncle Olin came up with the tarp in one hand and a sack of salt in the other. "Parker's the Hanging Judge down in Fort Smith. That's where they all go to hang."

Ma raised her hand at Uncle Olin. "Will you hush up? He's your own daddy, for Heaven's sake."

"Well, I was just telling you." He shrunk back and laid the cloth down on the dirt next to the hog and dumped a pile of salt onto it.

Buford finally blinked and said forcefully, "Pa was just tellin' you!"

The sheriff leaned over the porch rail. "What's that about night

19

rides, boy?"

"I don't rightly know," I said. "The marshal kept saying night rides down south terrorizing darkies and such. And Grandpa said he'd had bidnez with the Freedman's Bureau, and that made the marshal real excited."

The sheriff turned to Ma "Well, that'd be Klan, sounds like to me. Hiram wasn't mixed up in that was he? They are a secretive organization, what's left of 'em."

"Oh, don't be foolish," Ma said. "Pa's lived up here with me, Jeremiah, and the twins for almost ten years. He ain't been down in Tennessee or Arkansas in a coon's age. That's where the Klan's at. Not up here in Jackson County. Not Missoura. You know that, Cletus."

Sheriff Cletus nodded but didn't look convinced.

About then a buggy bounced into the dooryard, and we all turned to look. Mrs. Branson stepped out with her three youngest. They ran off to the shrieking game, yelling like the rest. It sounded like about five-hundred screaming kids by now, and my head didn't get any better with the question of a million blowflies still left to cipher out.

Mrs. Branson had the same wavy auburn hair as Miss Patricia, her firstborn. But Mrs. Branson was old and haggish, maybe thirty or thirty-five. Old enough for a mess of wrinkles and brown teeth which she made plainly visible whenever she quarreled with any fiercity. I once heard she'd bared her teeth and clobbered a storekeeper when her flour order came late. Nobody messed with old Mrs. Branson.

"Oh, Mrs. Clark," she said, stroking Ma's face. "I am so sorry to hear about Hiram." Just how she had heard, I wasn't entirely sure. But news like that traveled on good stock. "What can we do fer you? Bring along some meals and milk the goat? Patricia will be over the hill shortly. She's tendin' the oven. She'll be along by and by."

Ooohh… Miss Patricia.

The burlap sack slipped my hands.

Ma said, "Thank you, but there's nothing you can hep with right now. Jeremiah and Olin are finishing up this hog. Then we'll all go up on the porch for lemonade. I've still got ice down in the springhouse, I believe, and a little lemon powder. We're all just figuring on Pa, is all."

Uncle Olin and I lifted the hog off the chain and laid it on the layer of salt. Hungry flies bit into my arms and face – big horseflies and fat spring flies that had gorged themselves on hog flesh all morning. The busy insects didn't know pig from human, and proceeded to feed on me just the same. Buzzing and climbing into my eyes, mouth, and ears. A feeding and egg-laying jubilee.

"How far's Fort Smith?" I asked, clearing my face for the millionth time. "Can we hitch up the mules and drive down there today?"

"Three-hundred-and-fifty miles?" Uncle Olin wagged. "Take ya a month with them plow mules. Sheriff Cletus' old nag might make it in two weeks."

With some effort, Cousin Buford had dug a half-digested rat out of the hog entrails. He smiled and held it up before Mrs. Branson. "Look what he et, y'all."

Mrs. Branson belted him.

Uncle Olin flashed hot. "Git out of them guts, Buford. Right now!" Buford chucked the rat into the lilac bushes but didn't move from the entrails. Uncle Olin cuffed him in the back of the head but that's wasn't enough to move him. He evidently liked the sound of the sticky mush on his boot heel. Even I had to admit, it was a sound you didn't hear every day.

Ma shook her head. "Olin, how do we even know Pa's in Fort Smith?"

"Didn't Jay point south?" Uncle Olin replied.

"Mm-yeah. Could be south," Buford said, stepping up and down in the hog guts.

"Yes, but that don't mean they're headed for Fort Smith. Where's your brains, Olin?"

"But Judge Parker's the Hangin' Judge. That's where they all go. Ta the Hangin–" Uncle Olin cowered. "Well, I'm just telling you."

Buford looked up from the bloody pool. "Pa was just telling you!"

Ma stomped over and belted Cousin Buford too. "One more time," she said. "Just one more time, you brainless half-wit." Buford scrambled around behind Uncle Olin, who bent down to scrape flies from the hog flesh while I rolled the carcass. His big Bowie knife did a clean job and his thick leather apron was soon layered in blood, flesh and fly parts. The salt worked just capital. As soon as Uncle Olin scraped a patch, I salted it down. Then we'd scrape a little deeper to dig out the maggot eggs. I guessed we got most of them.

"What's all this about hanging judges?" Mrs. Branson asked. "My first inkling was Fort Leavenworth, up in Kansas. Ain't that only seventy, eighty miles? Wouldn't they take Hiram there?"

"That's for military men. Soldiers," Uncle Olin said. "Judge Parker, ya see… He's the—" He looked at Ma and shut up.

"They were military men," I said. "There was a colonel and that corporal that practically killed Grandpa with the butt of his musket. And they talked about Lawrence and some other place in Arkansas."

Uncle Olin looked up with a flourish. "Prairie Grove? Poison Spring? Little Rock?"

"Yeah, that one. Little Rock. They said someone had murdered two generals in two months. Shot in the head, I guess. But Grandpa said Northerners should just clear out of Arkansas and Missoura altogether, and that sort of thing wouldn't happen. Just let us be, he said. But it was them night rides in Arkansas that set the marshal off."

"That's Klan, I tell you," the sheriff repeated. "Night riders is Klan."

Uncle Olin's knife froze. "You sayin'… you saying… my daddy's a Klansman?"

"Well, the boy said he'd had bidnez with the Freedman's Bureau didn't he?" the sheriff said. "And we all know Hiram weren't no Lincoln Lover. So, exactly what do you think he was doing down there with them Freedman? Kissing their Yankee unmentionables?"

Uncle Olin started for the porch railing raising his Bowie knife to eye-level. "I'll cut yer rotten teeth out, Cletus. You call my Pa Klan again."

I jumped in front of Uncle Olin. We still had the hog to cut up and I wanted to finish that before Patricia rode in. She might not like the blood and guts. Plus, Ma said she was bringing cherry pie.

"Stop it!" Mrs. Branson hissed. She picked an axe off the chopping block and waved it at the men. "I'll take a finger off if I have to. Or worse. Now, stop it. You too, Cletus." She waved the weapon at the sheriff. Mrs. Branson was a hard-strung woman and I think Uncle Olin and Sheriff Cletus knew she could do what she said. They both knew the story of when Mrs. Branson staked a circuit peddler down and flogged him for poor quality tinware he had sold her the winter prior. Everyone did.

After a minute Mrs. Branson set the axe down. "We were talking about military men," she said. "Shooting bluebelly generals in the head. Isn't that what the boy said? That's sounds military to me."

"Well, then it could be that prison they got up in Leavenworth," Uncle Olin said, throwing up his hands. "I reckon they hang–" He stopped again. "They could have taken him there. And yer right. It ain't no more than eighty-mile up there. Could be there in a week if we rode hard. But we ain't got no money fer trips like that. And no dependable horseflesh anyways."

He dropped the leather apron into the dust. Only a few flies buzzed around us now. The job was pert-near done.

"Sounds right to me," Mrs. Branson said. She looked at Ma. "Don't you fret yersef about no Judge Parker. They ain't goin' all the way to Fort Smith to hang an old coot like Hiram. And if it's a military matter then Leavenworth would be the place for that. Wouldn't it?"

"But that's Yankee territory," Uncle Olin said. "We ain't going–"

Mrs. Branson turned to me. "Now Jeremiah, did your granddaddy say anything more about those night rides? Anything?"

The sheriff leaned in.

"Just that he had bidnez with them Freedman's. He don't like 'em, you know. Northern Aggressors, root and branch. And that Freedman's Bureau is the Northern hive, to his mind. Grandpa don't–"

"Just a minute!" Uncle Olin stepped up. "I know what they're talkin' about. I was on one of them rides after the war. Down near Little Rock – Woodruff County, I recall. It weren't no Klan work atall. Pa and a few other fellers was–"

Just then, Patricia Branson ambled up on a plow horse toting a brown paper bindle under her arm. Everyone ignored Uncle Olin. He snorted and hung his head.

"Hi Ma! Hi, Mrs. Clark," Patricia said, waving. She looked at me, blushed and tried to dismount the tall horse with her free hand. She nearly dropped the sack. Mrs. Branson and Ma rushed over.

"It's so nice to see a fresh young face," Ma said. "Jeremiah, git over there and hep with that pie. How old are you now, Patricia?"

"I'm thirteen, ma'am. But I'm fixin' to turn, you know. Jeremiah, you know... well we're the same age and all, and he says when I'm fourteen we ought to jes run off and get–" Patricia stopped and checked my eyes.

Ma exhaled hard. "Jeremiah, you cut up that hog right now. I'll git that pie." She looked back at Patricia and then at me again.

"You finish up and meet us on the porch," Ma said. "We'll have lemonade." She took the pie and set it on the front step.

I could cut hog flesh pretty quick, especially when the Branson's were over and there was pie.

Uncle Olin and I finished slicing and packing pork: layers of salt and meat in a big pork barrel. A layer of salt, then pork, then another layer of salt, and so on. We laid a big rock on top and filled the barrel with brine heavy enough to float a dozen goose eggs.

We threw the excess fat into a slow kettle over a small fire next to the maple tree. By sundown it would render into snow-white lard ma could use for cooking and such. Of course, I'd have to scrape cracklings off from time to time and throw them onto cheesecloth to cool. Cracklings and cornpone make a bully breakfast.

Now maybe I could sit next to Miss Patricia if she didn't mind a little hog smell.

I picked the cherry pie off the front step and bounded onto the porch. I wanted some iced lemonade real bad. But just as I hit the top step I noticed Patricia and Ma negotiating. I lost my wits and dropped the pie right there on the floor. Juicy red cherries splattered over the bare wooden planks. Everyone gasped.

"Jeremiah, boy! Be a little mindful," Mrs. Branson said scolding, baring her brown teeth and threatening to beat me with the porch broom.

"Yes'm."

"Aw, scrape her up and we'll eat it anyway," Uncle Olin said. "I like cherry pie!"

"But what about Buford's guts and—"

"Scrape 'er up, son. I'll eat that cherry pie any way she comes, just as long as I got a drop of this lemonade and a fresh jug to wash 'er down. I'll pick out the splinters and hog guts. Now, what are we going to do about Pa? Reckon it's Fort Smith or Leavenworth?"

Chapter Three

July, 1877

UNCLE OLIN AND MRS. BRANSON and Sherriff Cletus and Ma never did cipher out where Grandpa might be. And nobody else even knew he was gone. But Uncle Olin and Sheriff Cletus couldn't get Fort Smith and Judge Isaac Parker out of their minds. Grandpa must be down there, they reasoned, on account of Judge Parker being the Hanging Judge. It only stood to reason. So, they lit out for Arkansas on one swayback nag and a plow mule.

That left me and Ma back on the farm.

Which was practically an invitation for the bankers.

"Mrs. Clark," some nicely dressed men hailed from the porch door. I saw them from across the dooryard at the barn. "You home, Mrs. Clark?" The lead man banged on the screen door, which had no latch and rattled from the slightest touch. Mother didn't answer. I knew she was in there and wondered why she didn't come out.

I had mostly finished morning chores and stood in the open barn door in sloppy boots with a big wooden hay rake in hand. A mound of loose hay spilled out through the large door, giving the pullets something to peck through.

I grimaced back at the dilapidated structure. So embarrassing.

The whole barn seemed to be falling down at once. Half the shingles had blown off in a bad storm, and water ran down the inside walls. That made the stalls muddy and wet and the haymow reek of musty stank like a big mud hole in the middle of the hundred-and-sixty acres. I liked the oak trees up at the crossroads better. Especially when Miss Patricia was there. But Ma had two milk cows, six hogs, and a few goats that made this tumbling old pile of kindling their home. It was my job to milk and bed them every day. Plus weed the garden. Plus fetch water. And chop wood. And shovel chicken poop. Slaughter hogs. And plow, seed, and harvest the hundred acres out back. With Grandpa gone it was impossible. Ma couldn't hardly work and Uncle Olin didn't come around unless there was a frosted sweet cake or a bushel of barleycorn for his still. Or rye. My little sisters played in the creek all day which made the whole hundred and sixty acres mine to manage. Of course, that didn't leave much time for schooling and such.

But who needs schooling when yer going to be a millionaire?

The three men banged harder. They hollered for Ma. Still no answer.

"You looking for my mama?" I shouted from the barn. The men turned.

"Yessir," the lead man said, waving his bowler and lifting a lacquered cane from the porch planking. "Mrs. Mansfield Clark. She at home, lad?"

"I'll fetch her." I started across the dooryard as the men tipped their hats and smiled.

Bankers and politicians are such fine gentlemen. I never did know exactly how they made money, on account of them loaning it out all the time, and not even owning a plow to replenish the loaned-out funds. But I guess I was about to find out. Here they were on our own front porch.

I found Ma in her bedroom on her knees clutching a few old papers. She was sobbing and praying. I stopped short, not sure what to say.

"Ma?"

"I'm okay, son," she said. "I'm okay. I know what they want."

I felt like crying too.

"Just hep me up, Jeremiah. I'll go out and talk to them. Maybe we can—"

"Uncle Olin can talk to them when he gets back. Or I'll do it."

"He won't be back til August. Fort Smith is a fair piece and he only left a month ago. Black Jack ain't no riding pony, you know."

"Mrs. Clark?" the man hollered. "We need a few moments of your time out here. This is very important. Mrs. Clark? Hello?"

One man had even gotten brave enough to venture into the front room where I could see him picking up things and snooping around. Uninvited, of course. He had removed his gentleman's hat and peered around for Ma. Then he started opening drawers and looking at things. The other two chattered out on the front porch like kin.

Mother and I came out of her room.

"Oh! Mrs. Clark!" the man said surprised, as we entered the parlor and found him handling Mother's glass figurines, finery handed down from Grandma when she passed on a year prior. He bowed quickly and retreated back onto the porch with the others. Ma and me followed.

"What can I do for you gentlemen?" Ma asked, clearing her eyes. Her face stiffened to hear whatever news the men had ridden out to deliver. Was it about Grandpa? Had they found him? Was he in Randalls Flats? Maybe he had whipped those army rascals single-handedly and dragged their carcasses back to town. These men must be here to deliver the good news.

I leaned in eagerly, but Ma did not.

"Mrs. Clark," the lead man said. "My partner and I are commissioners for Jackson County, you know." He beckoned to his partner at the rear who bowed and raised a black gutta-percha cane to his brow. An odd clump of crooked hair lay atop his head. He smiled, somewhat akin to a he-goat – empty black eyes and unnatural chin whiskers under a stiff smile. I never knew a smile could be so cold.

"We manage the property taxes in this region. Felt it was a good time to discuss your standing in our county. You are such a key asset to our community, Mrs. Clark. In fact, your family has been for the last hundred years. Great granddaddy settled here, right? Word is, he chased off the Osage Indians with three flintlock pistols and a long arm. And that was before the modern muskets and repeating rifles we have today."

The men all smiled and raised an eyebrow. Canes rose and fell. The he-goat stroked his chin hairs and cocked his head to consider how important our great granddaddy was.

"Hmm, what a great man…"

Ma said nothing. It made me smile with them, but not Ma.

"Yes, the Osage. Heathens all. And what a great man Anson Cantrell was…"

The others piled on.

When their praises ended the men just stood there for a few seconds more. They all just shook their heads, smiling and glancing around – embarrassed and awkward, with no more fine words to add. I guess the praises didn't work because Ma just flicked her fingers as if to hear the real reason they came out.

"Why don't you just say it?" Ma said. She held up the wrinkled papers and frowned.

"Well now, Mrs. Clark. We, ah… We have a proposal for you," the commissioner said. "And I think you're going to like this. We've got it all worked out, right here in these fine documents." The man held up a leather binder.

Ma took a seat in her porch rocker and stared at the russet folder. I don't think she liked what was in there. But how could she tell?

"First, I'd like you to meet Mr. Wilhelm Schurz," he said, beckoning to the man at the rear. "He's the elder brother to the great Carl Schurz himself. Come down here to see our great work in the Southern states."

The man paused for effect, but Ma's dull eyes gave no sign.

"You must know…" he continued. "Certainly, you know the Secretary of the Interior… Carl Schurz." All the men smiled and wagged their heads.

Mother didn't seem to understand.

Schurz, the plump sweaty man with two large tapestry bags stood at the edge of the porch. His vest buttons were about to pop; I could see little white threads straying out from his fancy machine-stitched buttonholes. He too, like the others, juggled a dandy black cane and derby hat along with a gaudy pair of carpet bags. With such fine handbaggagery, he'd evidently traveled a fair number of days to be here, and gained some expertise in managing the clumsy gear. Hat, cane, sweat rag, bag-one and bag-two all changed hands like a juggler's act. Much more agile than the he-goat who stood like a wooden Indian stroking his chin whiskers and saying, "Hmmm, yes," and looking into the horizon for some important thing that might arise from there.

I wanted to poke a stick in his eyes to see if they were real.

The fat man was definitely real because sweat ran off him like a stuck hog.

"Mr. Schurz is an investor and politician from up north, Mrs. Clark," the lead man continued, nodding to the fat man. "He's come all the way to Jackson County to lend his expertise in Lincoln's Reconstruction. Mr. Schurz thinks—"

"I know what he thinks," Ma said. "And he'll do it over my dead body."

"Oh, Mrs. Clark," the man said, perfectly stunned. "I fear you take the wrong meaning. We simply—"

The fat man, Schurz wiped sweat and pushed forward to speak. His large tapestry bags never left his side, and making room for them created a wedge between the other two men. "Ma'am, do you have the financial wherewithal to cover your tax responsibilities?" he spoke with a thick Dutchy accent like the bluecoat soldiers from Saint Louis we all hated. "Taxes have risen substantially, you know. The South has quite a debt to pay. For the recent rebellion that is. There are rail lines and government buildings and telegraph wires and… Up North, we call it… 'Infrastructure.' Taxes pay for those things, Mrs. Clark. Now ah… I have studied your financial position with the bank executives, and… well, it is the blackest of conditions, I am certain. And so I have come all the way out here to offer a fine solution. My proposal will benefit both you and your neighbors alike. These are hard times, Mrs. Clark. I'm sure you understand."

"I am not interested, Mr. Schurz. Thank you for coming out, but we'll manage."

The commissioner stepped around bag number one. He stood slightly behind Ma, which formed a circle with the other men like a pack of coy dogs on a tasty morsel. "That's just it, Mrs. Clark. We've heard about Hiram."

Ma jerked around to face him. I think she expected news.

"He's no longer here to work the land," the he-goat put in. "We know that. We also know your brother and the sheriff are off looking for him, but we fear the worst for you and your progeny. We must look after the widows and orphans, and we just don't know exactly how you'll make it without Hiram. And with all those back taxes—"

"Hence the reason for our visit," the fat man – Schurz – resumed with a Dutchy flourish. "Let me show you my wonderful plan. Oh, you're going to love this!" He dived into his carpet bags while the other two men piled on more words. A lot more words.

Ma just covered her ears and hung her head.

"Take a look at this," the fat man urged, producing a thick stack of paper.

"You're going to need to sign something today," the he-goat added. He tapped the stack as if they were necessary for our very survival.

"Let's get this thing taken care of today. You know Hiram isn't coming back."

The men seemed to come in from every angle, hovering, swooping, and diving for a chance at Ma's buried face. She wasn't listening any longer but that didn't stop them. They wanted her attention real bad.

"Can't hold this property forever. Got investors looking over it every week," the fat man said. He frantically produced more pages which he tried to wiggle under Ma's chin. "Buyers lined up to Charleston. Practically fighting 'em off with a cane. Prime Southern real estate here. Another year like this and you'll be—"

"I'm afraid he's right. Your tax situation is quite untenable," the lead man broke in.

The he-goat raised his scrawny chin. "And, Mrs. Clark... There are some... ah base fellows of course... who ah... report you are a woman of wonton morals—"

Just then, a double-barreled shotgun exploded in the front dooryard not ten feet from the porch rail. Both barrels, practically at once. A deafening boom.

It was Mrs. Branson coming at them.

She emerged from of a white cloud with a nasty scowl.

Two more paper cartridges hung from Mrs. Branson's brown teeth. She tore them both and began ramming them into the weapon as she strode through the weeds, with cicadas and katydids skittering to both sides. Miss Patricia sat in the buggy covering her ears.

"You ornery rascals clear off," she said, drawing the ramrod from barrel number two. White smoke wafted out the barrels as she leveled it again. Mrs. Branson bared her teeth. "I ain't here for cakes and coffee."

BOOM. Barrel number one went off again.

The three men had tarried just long enough for Mrs. Branson to put a fresh load of buckshot from barrel number two into the porch steps. The massive eight-gauge blasted the two lower steps clean off. Splinters flew into the men's faces as a hot wind blasted my hair back. I felt the hot sting of pellets in my own ankle and dropped to the floor in pain.

The two skinny men skedaddled over the porch railing into the lilac bushes while the fat man grabbed up his tapestry bags and leaped over the front steps like a scalded dog. Papers, pen, and ink flew into air, abandoned by the fleeing men. Their buggy horse reared up and sprinted down the driveway past the barn without them.

Mrs. Branson tucked the weapon under her arm and stepped up to examine her work. Before long, the men had hailed their buggy and whipped the horse into full gallop. A cloud of dust trailed behind them.

"Don't worry, Mary. I'll get Slim to throw a few planks across them broken steps. Sorry I nicked you, boy. Sit down here, and I'll dig that iron out."

Chapter Four

I GUESS MRS. BRANSON got the best of them cotton pickin' scalawags. But they'd probably be back. Ma couldn't hold them off forever. And Uncle Olin still wasn't back from Fort Smith.

By the time I had finished my field work and chores, and limped up to the crossroads of Randalls Flats and Big Hollow the sun was big and red over the horizon. Nobody knew where Grandpa had been taken to and I had to stay home and work the farm while they looked. But at least I got to spend summer nights with Miss Patricia.

I could see a little fire under the oak trees already glowing. Patricia had evidently caught a prairie hen, plucked and cleaned it in Cottonwood Creek and had it turning on a spit. After twelve hours in the field with Rosebud and a four-foot drag harrow I could eat four prairie chickens and a half-peck of potatoes. But wild hens didn't last long in this territory, and I'd appreciate even one. I'd have to hold my appetite and share it with Patricia. She'd probably only want a scrawny wing and leave the rest for me anyway. Hopefully, she had a big pan of cornbread and some newly churned butter. If so, I'd eat the whole dern thing.

I liked sneaking up to the oak trees with her.

Mrs. Branson didn't let Patricia out after dark so that didn't leave much time to eat and talk a little before Patricia had to skedaddle home before sunset. Otherwise, she'd get it. So we watched that big red sun real close. But one thing was for sure, Mrs. Branson's sun always set a little sooner than ours. She'd started that about the time Patricia turned thirteen, and I wasn't exactly sure why.

"I'm sorry Mama shot you," Patricia said as I stepped into her little homestead in the woods. She stirred something in a battered old pot and turned the chicken on a spit.

"Aw, it ain't nothin'," I said. "No worse than… say… getting hooked by a plowshare or a hay rake in the backside. One time when I was—"

"Jeremiah, do you think your ma knows about us?"

"Us? Naw, old folks don't know stuff like that." But that little word "us" sure got my nerves up. What exactly did she mean? I wasn't sure when I started hearing that word; this wasn't the first time. But I guess it wasn't so bad. Miss Patricia and me had been best pals since we were babies in the cradle. Ma said we practically sucked each other's thumbs. Most folks just figured we'd be hitched in Holy Matrimony by age thirteen. So I guess that little word didn't rub me so bad.

I watched Patricia move from pot to chicken and back again. I wanted to touch her soft white hands and stroke her long auburn hair. My eyes followed her hips and shoulders and legs, and my feelings got turned all crossways. But then, my stomach was all knotted up too, and I couldn't tell which was which.

Problem was, Mrs. Branson didn't let Patricia even hold hands. That also started about age thirteen. Before then, we had played down in Cottonwood Creek every day, practically naked. I probably touched her every place there was to touch and didn't think a dern thing of it. And then all of a sudden, Mrs. Branson put a stop to that. No more swimming together. And no more playing in the woods after dark. She sure had some kooky ideas about her daughter. But I didn't want to chance another accidental shotgun incident so I abided them. And never knew what old Mrs. Branson might be planning. I'd heard about a fella in the next county who had consented to the very act of matrimony, all on account of a shotgun. I never liked shotguns that much.

"I just wondered," Patricia said. "Your ma looks at me funny now."

"It's hard to say with old folks. I just wish Uncle Olin and Sheriff Cletus would get back. It's been two months and I miss Grandpa awful bad."

Patricia asked, "Why didn't he just telegraph Fort Smith?"

"That's what Ma said. But Uncle Olin said, 'I don't spend my days waitin' on the advice of women and children. Me and Cletus will jes ride on down thar. Plus, I kin bust him out if it comes ta that.'"

Patricia just shook her head.

"Do you reckon they got held up by highwaymen?" I asked.

"No. I don't suppose many could get the drop on a war veteran and a sheriff both. Even a pair like that."

"Your Ma did. With that axe. Remember?"

"Don't be afraid of her, Jeremiah. She just wants me to be good."

"Yeah... She looks at me a little funny, too. I guess the elderly have their ways."

"Yeah. Do you think we'll ever be thirty?"

"Maybe. Or we'll get kilt in a war like our pa's."

"Yeah."

"Where the heck is Uncle Olin and Sheriff Cletus? Isn't two months long enough to get down to Fort Smith and back? I want some news. I want to know where Grandpa is and have him back. Nobody knows nothing, and they're all waiting on Uncle Olin. Do you think Grandpa busted out o' them leg shackles and run off? Or, do you think they really–"

"He probably busted out," Patricia said. She finished cooking and served up the chicken and rice on some old tin plates. She had found the abandoned tinware in the woods next to some old muskets and saber bayonets. The letters "US" were stamped on the bottom. We had to share a rusty fork of the same vintage – old junk Patricia had scrounged up from a big pile of such relics.

I liked to lay back in the tall grass and eat Patricia's vittles. It was worth picking off a few ticks and chiggers later. Sometimes she stroked my hair and fussed with my fingernails and such. Just as long as her ma wasn't watching. But I drew the line at toenails now because she once put little dabs of red paint on mine while I was sleeping, and I had to scrub them off with kerosene while she laughed and teased. But still, I liked watching that bright red sun over the hill when she fussed over me.

I laid back and watched her shapes and jiggles. That got me stirred up every time.

"Is your ma okay?" Patricia asked, working on her little chicken wing.

"What do you mean?"

"Well, those carpetbaggers and scalawags that bullied her. You know…"

"Aw, she's tough, I guess. But she complains about her tired heart. That last affair had her laid up for a week but I guess she's well enough now. But I jes know them bank men are coming back."

Patricia nodded. "Mother says scalawags are stealing Southern farms. They bring in Northern moneymen and buy 'em up cheap. From the widows that lost their men and boys in the war. Ma says you have to be tough or they'll take your wooden teeth. That's why she carries that big eight-gauge in the buggy. I seen her pull it out before."

"That thing is a cannon!" I said. "A twelve-pound Napoleon!" We both laughed.

"Isn't it funny?" I said. "We were both war babies, born only six days apart. I guess that's why we know cannons when we see them. Made when our pa's came home on furlough. Good Southern men, Sons of Missoura and loyal to the cause, Ma told me."

Patricia sat up and leaned forward for some wild strawberries she had picked and I admired her little arms and shoulders. Just like before I wanted to touch them and lay down in the grass and kiss. I wondered what it would be like to make a war baby. I still wasn't exactly sure how. And would I die afterwards like our pa's? It made me wonder about the whole affair: babies and all… but I knew one thing. I'd kill a whole passel of Yankees before they got me.

Grandpa's old three-band musket came swiftly to mind, and Yankees dropping like rats in a chicken coop. Me, clad in a new gray shell jacket with grandpa's three-bander, picking them off one by one, smiting them hip and thigh, and routing the aggressors from our homeland. I forgot Patricia next to me. It was just me and the Northern Hordes locked in bloody combat. State's Rights! The Constitution! I shouted in my mind.

Until Patricia shook me by the arm.

"Hey… Do you think she'll lose the farm? With your grandpa gone and all?"

That was a spookish idea.

I stood up, indignant. "I'll kill every last one of them before it comes to that. And Mother says it will be over her dead body. I don't know exactly what that means, but I'm pretty sure she'll take up arms. I'll start another war if I have to."

"Can your Uncle Olin help? Can he talk to them?"

"He's practically no good to nobody. He's got his little shack and corn liquor still down in Randalls Flats with the other poor whites and negros. Half negro himself, I guess, living down there like he does. He don't work more than he has to, and don't much care what happens to Mother and the farm. Grandpa yells at him. Says, 'You tramped from Topeka to Tallahassee and back: three thousand miles, and half of it barefoot, and you can't clear a forty-acre patch today? Get off that porch and get a plow strap in your hands, boy! You done wasted yer possessions with prodigal living.' But Uncle Olin says he been down on his luck and just needs a little Soothing Syrup from time to time."

"Soothing Syrup?"

"Laudanum."

Patricia nodded. "I guess when you marry your own half-sister, that's the type you are. It ain't that uncommon but I still think it's creepy-crawly. I would never marry my stinky old brother. Not even for a hundred dollars! He never washes. Ever."

She turned to me and smiled. "I like it when you wash down at the creek, 'specially after a week of plowing. It makes you smell so fine. I like to lay next to you and smell that creek water and rub rose oil in your hair."

"And paint my danged toenails while I sleep!"

She smiled and twirled a little wildflower between her fingers. I wanted to hold her real bad. My urgings were getting hard to ignore. But

I'd probably wind up with another buckshot wound.

"Those bankers made Ma cry," I said. "That made me really mad. Did you see 'em hounding her with those papers? You were in the buggy, right? I wanted to crack a log over that fat man's head. That Dutchy from up North. They just kept at her like a pack of red devils. I guess they wanted her to sign something, but I don't know what."

"The mortgage, Jeremiah."

I shook my head. "What's that?"

"I'm not sure, but like a paper that says you own something."

"Really? They want our old place? What the heck for?"

"They want all the places down South. They're cheap. Northern bankers have thousands of dollars and they could buy the whole South if they wanted to."

"What would they do with our junky old place?"

"Cotton," she said. "Ma says they have all the textile mills up North, and now that we lost the war they want all the plantations too. It's called Reconstruction. President Lincoln thought it up. And they started it when we were babies. Cotton is King, Ma says. So we're pretty important. We got Cotton and they don't. But them Northern bankers want it all. Like the cankerworm they are always hungry. That is how Yankee's think, Ma says. She says Yankeeism is a lunatic disease they got when they were born. You know... like rickets. It makes them want everything other folks have."

"I'll tell you one thing," I said. "If that Dutchy with the tapestry bags ever comes sniffing around again, I'll crack a board over his skull and throw him down the well. When I grow up, I'll never be like that."

"What are you going to be like?"

"A millionaire. Like Ma says. But a good one. Everybody will like me then."

Color began forming over the horizon.

"I just want to go out west," I said. "Out into the territories. Out of this place."

Patricia stood up. "You need to fight for what's yourn, Jeremiah Clark. Can't run away from bankers forever. Fight them on your own ground. At their own game. That's what I think."

"I'm not running. I just want to go where there's no bankers and no county commissioners and no soldiers that capture your own granddaddy when you're out plowing another man's field. Out west. You know... There's gold out there. I could get rich and buy you a big house and parasols and nice shoes. I hate cotton and hemp and sorghum, and I hate this old place. I don't want to be poor no more. Not like Mama and Uncle Olin and Grandpa."

Patricia nodded.

With only an inch of sun left, Patricia obediently bundled up the tinware, pot, and fork. She stashed them under a pile of brush, hiked up her skirt, waved goodbye, and started on the three-mile run for home. Her little feet never missed a rock and never wearied.

I stood there watching her disappear into Big Hollow like a little fawn bouncing over hills and swales until she slipped out of sight.

And then I breathed.

Chapter Five

"HEY, CORNPONE!" UNCLE OLIN hollered from the saddle, still a stones-throw down the south road. Black Jack had just about figured out he was home and brayed loudly then started for Cottonwood Creek – a diversion that would have taken Uncle Olin a quarter mile out of his way. Uncle Olin wasn't about to permit that. He gathered up a cheekful of tobacco juice and spat into Black Jack's left eye. The animal shook its big black head and romped up and down before settling down. Dust filtered down around him.

"Thar now! Ya ornery varmint. Git back on the road!" Uncle Olin yanked the reins toward the narrow lane, letting out another stream of language powerful enough to alter the animal's intentions. Mule and rider herky-jerked up into the front dooryard just as the sun peeked over the eastern fencerow. Together they were one foamy mass of lathered sweat under a quarter inch of trail dust.

Uncle Olin's green eyes blinked out from under the brown layer.

"I said, 'Howdy there, Squirt.' Ain't you even got a good word fer your favoritest uncle? And after I rode all the livelong way to Fort Smith and back on this ornery beast?" He smiled and blinked back the smothering dust like a pair of puppy dog eyes under a brown woolen blanket.

"Oh, hi, Uncle Olin!" I said, forcing a smile. "I thought you was an old hermit come to beg bread off us." But I knew better. I just wasn't happy to see him come up without Grandpa. I knew it meant bad news right off. News I knew was coming anyways from the very first day. Them soldiers wanted to get Grandpa hung real bad, especially Marshal D.P. Upham. He was in a hurry to hang somebody. I could tell. And I reckon Grandpa fit his liking just fine. Now Uncle Olin was back, and Grandpa wasn't with him. That meant only one thing. I might as well crawl into the root cellar and bawl.

And that wasn't the end of it.

Ma was in trouble with the bankers again just like I knew she would. Her heart ailed her practically every day now, so much that she napped about four hours every afternoon. Uncle Olin's wife – his half-sister – had run off with a boot peddler and left Buford with us on her way out. Cousin Buford had broken or stolen all my stuff since she left. And now, Grandpa was as good as hung.

I just kicked the dirt.

"Hey, now. What's the matter?" Uncle Olin said, dismounting the fitful mule.

"Aw…"

"I brought you a lemon drop from Fort Smith. Looky here!" He fished around in his dusty pocket and produced a slightly yellowish lump of hard candy. A big one. After blowing and dusting it off he passed it over with a grin.

I licked it a few times. It tasted of mule sweat but sweet enough to tolerate.

"Where's Grandpa?" I asked, hiding my tears and sagging mouth.

"Well, alright now…" Uncle Olin said, frowning and twisting his head one way and then another. "I don't rightly know just yet. But now don't you commence to cryin' over that. I ain't got no news so that means we don't know just yet." He laid his hand over my shoulder and squeezed a little. Not so much that I'd run off, just enough to let me know he cared.

"I guess your old Uncle Olin ain't licked yet," he said, whipping up another big smile and a flat-foot dance jig to go with it. Lightheartedness came easy to Uncle Olin. Half his teeth had dropped out, and the other half were hanging on for next month, but that never stopped him from smiling and laughing with folks. He loved to play. And I guess that made me feel a little better. That, and the slightly tainted lemon drop rolling over my tongue.

"So, do you know where he might be?"

"I know he's not in Fort Smith. And that's a relief. You know old Judge Parker… He's the–" He stopped and looked around for Ma. "I'm just glad he weren't there. Now we can try some other place. I reckon that axe-wielding Mrs. Branson had an idea or two when she mentioned Leavenworth. Maybe we'll have her over to the house and find out if she knows anything more than how to lop fingers with a broadax." He wedged his shoulder up under my chin and feigned a few boxing jabs, dancing around and spitting like an Irish highlander. "And maybe bring that pretty little offspring of hers? Huh? Yeah?"

His eyes raised with a taunting smile. "Yeah, I know you and her got a little whoopie going on."

"I ain't so much as kissed her! Mrs. Branson don't allow it. You know that." I said, taking a swing at him. But he stepped aside and let me stumble forward.

He started bobbing and laughing, jabbing at my chin.

"Jay and Pea, sittin' in a tree…" he sang with a little taunt. "K-I-S-S-I-N-G." When the taunt ended he stumbled around laughing and falling down.

By now I could not stop the emotion. I felt like bawling, but I also like laughing too – all mixed up in one big ball of beeswax. I tried to jump on Uncle Olin but he was faster than a water spider on Cottonwood Creek. He sprawled over the dusty road avoiding my lunges. And then came in for a gut punch and an ear slap.

We could have been brothers.

"Hey," he said, stopping to think hard. "I made up a good one while I was on trail from Fort Smith. It goes like this…" He looked up. "Wanna hear it?"

"I guess," I said, brightening up a little.

"Okay. Okay. Here she goes… Tra, la, la, boom dee, aye…" he sang out, blinking his eyes under the layer of dust. "I'll take yer pants away… And whilst yer standing there… I'll take yer underwear!"

Uncle Olin busted out laughing and rolled into the dooryard like a monkey. He laughed and choked up tobacco juice. A big wad came flying out as he doubled up in a coughing spell. Half the brown juice came out his nose.

"Oh, yeah?" I said. "Well, here's one for you. Yahooo, mountain dew. Somebody pooped in Olin's shoe!"

Uncle Olin tried to act hurt and offended but could not hold back his big black smile and smothering arms.

Then he mussed my hair and looked into my eyes, "Jay, he weren't there for sure. I searched the whole dern town. Asked at all the saloons and cribs. Stopped citizens on the street. Talked to the county sheriff and the colonel in charge. They never brung him in. No Cantrell's waz never hung in Fort Smith, leastwise not for over a year. So we know that much for sure. I say we get Ol' Lady Branson down here and do some ciphering. But I don't want you dragging around like a redbone hound. You understand? We will find him. You have my word."

He searched my eyes thoughtfully. Truth flowed out from him. "We will find him."

"Olin, you're back!" Ma said, coming down off the porch. She had just gotten up and still wore her night clothes and lacey cap. She rubbed her eyes and reached out to hug him. But then… "Agghh!" she shrieked. "You're a lathered-up mule, your own self. Get over to that horse trough and clean up. Stinky old skillet licker!"

Uncle Olin headed for the water and dunked his head. A natural spring kept the hand-hewn sandstone full all the time. We used it for Saturday night baths and drinking and such. Ma wanted it piped up into the house but Grandpa said running water was for idlers and city folk without the common gumption to step outside to pump it. He said he'd once lived off a single canteen for a week down in Pea Ridge during the war when all the cricks was polluted with human waste from twenty-thousand soldiers on the march. And why would anyone need more than a canteen's worth in a week's time anyways?

But I liked Ma's idea: pipe the water inside.

"Where's Cletus, Olin?" Ma asked. "I heard all about Pa and Fort

Smith in between your little rhymes and monkey acts but what happened to Sheriff Cletus? He's got another three miles before he's home. Is he back a-ways behind you?"

Uncle Olin whipped his head around to clear the water. Large drops flew off his long hair and drained down his thin muslin shirt making little furrows in the sheet of dust. He looked at Ma and then let his head down.

"Well?" she asked.

"Well, he weren't no victim of the blue-tail fly."

"What's that mean?" I asked.

"He wasn't thrown from his horse," Ma answered.

"Cletus was killed, Mary. Shot and killed by a mess of bushwhackers."

"Oh!" Ma grabbed her mouth and shrieked.

"That's right," Uncle Olin said. "That's the honest truth, if you must know. It weren't more than ten miles outside of Fort Smith. Shot right off his horse and drugged a hundred yards. 'Course I wasn't about to sit idly by while they done the same kindness for me. I dug out for town just about a pistol's distance from the lot of them."

"Well, where's his—"

"I don't even know," Uncle Olin said. "Went back the next morning with the marshal but there weren't nothing but a few blood stains in the sand. Coyotes and varmints carried it off, most likely. Badgers, maybe? I don't know. The marshal didn't even spit. He just rode back into town. Said paperwork was piled up to the rafters. Lots of bushwhackers and ruffians, he said. Can't track 'm all. Sorry for yer troubles."

"Oh, that's awful," Ma said. "So, Pa wasn't there neither? In Fort Smith?"

"Nope, not hide nor hair. Never even rode in."

Ma fiddled with her night dress. "Things haven't been good here, Olin."

"What? Yer making it, ain't ya?"

"Not without Pa, and with only one mule. Pa was bringing in two, maybe four dollars a week with them mules. We ain't had that in two months. Pretty poorly here now."

"Well, don't worry; I'm back now, and the boy and I can earn a few greenbacks or rustle steers if we have to. We'll turn bushwhacker ourselves if it comes to that." He looked at me with a half-ready smile, hiding it from Ma.

"Now, Olin—"

"Aw, Mary, don't ya know when I'm—"

"No, I don't. Now get a bath before you spook the livestock." She turned and stamped up the porch steps.

Uncle Olin and me did some jobs over the summer. Some of the farmers had taken to a double crop rotation to bring in extra money, and that gave us some work plowing, planting, and picking.

"Never seen land under such a high state of cultivation," Uncle Olin said. "Almost like before the war."

That meant we had a little work left over from Grandpa's dealings. And of course, everyone knew he was gone and knew we needed something to live off of. I just wish we could have raised some traveling money a little faster. I wanted to go north like Mrs. Branson said. But Uncle Olin said it would cost forty dollars to travel all the way up there. And there weren't no way we could make that kind of money in one summer. Not with the twins to feed and the bankers lurking about like painted devils scalping citizens for tax payments. Ma said she couldn't even pay the penalties on the back taxes so she stopped paying them altogether. Of course, that made the Yankee devils even more hostile. Mostly because she wouldn't so much as open the door for them anymore. She'd just sit inside while they banged on the screen door and hollered for her attention. The whole thing got nasty. Sometimes Uncle Olin poked a shotgun barrel out a knothole just to see what they would do.

But I had a great idea.

"Uncle Olin, why don't we jes borrow forty dollars off them bankers?"

We had just finished raking a hundred acres of timothy-grass into windrows, and were within two or three miles from home. We each carried a big wooden rake over our shoulders and tramped up the lane toward home – practically wrung out. Every mile or so we passed another burned-out farm with raggedy barefoot kids and a rusty plow and a dead mule in the dooryard. Sweat practically shot out our eyes but the sun had already set and a cool breeze began to blow. Summer would be over soon and after harvesting most of this work would end. I wondered what we'd do then, without Grandpa.

"Ha! Bankers only loan money ta them that don't need it, son."

"What's the point in that? Ain't that why folks borrow? Cuz they need it?"

"Well sorry, that's just how it works. If you need money real bad, like we do… you can't get it. It's only for them with 'town' jobs and such. My advice: don't get tangled up with bankers and moneymen. It's a ruinous affair, and you'll end up in the poorhouse. That is a certainty of which I will stake my reputation on. The way they've treated your Ma is an insufferable sin. Money does that. And it affects the weak-minded Yankee more than most."

"Humm," I said, mostly doubting everything Uncle Olin ever said. He seemed to believe it but it still sounded like a bucket of rinse water to me. What else would bankers do with the money, 'cept loan it to poor folks?

We walked past another burned-out farm which Grandpa said Jim Lane's Jayhawkers had burned the year I was born. He and Uncle Olin had been fighting the war down South and there were no Southern men to stop them. He said all the burned-out farms were marked out as abandoned lands now, and that the government was about to get 'em all. Some were now darkie farms, but most not. Just burned out and empty, and about to get taken by Yankees.

Ma said our own house was also robbed four times during the war by murderous, abolitionist Jayhawkers, and even once by Missoura bushwhackers – our own countrymen. She told the abolitionists we weren't slaveholders but they robbed us anyway and undertook to burn our corncrib and smokehouse to boot. Then Order No. 11 came and she had to leave the county, that is, until she found a way to sneak back in. When I was a baby we had nothing left but the bedposts, and if the freesoilers came back again they'd likely steal those, Ma said. But she made do with things she'd hidden in the dirt in oilcloth. Practically everything we owned today was hid from the Kansas raiders in the back hedgerow at one time or another. Dirt can't eat through linseed oil and lampblack, Ma had said. And even if John Brown came back from the dead he couldn't find half the things she had hid back there.

Need a jar of peach preserves? Or sixty rounds for a .45? It's likely back there somewhere.

Uncle Olin eyed the wrecked buildings and shook his head.

"Naw, they won't loan you money," he said. "Not with your Ma so far back on her taxes. I told her to let the whole kit-n-caboodle go down the sinks and move out with us. But ohhh no, she—"

"What? Leave home?" The whole notion sounded so stupid I couldn't even imagine why he even brought it up. Leave our own home and move down into the shanties and slave shacks? It just didn't make a lick of sense.

"It's just dirt and lumber, Jay. Don't get attached to it. Jesus didn't have a place to lay his own head." Uncle Olin chomped on a new plug of tobacco without so much as a sniff. We walked along silently.

Crazy notion.

Within minutes a figure appeared along the horizon, coming in from the eastern Wire Road. That was a long road with telegraph wires I'd never been to the end of. Thirty miles, maybe? Ma said it led to a town where a building had a big steam wheel, and they operated little pulleys off it and stamped out iron farm implements – like a mechanical blacksmith made of iron itself. But I didn't know where that town was. And did not even know how a machine could do that. Machines can't think, and they don't have arms and hands so how can they stamp out iron parts? And at thirty-odd miles away I wasn't about to find out.

Wavy summer air blocked my view down the road.

But I could see a man on horseback. And he was no country feller; I could tell that much from his style. Good rider. Easy gait on a powerful animal. Not from around here. Even his clothing told that much. Lots of strange fellows lately. Lots of carpetbags. Lots of Yankees.

The horse and rider were still a half mile off when something rose up in my stomach. An awful gut-achy feeling. Like nerves before a barn dance. But bad nerves, not the good ones you get from dancing with your favorite girl. No, this was bad.

And then I knew it.

The rider was one of them.

Chapter Six

"JAY, GO CLEAR OUT the barn for this bluebelly. I'll be along with this piece of trash directly." Uncle Olin jerked a rope tied around the soldier's neck.

The one I'd seen on the Wire Road.

It felt awful to look at the man, stumbling along half dead. Maybe I shouldn't have told Uncle Olin he was one of them. Them that took Grandpa.

But there he was, riding right down the Wire Road as clear as day. And it wasn't ten minutes before Uncle Olin had him bushwhacked and captured. All I saw was two boot pistols and a Bowie knife flash from hand to hand, and then the man was on the ground. That was it. Uncle Olin had slipped around a little knoll and whacked him over the head. It was so fast, Uncle Olin could have been a painted devil himself.

The man stood before me bucked, gagged, and tied with his own saddle strings. He looked me in the eye, and I knew he was the one. Dressed in a dusty blue federal sack coat and trousers, neat and tidy, but trail-worn, and now bleeding down the forehead. And tied to his own horse's tail, a nice government remount onto which Uncle Olin had just mounted.

"Go on, Jeremiah," he said. "I'm going to run this Billy Yank around a while before I bring him in. Wear off some Yankee fat. We'll fetch a few good Southern boys and hold court right there in your ma's barn – Confederate style. I reckon there's a rafter strong enough to hold him when we're through."

Uncle Olin looked back at his prisoner. "Strayed a little too far south did ya, Billy Yank? Well, we know just what to do with ya now." He laughed and kicked the pony off the road into the brush.

I ran on ahead like Uncle Olin said, but still felt terrible. Why had the man come back? For more Southern men? If so, why come alone? And what about Marshal Upham? Was he waiting in the bushes to capture Uncle Olin like he had Grandpa? Maybe this man was just bait. A trap. But that didn't make sense neither. Nothing made sense any more. Sweat poured down my face and my mind tangled up with a thousand conflicting questions. Would Uncle Olin kill the man, or would he be bushwhacked too? Would the man be dead before Uncle Olin got him back to the barn? Did he know anything about Grandpa? What if Uncle Olin stringed him up before he could tell us. Would the Southern men scalp him and burn him like Uncle Olin said they would?

I just wanted to get Ma and find out what to do. But she was still a mile off, and that mile took seven or eight minutes at a dead run.

Ma and I stood at the barn door when Uncle Olin finally trotted up the road. I was still panting when we spotted him on the man's horse with his prisoner stumbling behind – practically dragging and half-dead. Uncle Olin shouted at the soldier but I could not make out his words. Minutes later, he sauntered in and stopped at the barn door. The man fell into the dust like a paper sack.

Uncle Olin smiled and nodded back at the bedraggled figure.

"Caught your man, Mary. Jay says he's the one. Or at least one of 'em."

Ma lifted her hand to her face and studied the man. She showed no emotion.

"Stupid fool rode in alone. There's no one else out there. I circled around three times. He was all alone."

The man opened his good eye. Blood trickled out his busted lip. "I... I came to–"

"Came to capture more rebels, I know," Uncle Olin shouted and pressed a foot into his neck. "Well, ya got captured yerself, didn't you Uncle Billy? Got the rules all turned around, now don't we?"

Uncle Olin nodded to me. "Get him in the barn, boy. I'll ride into town on this fine new government horse of mine. I know just the fellas for this job – Quantrill's old raiders – loitering down at the sawmill about every day. They'll know what to do with him."

"No, bring him into the house," Ma said. "And cut him loose and bring me a bucket of water from the trough."

Uncle Olin's lower tooth hung out. "Mary, you ain't–"

"Be quiet, Olin. You will not abuse this man any further. I know those Quantrill border ruffians. Ignorant, debauched, semi-savages. Hate being on the same side of the road with 'em. Greasy little rats."

"But Mary. You don't know what type of man he–"

"I said untie him. He's entitled to a little decency. If he took Pa, he'll tell us, and then you and your little friends can have a fandango. I guess he earned it."

The man looked up at Ma and tried to thank her. She just hardened her eyes and turned toward the house.

At least she didn't step on his neck.

"Awright, Jay. You heard the Provost Marshal. Judge, jury, and executioner, right there in one ninety-pound female. Go on… trot him in there." Uncle Olin threw up his hands, shook his head, and trudged in behind us.

"Sit him down at the table," Ma said.

The twins had heard the commotion and came running in from the woods. "We got company, Ma? We wanna see. We don't get much company. Do we get lemonade?"

"Git!" Uncle Olin said. "This ain't no time for younguns pestering about. Git you a piece of bread and git! Brats." He smacked them around until they headed for the door.

"That's right, go on," Ma said, but hugged them on their way out. "And Jeremiah, fetch that pan of cornbread and jar of buttermilk."

The man sat at the rough wooden table. Little drops of blood fell from his open lip; his hair fell down over wet eyes.

"Stop bleeding on my table!" Ma screamed, and threw a rag at his chin.

"What are you doing with that panbread?" Uncle Olin complained. "That's our supper. You ain't handing it over to that filth. Besides, he's going with me in a minute or two."

"I certainly am. Jesus said if your enemy thirsts, give him drink. If he is hungry, give him meat. I can do no less." I looked at the pan of cornbread and wanted it myself. My guts wanted it real bad, especially after that fieldwork. My stomach growled and every rib begged for food. But Ma was giving it to this man instead. She looked at me sadly.

"Begging your pardon, ma'am, but I'm not your enemy. I came to—"

"Shut up, mister! You are my enemy. You are a man-stealer and Heaven knows what else. Now clean up that lip and eat. We're going to have some words before my brother gets you out to the barn. I hope you die. You hear me? Die!"

That made Uncle Olin happy. He had taken the man's old horse-pistol and was proceeding to load it. He sat across the table with a powder horn and some percussion caps. Ma sat down at the corner, almost touching the man. He looked pretty hungry, and soon devoured our supper and buttermilk all by himself.

"Mister, what do you know about my father, Hiram Cantrell?" Ma asked.

"Well, that's what I came to tell you." He looked at Uncle Olin with no affection. Uncle Olin had loaded and capped a few cylinders, and waved the gun around with a smile. He wanted to get the man out to the barn pretty bad, but now the new weapon occupied him happily.

"He's up at Fort Leavenworth right now. U.S. Marshal Daniel P. Upham has him in custody and he's planning to hang him next month."

"On what charges?" Ma asked, unflinching. She had a poker face when she had a mind to.

"Ma'am. It's a long story and hard to explain."

"Well, you best git at it, Uncle Billy!" Uncle Olin said. He was fiddling with the lever action, packing the last ball into a chamber. The man eyed it uneasily.

"You've got to understand Marshal Upham, ma'am." I guess he

figured it was safer to address Ma than Uncle Olin. "First off, he's a Radical Republican. And wild for Negro franchisement. So that tells you a little about his character. A Lincoln Lover, I believe you folks in the South say. About as radical as they come, but somehow got himself elected to the Arkansas House after the war. He's a reconstructionist, and has led the state militia down there for about ten years. Even made Brigadier General."

"Reconstruction's over, Mister. The South has been redeemed," Uncle Olin said.

"What's that mean? Redeemed?" I asked.

"Be quiet, Jeremiah," Ma said, turning back to the man.

Uncle Olin waved her off. "No Mary, he needs to know what happened down here. He's old enough. Jay, after the war them radicals got the idea to make citizens out of the slaves. Was that in '68, Mary?" His eyes widened as though it were the worst act imaginable.

But I still didn't understand.

"Of course, they declared us criminals and took away the vote. You were just a boy. Two years later they gave it to the blacks. So when ya shake it all out, rebels lost the vote to the Negro! It's the bottom rail on top, and you're going to have to fight for jobs against them same blacks, Jay: plowing, planting, and harvesting. Root, hog… or die; all the freedmen want dem jobs. And they expect to be paid now."

"But what's redeemed?"

"Southern rule. Redeemed from Northern tyranny. The radicals is pretty much throwed out. All the Southern governments are run by us rebels now. The way it ought to be. And the South will rise again. You mark it down!"

"They called you rebels for a reason," the man said, unafraid, but still eyeing the loaded pistol. "You seceded from the union. That's traitorous rebellion, and you're doing the same thing all over again with the freedmen. Treason must be made infamous and traitors impoverished."

"Mister, yer about one minute from testing the strength of a new hemp rope," Uncle Olin said, waving the gun and throwing an eye toward the barn. "My sister ain't big enough to hide behind forever."

"I'm sorry; I'm only trying to explain. They took the vote from Confederate men for rebellion to the union. Simple as that. And Daniel P. Upham is the man to reconstruct your rebel actions in Tennessee, Arkansas, and Missouri. And he's as rough as they get."

"Humph. Reconstruction. Them radicals took more than the vote," Uncle Olin complained. "Freedman's Bureau grabbed up rebel farms and gave them to the blacks too. All them little Freedman villages you see… that's confiscated lands! Took from our friends and countrymen. And we will get them redeemed too. One way or another. Bring in the Klan, if we have to."

Ma nodded. "Don't you think that was the reason for the KKK in the first place?" she asked. "Just good Southern boys trying to get their lands back, and the vote?"

"No, ma'am. It was not. They wanted another civil war. And blacks back in chains where they belonged. Or, so they said. You must know that. Living down here and all. Some of them ain't good boys, ma'am."

She nodded in partial agreement.

"Upham's been battling the Klan for ten years, and he's a madman by now. Half-deranged, he pulls up the wheat with the tares. Not exactly right in the head if you ask me. Grant appointed him U.S. Marshal for the Western District court so that gives him ten times the power he had when running the Arkansas militia. And he reports to Judge Parker down in Fort Smith. I think you know what that means. He'll hang your pa for sure."

"Aw, he weren't even down there," Uncle Olin grunted. "You been a liar from the beginning."

"Like I said, Fort Leavenworth."

Ma's poker face cracked. "What's Hiram done? We live way up there in Missoura, so what's an Arkansas marshal want with Hiram?"

"Upham's bringing in every ex-rebel who's ever lipped off in public. And most of his charges stick like beef tallow. Especially with Judge Parker. They don't call him the Hanging Judge for nothing."

"I still don't understand what Hiram did?"

"Like I said, ma'am, it's a clean sweep. But as for the charges?

Well… murder, Upham says. Goes back to 1863 – fourteen years ago – when Upham's cousin was killed at the raid on Lawrence, Kansas. He was just a recruit then. Just a boy. I was there, so I know the particulars, but not many do."

Ma reached over and dabbed a little blood from his lip. "Can you break it down?"

"I don't know. Maybe…"

"Well, so far all we have is Upham prosecuting ex-rebels who just want the vote back. How does that relate to Hiram?"

"Night rides, ma'am. Hiram was on some. At least one we know of."

"I don't believe it."

"Ma'am, I think it's true. Woodruff County, Arkansas, 1868. Maybe others."

"I don't care what you think. Pa wouldn't do that. He's not Klan. Never agreed with them."

"It doesn't matter. Upham's building a case right now up in Leavenworth."

"And you helped bring him in."

"Ma'am…"

"Mister, you rode with Upham and you arrested my pa. This boy's only granddaddy. Without knowing anything about him."

"Ma'am, I was just doing my duty. I'm a private soldier. Do you think I had a choice? I would have been court-martialed and shot for insurrection myself."

Uncle Olin cocked the pistol and pressed it into the man's skull. "But it's all the same in the end, ain't it, Uncle Billy?"

"You may not like me, but you need me nonetheless," the man said nervously. "I'm the only one who knows Upham."

Uncle Olin snapped the pistol up, uncocking it in one swift motion. "We'll find out about that, Uncle Billy."

I leaned over and asked Ma, "Why does he call him Uncle Billy? Is he kin?"

"General Sherman's nickname," the man said. "Uncle Billy. The men loved him. Everyone still loves him. He prosecutes the Indian wars now."

"You mean Sherman's Bummers?" Uncle Olin said. "They loved him. The ones that burned every house and farm from Atlanta to Savannah? No... not everyone loved Uncle Billy. Now you had better have some more information about my pa, Mister." He twisted the pistol up in front of the man's face again. "You're talking in circles, and half of it don't make a lick of sense."

"Put the gun away, Olin," Ma said. "You're starting to look like a fool." Olin turned up his nose at her and threw the pistol down. I wanted to pick it up, but Ma would probably yell at me too.

"How is it that you ended up down here," Ma asked. "Do they let private soldiers wander about like that?"

"I'm mustered out. I quit Upham."

"After you brought my pa in? This boy's granddaddy and only provider?"

"Ma'am..."

Ma cringed. "I am sorry. There was no call for that."

"Yes, ma'am. I quit Upham as soon as we reached Leavenworth."

"Why not take him to Fort Smith?" Uncle Olin asked. "I spent a week down there, and Pa weren't even there. Spent every cent we had gettin' there. Sheriff Cletus got bushwhacked and kilt. You said Upham reported to Judge Parker, but they hadn't heard a lick about no Hiram Cantrell."

"Well, that's true. He does report to Parker. But the Fort Smith courts are jammed up. Too many criminals."

"Southern boys, you mean?" Uncle Olin said. "Still loyal to the cause?"

"No, still loyal to lynching blacks and harassing law-abiding citizens. Night riders. Hooded thieves and murderers. Cow skulls, bed sheets, and torches. Burning crosses. Kidnappings and beatings. Gunmen at voting booths. All that. It ain't just the Republicans that are radical. This whole territory is on the brink of a second civil war."

Uncle Olin gnashed his teeth. "I might just join 'em for the likes of you."

"Then you'll meet Judge Parker personally. I tell you, they are putting an end to that violence. President Hayes wants it finished. The whole country is tired of it. But you good Southern boys just keep it up. Stirring up hatred and terrorizing free men. Ever hear of the thirteenth amendment down here?"

"And my pa's one of them? A hooded terrorist?" Ma asked.

"I don't know…"

"But you brought him in."

"Yes, and I quit too. There are… questions."

Ma lifted her head. "Questions?"

"Things I need to sort out. Details about your pa. From his days with Quantrill and Bloody Bill. And after the war from Woodruff County, and Pulaski County, Arkansas. Evidence to sift through."

"And?"

"Give me some time, ma'am. I'm trying."

"Fair enough," Ma said.

Uncle Olin slammed his chair into the table. "Well, that's all tolerably nice. While you two are ruminating all nicety-nice, I'm going down to the tavern for some supper. You better have something convincing by morning, Mister. Or I'll be back with some friends. With some of those 'criminals,' like my pa." He dragged the pistol across the table and walked off with it.

I managed to scrape up some beans and cornpone, and headed for bed. I didn't really understand everything the man had said. It just sounded like the Civil War had never really ended, and some were still fighting it. But I guess that made sense, especially if they took away their vote. And with Northern carpetbaggers coming in by the trainload and taking folk's land, and Southern scalawags letting them do it. I guess I'd fight too. But I wasn't exactly sure what to fight for. Not like Uncle Olin. He knew. And maybe Grandpa knew. But he said he hadn't been down South for ten years. But still, what about those notches under his lock plate on the old three-band musket? What did that mean? It just confused me even more, so I went to bed.

When I stumbled out the next morning, Ma and the man were still at the table. Still in the same places. Talking quietly and smiling. The man warm and chatty. Mother fiddling with a dish rag and wagging her head, jabbering like a schoolgirl with a new hat. She didn't look wrung out and worried like before.

Pink lips. Bright eyes. And bouncy.

They had drunk the whole crock of buttermilk, and Ma had baked cookies. Most of those were gone too. Mother and the man looked up as I lumbered into the kitchen and grabbed up the last few.

"Oh, Jeremiah!" Ma said with a smile.

"Yes, Mother?"

"Hitch up Rosebud and Black Jack. You're going north with Mr. Martin."

Chapter Seven

MOTHER MADE UNCLE OLIN give the horse back and apologize. And the pistol. But I wasn't exactly sure how because Uncle Olin carried a big Bowie knife and two boot pistols, yet Ma still made him do things anyway. She had a manner Uncle Olin couldn't work against. For one thing, she talked better than him and outsmarted him whenever they argued. Uncle Olin knew she was wrong, but could not figure a way around her bad cyphering, so he just gave in. Ma says I'm pretty smart too. But she says I can get a little too bullheaded when I get an idea in my head, just like my pa.

Like going west. "Get that idea out of your stubborn head before you get yourself killed," she had said. That's no place for a sweet boy like you. But she didn't know I was practically a man.

Uncle Olin put up a fuss but finally said he was sorry for pistol-whipping the soldier and dragging him around like he did. Although it might have done him a little good, he said. But maybe it was Mrs. Branson's threat that finally did it. Ma and old Mrs. Branson had ganged up on Uncle Olin and threatened to tie him down and shave his head. Ma said his hair was a long greasy haven for lice and vermin, and that a good shave was the only sound remedy for it. Never know what you might find in there, she said. Mrs. Branson agreed and they both came at him with lightning bolts in their eyes. That's when Uncle Olin finally agreed to give the horse back and come along to Fort Leavenworth with us.

We started north four days later.

Eighty miles to Leavenworth City.

Rosebud and Black Jack plodded along the dusty road for eight hours, and yet the federal had not loosed his tongue once. Neither had Uncle Olin. Mr. Martin, the bluebelly soldier, seemed happy to sit and watch the prairie grass go by. Not mad, not fuming, just quiet and content, although he favored his wounds from time to time. I drove the mules, and he sat next to me on an old buckboard wagon Uncle Olin had given five dollars for. It needed a little work but traveled fine except for a little sag in the right rear corner and a clunk in one wheel. Uncle Olin had given the wagon a good going over before we left and said it would get us there, but he didn't like that clunk one bit.

Uncle Olin lay in the back on a cotton quilt picking a new banjo he had also traded for. I think he gave a pistol and six rounds of ammunition for the banjo and a mouth harp. But I'm not sure how, seeing that pistols outnumbered banjos by a goodly number.

He frailed the yellow strings with his thumb and fingers, producing a little rhythm, and occasionally popped a thumb onto the calf-skin head for effect. The man he traded with taught him that, I expect.

After some time, Uncle Olin cut open a can of peaches, slurped them up, and tossed the can onto the roadside. Clink. I looked out and wanted some of the peach juice that might still be in the can. That and a biscuit would go good on a trip like this. But I was too embarrassed to jump out and get it with the federal sitting next to me.

Bum-ditty, bum, went the banjo strings – sounding out a little tune of Uncle Olin's particular liking. Uncle Olin sang out the tune from his spot on the quilt.

"Jack O' Diamonds, Jack O' Diamonds, I know you of old. You've robbed my poor pockets of silver and gold. It's whiskey you villain, you've been my downfall. You've kicked me, you've cuffed me, but I loves you for all."

For miles and miles. Over and over again.

And, "Rye whiskey, rye whiskey, rye whiskey I cry. If I don't get rye whiskey, I think I will die."

And still the man had not spoken.

"Fourteen thousand and eighty," Cousin Buford finally cried out without looking up.

"Will you stop that!" Uncle Olin yelled. "I'll put you out of the wagon and you can walk to Leavenworth City. How would you like that? What do them numbers mean anyways? It's monkey talk. Now shut up or I'll put you out." Buford shook violently.

"He's counting the number of yards since we left," the man finally said.

"Yards? Like a man's stride?" Uncle Olin asked. "It ain't no such thing. Just monkey talk is all." He went back to his banjo picking, still annoyed.

"No, that's what he's doing. Watch his eyelids. Each spoke of the rear wheel is seven and a half inches apart at the iron tire. Except for that missing one. He blinks at each missing spoke and ciphers the number of inches, and then converts it to yards. 14,080 is the number of yards since we left your sister's house."

"How do you know? You some kind of wizard?"

"There are 1,760 yards in a mile, and we're about eight miles out. It's just simple mathematics, taught in all the schools up North."

Uncle Olin sneered. "Oh, it's Yankee schools now... Monkey talk, if ya ask me. I'll slap him off the wagon if he don't quit."

But I think the man was right. Buford could somehow count the miles from that wheel. He just blinked and added up the yards we traveled. I wondered if a machine could do that somehow. Probably not. Machines don't think. But neither did Buford, so it was a puzzle.

Ma had traded for some of those same Northern ciphering books, and made me read them. She told me to be smart like the Yankees, not ignorant. But not act like them because they don't know no manners and don't respect the rights of common folk. But still, be smart like them. It's the only way to get ahead in life, she had said.

"Reckon we'll be there soon?" I asked. "Eight miles is a fair piece."

"Naw, it's a long drive up into Kansas," the man said. "Five days and a bit. Seventy-five more miles. Maybe eighty. And we'll be going up past Westport and Kansas City."

"What if we traveled all night?"

"Can't push these mules, not unless you want to ruin them. Rosebud and Blackie are good for about fifteen or sixteen miles a day. Slow and steady."

"His name's Black Jack. So we'll have to camp?"

"That's right. Your mother packed all the provisions. And sorry... Black Jack."

I wondered where she'd gotten the money because Uncle Olin said we were flat broke. But somehow he had traded for this wagon and the banjo. Plus, we had provisions for the whole trip, and Mother had fabric and thread to sew two new shirts. And Uncle Olin slurped peaches out of a can. And I saw a new twist of tobacco and two new clay pipes. Heck, there were things in the wagon I had never seen before. Like that quilt. Things costing fifty cents, a dollar, maybe even two or three. Where had it all come from?

I looked over at the man.

"Will we see Grandpa when we get there?"

"I hope so. It's been a fortnight since I quit out of Leavenworth, but I reckon he's still there. Been four months since his arrest. The justice system runs slow. Especially when... well, when there's a lot at stake."

"You mean when there's a man to hang?"

The man turned to me with a bad look. "That's right, Jeremiah. When there's a man to hang. I just hope we're not too late. I know right now that you'd just as soon lynch me, like your uncle."

Uncle Olin peeked up from his banjo and muttered, "Dern right."

"No sir," I said. "I just want Grandpa back. Mother says you're going to help us."

"Like I said... If we're not too late."

"What's your name, Mister?"

"Beelzebub," Uncle Olin muttered under his breath.

The man ignored him. "J.T. Martin," he said.

"If you're out of the army, why do you still wear those blue duds? Ma says that's what got you into trouble so quick down here. She says you're a danged fool for coming in dressed like that. And that you ought to take better care of yourself, especially your hands and skin."

The man laughed. "I guess so. My pa's one of the main army contractors for these trousers, shirts, and sack coats. I've worn his clothes all my life in one style or another. But I had to get out of Leavenworth quick."

"Going to hang you too?" Uncle Olin snapped. He was bored with the bum-ditty, bum-ditty, bum and wanted to pick a fight. Now that we were out of Ma's reach.

The man looked back. "I'm going to tell you a story, Olin."

Uncle Olin raised his eyes. "Well, you ain't said two words worth listening to since we left out so you best spin a good one. We'll tolerate you for a few more... yards." He looked at Cousin Buford and wagged his tongue. "Yards. Monkey talk is all."

"Why thank you, Olin, much obliged," he said. "Okay. I'm going to tell you about U.S. Marshal Daniel P. Upham's younger cousin. A little story about Lawrence, Kansas and Quantrill's partisan raiders back in '63. It should help explain Upham's madness for the secesh."

"What's secesh?" I asked.

"Secessionists. Folks who seceded from the Union. Confederates," the man answered.

"Well, I was there in '63, Mister, so you best not be fibbin' the boy or I'll know."

"And you'll slap me off the wagon?"

Uncle Olin rolled his eyes. "Git on with it, Uncle Billy."

"Wait a minute," the man said. "You were in Lawrence in '63? How old were you then, Olin? Was Hiram there with you?"

"Danged right, we was both there. Wouldn'a missed that show. I think I was sixteen or seventeen, cuz I went into the war with Pa when I was fourteen. That means Pa was about... oh... thirty at Lawrence. One of the old ones. But he wuz still a hard fighter, even at that age."

"Alright... Let me tell this story. Upham's cousin, Asa Upham was in my regiment – a new recruit, only fifteen years old – right out in

Lawrence, Kansas. We were part of James H. Lane's, U.S. volunteer militiamen."

Uncle Olin curled up his nose. "Ah, Jim Lane – King of the Jayhawkers! Scalpers and man burners. Probably killed more men than Quantrill ever did. Stole a lot more horses too."

"Yes, Jim Lane. We were just recruits. Actually, Upham, Asa and me all served in the same unit. I was only sixteen at the time, and toting a musket and traps one quarter my own weight. Asa and I were pals – he from Dudley, Massachusetts and me from New York. Daniel was more of an officer type, and didn't consort much with recruits. But I knew him well at the time."

Uncle Olin dropped the banjo and stared at the man. "Just a blamed minute, Mister. Your pa was J.T. Martin? From New York? The millionaire army clothing contractor? And you joined the infantry? That don't make no sense, a rich boy like you. I'm sure papa could'a found a three-hundred-dollar substitute for all his prissy sons."

"It's true, Olin. There were no substitutes for the Martins. I left home at age sixteen and signed up to fight rebs. My first fight was Lawrence, Kansas. We'd been camping near the little town–"

"Squatter colony, you mean," Uncle Olin interrupted again. "Lawrence weren't nothin' but a squatter colony of hired paupers from New England. German Dutchman, Hessians, hirelings and abolitionizers," he snorted.

"Near the little town..." the man continued without pause. "Learning to drill with the new three-band muskets. Model 1855's, I believe. None of the boys like me were expecting to fight; we were just drilling and learning to be soldiers. But that all ended on the morning of August 21, 1863, when we suddenly became soldiers. Quantrill's Raiders rode in yelling "Remember Osceola" with over three hundred guerrilla fighters against our little force of forty. And half those were green recruits like Asa and me. It was a bloody massacre. All the Lawrence menfolk were gunned down, still in their bedclothes, all except General Lane and a few dozen militiamen who escaped with their skins."

J.T. continued with a lost look in his eye. "The boardwalks were stacked with bodies, and the partisan raiders owned the town. Ditches ran with blood and buildings burned around us. It was a slaughter but I somehow made it out alive. God only knows how."

Uncle Olin smiled. "I remember that little ride. Us rebels whooped ya good, prissy little Yankee Boy. Best day of my young life!"

J.T. ignored him. "Turns out, Asa Upham had been shot through the finger while still in his tent at the recruiting camp, but was quite animated just the same. Happy to be alive, I guess. He had had a premonition of death that very morning, and when it didn't happen you couldn't hold the boy down with a Texas boulder."

I leaned in for more.

"By nightfall, we all hunkered down next to a corn crib at the edge of town in a bone-deep exhaustion. But not young Asa; he just wanted to show off his bloody nubbin finger. The boys started throwing up breastworks against the possibility of another attack, rolling in big rocks and logs for any protection they could muster – anything that would turn a bullet. Two dozen frightened citizens clustered around, hoping from some protection from the Army. Asa had a dirty shirt wrapped around his hand, and every so often he'd pull it off and showed off his war wound. His first amputation! He kept upholding the courage of Massachusetts men and how all the folks back home would admire his badge of courage."

Uncle Olin slammed his fist on the wagon. "Come on... Git on with it, prissy boy. You ain't said a dern thing about Upham, 'cept little Asa and his bloody nubbin finger. Is that the story?"

The man stared back at Uncle Olin. "Every once in a while a potshot came out of the empty prairielands and knocked a man down. It must have been five-hundred yards judging from the muzzle flash. Those rebel riders were pretty handy with rifles, not just revolvers. And of course, they were hidden in those little ravines so we couldn't hit them."

"And you didn't go after them?" I asked.

"Lord, no! They would have scalped us out there in the darkness. We were down to fifteen men, and just wanted to stay alive. By now, they were firing double charges to make sure we knew they were still there. One hundred-and-thirty grains of black powder. A few more recruits were killed by those long shots – anyone dumb enough to stand up above the breastworks. But still, young Asa couldn't stop shaking hands and congratulating survivors and showing off his shot-up finger. He trotted around like it was a New Year's Ball. Shaking hands, laughing, and smarting off with the boys.

"And then he just fell down. Dead. Shot in the head."

Uncle Olin wagged his head with a flourish. "Smart-aleck got what come to him, huh?"

The man clenched his teeth. "Of course, Daniel Upham ran over and fell on the boy's neck – his younger cousin. He cried all that night and cursed the rebel partisans out in the treeless prairie. He wanted to get at them real bad, and it ate him up. Two days later, young Asa was buried out there in the west side of Lawrence."

"So, he was dead and buried," Uncle Olin said, evidently pleased.

"That's right. But Daniel Upham practically went lunatic over those guerillas. It was mostly those sharpshooters he hated so much, for how they killed young Asa, just a boy with a badge of courage he wanted folks to admire. Upham never forgave those rebels. Never recovered. Not since that day in Bleeding Kansas."

"I don't understand, Mr. Martin," I said.

"Call me J.T."

"Okay, J.T. I don't understand why–"

"Why I'm telling you this?"

"Yes. What does that have to do with us? With Grandpa?"

"Son," he said softly. "Do you know what your granddaddy did during the war?"

Chapter Eight

August, 1877

FORT LEAVENWORTH WAS THE farthest I'd ever been from home. Almost a hundred miles and into a whole different state. Kansas. Travelers on the road said the mountains of Colorado were just west of here, but I looked and could not see them. Only flat plains of wavy brown grass. This was nothing like the green hills of Missoura.

I wondered about the goldfields and riches folks claimed were out in Colorado. Idaho Springs, some said. Others said Telluride, Breckinridge, Colorado City. All manner of wild stories came down this road. Stories of millionaires, lucky strikes, picking nuggets right out of the streambeds. And Injuns everywhere you looked. That's why Sherman had to fight them. To make it safe for folks on the Santa Fe trail.

But all I wanted was Grandpa back. Maybe then I could go west.

J.T pointed. "That's your muddy Missouri river, Jeremiah," he said. "Too thick to drink, too thin to plow. Leavenworth City is just yonder, and the military prison is up on the brow of that hill. Hope you're ready for this."

We lumbered along with every mile filling my guts with dread.

Uncle Olin finally pointed to a corn field near a copse of trees. "That's where she sank. Back in 1856."

We all strained to see.

"What sank?" J.T. asked. "You're pointing to a corn patch."

"The riverboat, Arabia. Right there in that corn field. You'll find 'er at the bottom of that little patch. Two hundred tons of manufactured goods headed for the frontier mercantiles. And now just sittin' there at the bottom of that corn field."

I looked over the stubble of newly harvested stalks. There was no steamboat, no river, no road. Another one of Uncle Olin's crazy notions, I thought. Nobody said anything. We just looked, but there wasn't nothing to look at.

J.T. finally turned to Uncle Olin. "The river's a hundred yards away, Olin!"

"Changed course in the spring of '57, when I was a boy. Pa brung me up here to see the old side-wheeler out in the wet field where the river'd been the year prior. I weren't no older than Jay's bratty sisters. Big smokestacks stuck right out of the mud. 'Til the river silt filled in. Take my word, she's down thar somewhere smokin' at the bottom of that field."

Uncle Olin squinted into the field again. "This weren't no rowboat neither. With two-hundred-tons of dry goods, that boat must a weighed ten times that. Kids had tied ropes to her stacks and was swinging off 'em like trees – twenty or thirty feet in the air. Dangest thang I ever saw." He pointed again. "Right there next ta them trees."

We all studied the corn field and trees as Rosebud and Black Jack clopped past. Uncle Olin went back to his banjo. Bum-ditty-bum.

The commotion ahead now demanded my sole devotion.

The steamship Arabia left my brain as quick as it went in.

The looming Leavenworth City invited entirely new notions of getting shot or molested or captured. Uncle Olin reminded me that we were Southern men, and Kansas was Yankee abolition territory. All of it. Every last inch. Awful things happened to Missourians here, and our folk don't travel past the western border. Was Grandpa bad enough for a place like this? I supposed when they hung Missoura folk this was the type of place where it got done. Either here or out in the back country like Big Hollow. I remembered stories of a man hung down in Big Hollow one dark night. Folks said he'd "done up a girl" and her pa would not stand for it. The father brought in his old mess pals and reminded the man of his manners with a certain length of hemp rope. He hung there all night, is how it was told to me.

But I reckoned this was the type of place they did it in the daylight.

Honestly, I didn't know enough about any place to know if this was good or bad. Or if boys like me were routinely shot and killed. Or whether folks came here to hang or whether it happened in every town. But this just about looked bad enough for it.

Gunshots echoed off unpainted buildings as rowdy men harassed a citizen. "Probably from Jackson County," Uncle Olin said. Rosebud flinched and fought the reins. Mule teams and wagons crammed the dusty streets which made her even jumpier. Horses raced through with little regard for citizens crossing before them. Men stumbled out of a Can-Can saloon as a carnival barker drew more in. A building at the edge of town burned without notice. This was nothing like Randalls Flats, but they didn't hang folks down there neither.

I tried to think of something other than hanging but it didn't work. It was as if I saw ropes and scaffolds everywhere. Hanging, I thought again and again. This must be the place for it.

"There's your prison up yonder and across the river," J.T. said, pointing to a stone wall and wooden stockade a few miles off. I could see little wooden guard shacks on stilts at each corner. The buckboard rattled up the south road, and I could do nothing to speed it along. J.T. had the reins, and would not let me run the mules. "We've crossed the great Missouri. Be there soon."

My heart fell. "But what if they got Grandpa? And—"

"In that case we're too late," J.T. said. "I was hoping to get up here before the hearings started. If they're over then we're too late and we might just as well go home."

Uncle Olin looked up from the battered old banjo. His relentless tune had gotten on my nerves. "You reckon Upham's up there prosecuting the case?"

"Yes Olin, he is. But he'll be in a hurry for Arkansas. Plenty of local business in Little Rock. He'll rush this through if it's not done already. Fort Smith is his territory. He's just up here because they were backed up. Too many criminals in Missouri and Arkansas."

"Humm," Uncle Olin said. "I'm not in a big hurry to run into that man, myself. I just come along to–"

"Why's that?" J.T. asked. "You know Marshal Upham?"

"I do not. No, sir. But I know a little about them night rides he's all-fired hot about. I understand he's got Pa on account o' them. Or some other shooting affair."

J.T. turned to face Uncle Olin. "Down in Arkansas? You know something about this case?"

"Nosir. I just know what went on down on the border in '68, that's all. I tried to tell the boy here, but nobody–"

"Wait, look!" I grabbed J.T. by the shirtsleeve. "See that flag up the hill. Y'all see that?" A flag on the fort stockade waved at half-mast. Next to it, a bugler floated a lonely tune out over the town below. Low and mournful. My gut tightened and my face turned hot. Even my legs wanted to bolt for the fort, still a mile off. But they soon turned to water as the bugler ended his mournful call. "Do you think–"

"It's probably not what you think," J.T. said. "Now just calm your nerves, Jeremiah. You're on edge. We don't know anything so let's just wait until we get there. We're going to have to check in with the provost marshal and schedule a meeting. Can't just barge in. You may not even see your grandfather for a week. You're just going to have to be patient. We've got to do this right."

"My pa ain't never been hung before," Uncle Olin said, clearing an old wad of tobacco from his cheek. I think the wad had been in all day, and he seemed rid of it. He spit loose flakes into the wind. Only a few got on me. "Don't reckon today's the day he'll hang neither. We seen ropes before we seen Yankees. Besides, even if they did git him, Pa would make a right pretty corpse. All Southern men make pretty corpses. Remember Captain Anderson with his bullet holes on display? That was a pretty corpse. Seen it myself. Bullet holes and bloody shirt. If I ever wake up dead, I want a passel of bullets holes for women-folk to admire and cry over my–"

"Shut up, Uncle Olin!" I screamed. "Just shut up about pretty corpses and–" And then I expected him to smack me in the head for backtalk, but he didn't. He just shut up and sat there. We all did.

After a time, Uncle Olin finally opened his mouth, but not proud like before. "Nope, that hangman won't get him; not 'til I told my part of the story."

"What makes you think they're even waiting for your part of the story?" J.T. asked.

"Reckon it's the only right thing." He sniffed. "Me being kin and all. And marched all over the western states together. Reckon I know what my pa done and what he ain't done."

"Well, your testimony may be helpful, Olin. But you're going to have to cut your hair and shave before they'll even let you in. I'll have a new suit sent out. What size are you? About a thirty-six?"

"Thirty-six what?" Uncle Olin twisted up his lip. "I don't even know what you're talkin' about."

"I'll take care of it. Tell me what you know about those night rides in '67 and '68, after the war. That's Upham's charge against Hiram. I need to know everything you know."

Uncle Olin lifted his head a little higher. "Want to talk to the rebel now, huh?" He rolled his head and cast an eye toward J.T. "Pa and me was just helpin' out, really. After the war…" He lifted an eyebrow to make sure J.T. was still listening.

"Go on. Just helping out…"

"The whole mess was on account of them Freedmen."

"Freed blacks?"

"No, you ignorant Yank. Freedmen's Bureau. Government men. Federals, down in Arkansas with no business but to try the patience of good citizens."

"Alright, I'm following you. That was Daniel Upham's jurisdiction."

"Well, it got started right after the war, when they come in and took lands what belonged to our colonel."

"President Johnson's administration?"

"No, the Freedman's Bureau. I just said. You are one ignorant–"

"Well, yes. But President Johnson was behind that. He laid into those plantation aristocrats and rebel officers pretty badly. I supposed your colonel was one of them."

Uncle Olin nodded. "Okay, well them Freedman's decided to clear out the farm buildings and put a darkie school in one of his tobacco barns. The colonel's own barns, you understand? In Augusta, Arkansas. And then a month later the land was marked off in forty acre lots and given off!"

"To the coloreds?"

"That's right. Of course, there weren't hardly no livestock after war but they confiscated mules and give them to the darkies too."

"Forty acres and a mule. I know the policy. But it wasn't as widespread as–"

"But that ain't the half of it. Colonel Raines was a U.S. senator. Of course, that's why he got the job of colonel in the first place. The commander of our regiment, that is."

J.T. shook his head. "And the Radicals refused to seat him in Congress after the war? And refused his right to vote, right?"

"That's right. So Pa and I was just there to see things straightened out. We rode with Colonel Raines during the war for a time. And what they done was wrong. Bald-faced wrong. That's your Yankee bayonet rule."

"And you two did what? Exactly? In that private war of yours?"

"Well…." Uncle Olin lifted his hand to his lips and studied the shops along the street. "We did what any good Southern men would do. What they all did."

"That's what I was afraid of… Take the reins, Jeremiah. And turn left up that hill and across that bridge at the other end of town."

"Is that the road to the prison?" I asked.

"No, Olin's going to get a hotel room before they fill up. We'll head out a little farther to the prison."

J.T. looked back at Uncle Olin. "You know, your colonel could have gotten President Johnson's pardon. Twenty-thousand were given out to Confederate officers and politicians. He could have gotten one too."

"Pardon from what? Exactly?" Uncle Olin asked.

"Treason to the Union. For the rebellion, of course."

"We ain't no traitors, Mister. Don't need no pardon for anything we done." Uncle Olin narrowed his eyes on J.T. "Colonel Eli Raines weren't no traitor, neither. And we weren't about to swallow the dog like no yellow cowards."

Uncle Olin turned his face away. "We're men."

"Alright, so he didn't get his pardon. So, what became of him? Did he get his land back?"

Uncle Olin wouldn't look. He just picked slivers off the wagon boards. "I ain't talkin' no more. We ain't no traitors, and we ain't no cowards. That's all."

"Fair enough, Olin. But I'm going to need to hear the rest of that story. After you get your mind straight on it. Alright?"

Uncle Olin didn't answer.

We let Uncle Olin off at a little boarding house at the other end of town. J.T. had tried to apologize for calling Colonel Raines a rebel and a traitor but it didn't work. Uncle Olin wouldn't say another word. After J.T tried again, we finally left Uncle Olin and turned the mules up the hill.

The evil hill.

My gut tightened again. I did not want to go anywhere near that ugly prison. I just wanted Grandpa to come out and go home with us. And maybe Ma could come too. Maybe we could all live in the boarding house until the whole mess got sorted out. Why did they have to keep him in that awful place?

But J.T. wouldn't stop. He just pulled right up to the stockade and set the brake. Rosebud and Black Jack shook off drops of white lather.

A big wooden fence surrounded the prison. Over six feet tall. I walked around and found a knothole big enough to look inside. Men were working, marching, yelling, sawing, lifting, running. Like a wasp's nest. I could see that much straight ahead. But no Grandpa.

"Come on, Jeremiah. Let's check in with the provost marshal." J.T. pointed to a wooden structure with writing on it. "Right over there."

"No. I want to see Grandpa. Right now. If he's in there, I want to see him."

"It's not done that way, son. I'm sorry. Let's—"

"Hiram Cantrell!" I yelled through the knothole. "Anybody know Hiram Cantrell? Hiram Cantrell!"

No answer.

J.T. grabbed my neck. "Stop it! You'll get us arrested. Now let's—"

"Hiram Cantrell!" I yelled louder, with my lips pressed into the knothole. "Hiram Cantrell!"

A man with three stripes on his sleeve walked over. "What's all that hollering about? What do you want, boy?"

"I want to see Hiram Cantrell. Is he here?"

"Of course he's here. We're just headed for fatigue duty. But you can't—"

"Mister, I want to see him. Where is he?"

"Come on, Jeremiah," J.T. urged. "We'll see him soon enough."

I yelled into the knothole again, this time twice as loud. "Hiram Cantrell! I want to see him, or I'll get the mayor."

"You'll get arrested," the soldier said. "That's all you'll get." He kicked the fence and walked away.

I yelled for Grandpa again. Other soldiers in the yard turned to look.

"Awright, awright, boy… you weary me" The soldier glared back. "Hold still a minute. I'll fetch the detail." The man stomped off and began yelling out commands in the dirt yard. "Detail, Right Face!" A short pause followed as boots tramped in unison, and then, "Right Oblique, March!" Another pause, and more boots landing in perfect time. "Forrrwaaaard, March!" the man yelled.

The stamping boots approached the knothole.

Ten men marched in lockstep neatly past, each with his right hand on the shoulder of the man ahead, and an iron ball and chain in his left. Heavy chain links and shackles connected the men's ankles. Each wore black and white striped jackets, pants, and hats – all exactly alike.

"Detaaaail, Halt!" the voice bellowed thickly.

And just inside the knothole stood Grandpa.

Chapter Nine

"**D**ARNED NEAR EIGHT O'CLOCK already. Upham should be here in less than an hour." J.T. tucked his pocket watch into his vest, slid a crisp white napkin under his collar and looked over the table. He flattened the cloth neatly against his breast with no urgency, no ravenous attack on the steaming plate below. Just practiced efficiency. The fricassee would wait for him. And that meant properly arranging the napkin, a few pieces of silver and his hand-carved chair up to the table. Those were Yankee manners. Wholly unfamiliar in my territory. But I tried to follow.

And then he prayed that the Spirit of God would hover over the face of the deep as it had at the very foundation of the world when all creation was in disarray. Only then, he prayed, would men see clearly to execute justice. "Remove the scales, O God. Open our eyes and make our paths straight. Justice for Hiram Cantrell. Peace for Jeremiah Clark. Strength for Mary and her daughters. Amen."

The little rooming house had eight round tables with lacey white coverings, nothing like the stout wooden benches in the Jeff Davis Tavern in Randalls Flats that Uncle Olin liked so much, spattered with grease and alcohol, with dogs underfoot barking and fighting for table scraps.

There were red window curtains with lace and fancy stitching.

The house mother rushed between the tables and kitchen, also with practiced efficiency. Her daughters appeared from time to time with water and rolls. The younger one smiled each time she skipped from the kitchen and each time she reentered. Her head wagged a little with each smile, which seemed to flip her hair ribbon a certain way, effective enough to interest me and jangle my emotions. Do hair ribbons know what boys are thinking? Do they flip one way and then another so as to manipulate the male eye? I did not know. But I did know that that hair ribbon alone was more interesting than J.T. and all his table manners.

But still, I missed Patricia.

"I made a lot of mistakes with Upham," J.T. said. "You listening?"

I turned back to J.T. "Yes. And there's one thing I don't understand."

"What's that?" He asked.

"Why did you ride with him? Upham. You don't seem anything like him."

J.T. shifted. The question set him back. "Well… back then I was full of vim and vinegar, and he had a mission. Upham, that is. Honestly, that attracted me. In fact, the Radical Republicans possessed so much passion for the equality of blacks that I could not resist that mission. It was everything I wanted. Travel to new lands, abolitionist work, freedom for every American, and execution of Lincoln's grand plan. Or… what was left of it after President Johnson got aholt of it. Anyway, it felt like all of America wanted Lincoln's plan to come to life, if nothing else than to honor him after that awful assassination.

"So I took off for the mission field.

"And landed in Fort Smith, Arkansas.

"A proud Lincolnite. To the land of white supremacy, bayonet rule, and Jim Crow democracy. A complete shock to my Northern upbringing.

"Jeremiah, do you know how many black laws the Southern states have invented since the war? Well I do, and it knocked the gall right out of me. But not Daniel P. Upham. No, not that man. When all the other Radical Republicans lost interest in the fight, Upham did not. He always said, 'There is one law governing the white man and the black

76

man.' That's what the fourteenth amendment in '68 was all about. Did you know that? The same law that protects the white man shall protect the black. The same law that punishes the white man shall also punish the black. One law for all men. That's pretty radical, I guess."

I nodded, but didn't understand what that had to do with us. Did they really have to arrest Grandpa and beat down Ma and burn down Southern farms just so somebody could vote?

J.T. continued. "It sounded so wonderful, but President Hayes has already given up that fight and he's pulled federal troops out of the South. After all, it's been nine years since that amendment and the South has pretty-much defeated the radicals and gone back to the status quo: slavery by another name: sharecropping. I'm not saying Upham loves the Negro but one thing is for sure, he has got some kind of fire against you Johnny Rebs." He shook his head and grimaced.

"But you quit him," I said. "You quit Upham to help us, right?"

"That's right."

"Will you ever go back?"

J.T. paused. He rubbed the table cloth and buttoned and unbuttoned his shirt sleeve twice. "I don't know; I might. Who else is doing this type of work? You know, there have been a hundred unsolved murders since the war in Taney County alone? Arkansas is a mess. And hundreds more in Woodruff County and more in Pulaski. And for every murder there's twenty floggings, beatings, bushwhackings, and kidnappings to go with it. And that's in every county in Arkansas and Tennessee, not to mention southern Missouri. I heard about Sheriff Cletus."

"Upham hates us," I said.

"I doubt it. But sure, Upham's got a rough side. Still, he's done a lot of good for your people: enforcing reconstructed governments, disbanding the so-called law-and-order leagues, catching renegades, desperate men, Klansmen, rebels. You know: gunmen, lynchers of blacks, and the like."

"Like my Grandpa?"

J.T. looked away, returning to his chicken. He didn't really answer. Just mumbled a little and shifted in his seat.

"We'll discuss that," he finally said. "But first, I want to prepare you for after dinner. Upham wants to meet with us – probably to sniff out a strategy or get me back in his holster. You need to know a few things before he arrives." J.T. paused. "Well, like that yelling through the knothole business. Your grandfather is paying for that right now."

"What do you mean?"

"Ever hear of a hot box? It's a little wooden box just big enough to stand up in. So don't do it again." He started on the meat and potatoes, letting the warning reach its depth. It was not really a scolding, not harsh, but stern enough.

"There are other things," he said. "Don't take me wrong, but there are some things you need to change if you're going to operate in this Yankee town. It's not Randalls Flats up here."

"Like what? I can't afford suits and fancy stitching."

"Little things that Northerners do."

"Like what?"

"Okay, for one, don't clear your nose indoors without a handkerchief. It's a repulsive act. I'll get you a set of handkerchiefs if you don't have them. That stuff flies all over the floors, and folks walk through it. You understand?"

He set his fork and knife down and laid his hand on my wrist.

"Also Jeremiah, don't wipe your hands on your pants when you eat. Use the napkin." He nodded to the neatly folded cloth I had never thought to pick up. Actually, I never knew the difference between napkins and handkerchiefs, or why you'd care to use either when trousers and shirt sleeves were readily at hand.

"And up here, you're going to have to bathe regular. I know your Uncle Olin says once a year is good for him. But Northerners have different customs. You can bet these Leavenworth prosecutors bathe regular, and you don't want to give them a reason to think less of you. Every two weeks will keep you fresh and clean. Or, once a week if you feel the need. Remember, you will be in the company of gentlemen. Later we'll work on grooming and fingernails."

"You'll have me resembling a riverboat gambler. Should I get a silver-headed cane?"

"You're just going to have to figure something out. Never give these people an occasion to discount you on the basis of appearance. They will do it if you give them the opportunity."

"Is that why tapestry-bag men hate us? They remind me of the blowflies in a hog we slaughtered the day Grandpa was arrested, laying their maggot eggs in the South. Ma says they should just go home."

"Jeremiah, carpetbaggers may be the lowest form of humanity. I'll grant you that. Opportunists, corruptionists, and looters. Well, many, I should say. But some are genuinely trying to fulfill Lincoln's dream: to bind up the nations wounds. It requires a lot of capital to revive the South. A lot of hard work and investment. Half the infrastructure was destroyed after the war. Cities were in ruin. Richmond was a brick-heap. Jackson, Mississippi was an empty chimneyville. Remember that? Think about that before you judge them harshly. But yes, some are just here to get rich off the hard luck of others."

My eyes narrowed to a squint. "Sounds like the ones after Ma."

"Maybe. Jeremiah, the love of money is the root of all evil – having money isn't evil – but loving it is. You understand the difference. It is a stench to God. And they will get their reward. Lincoln used to say, if you turn your back on the truth and burn your britches, you'll have to sit on the blisters."

He laughed. "But you may need to work with those kinds of men. So be as wise as a serpent but harmless as a dove. Understand?"

"Mother says to learn the Yankee talk. She says—"

"We'll work on that. But there are some other things I want you to know about this town and the prison system. And military justice. I know a few things and I want you to remember them while we work to free your grandfather."

We finished eating and J.T. left the table neat and orderly. He reached into his vest pocket, checked his watch, and handed me a small booklet. "Beadle's Dime Book of Practical Etiquette for Ladies and Gentlemen."

"Read this," he said, pointing at the subtitle. "You see: it's a guide for true gentility and good-breeding. These Beadle books are all-the-go now."

J.T. and I took a seat on the red-velvet upholstery in the boarding house parlor. It was a quarter til nine, and Upham hadn't shown. I was glad of that. I liked J.T's vision of the new America and liked listening to him. Everything had changed since the war, he claimed. Changes he said were essential for growth: Industrial Capitalism. A new brand of Christian churches and evangelizers spreading the good news of Jesus Christ in new and different ways. New manufacturing methods. Travel and lower shipping costs. Railways stretching a thousand miles. Goods and services sold to customers in completely different states. Or across the ocean in England, Germany, and France. All this was opening up, and the individual farm life was evaporating, he said. "We are all connected now. Not individual communities. Or individual yeomen farmers. It's a network of productive citizens across an entire continent. We are the great United States of America. A new Christian experiment inspiring the world."

It felt so exciting to hear him tell it. Maybe I could be a Northern man, if I tried.

And Uncle Olin didn't hang me for treason.

"Do you think I could go west?" I asked. "There's gold in California."

"California's played out. Consider the silver mines of Leadville, Colorado. Or gold mines in Idaho Springs, that's also in Colorado despite the name. But that's awfully hard work."

"It can't be no harder than working Rosebud and Black Jack for beans and biscuits. I'm not much good at that, so I might just as well go."

He smiled. "Out there they have a saying: whiskey is for drinking and water is for fighting over. It's a hard country, but you can get out there in a weeks' time and take a look. There's a rail line into Denver City, and another down into Colorado Springs and Colorado City. That would be the place to start. But Jeremiah, that's all Yankee territory just like here in Leavenworth. Remember what I said earlier. You'll have to learn to operate in Northern society or you won't make it out there either. It could be worse than mule skinning."

I still wanted to go.

J.T. pointed to a stack of newspapers and said I should pass the time until Upham showed up. The Harper's Weekly had mostly political articles and stories, but I liked the Humors of the Day and advertisements in the back. There was a whole mess of ways to get rich, but mostly in New York or other places back East. For instance, I could make fifteen dollars a day selling parlor games, or gold pens, or playing cards, or whisker liniment. But New York was on the other side of the moon, so I just read the Humors and laughed. They were so funny!

An unwelcome visitor is like a shade tree; you're happy when he leaves.

Man is born of woman; and he may often die of her.

One of our city confectioners advertises broken hearts for three cents a pound!

Difference betwixt a soldier and a sailor: one tars his ropes, the other pitches his tent.

Don't tell secrets in a cornfield; it has a thousand ears.

A man being led to the gallows saw a crowd running on before him. "Don't be in such a hurry," he said. "Nothing will happen without me."

And that's when I quit the humors and went back to the get-rich schemes. Maybe I could make a million dollars selling blood purifier pills or cocaine remedies. It seemed so easy. Become an agent for the New Wizard Apothecary and payments in gold came in by train. I believed I would like that.

By-and-by a man entered the parlor, looked around and turned toward us. "John Martin?" he inquired. I put the paper down and looked up.

"That's right. John T. Martin. You Upham's man?"

"Yessir. Andrew Blackhouse. Mr. Upham was unable to attend.

He sends his most sincere apologies. I am here in his stead. How can I help you Mr. Martin?"

"Help me? I didn't call the meeting. Upham wanted to meet with me."

"But surely you have concerns. Questions?"

J.T. dropped his hands. "Sure. How is Hiram Cantrell's health? In good spirits?"

The man paused in surprise. "Oh, surely you've heard…"

"Heard what?" J.T. asked. "I am here to look in on him. I just want to make sure he is bearing up. I understand the U.S. Military Prison can be an austere institution. Is he faring well?"

"Oh he'll never see the Happy Land of Canaan. He's to be hung. Next week. I'm sure of that. Yessir, the hemp is already grown and cured that'll adorn his neck. We go through a passel of rebs every week. Every one guilty. Every one hangs. Operates like a fine Waltham watch, I'd say." The man opened his gold pocket watch and admired it coolly. He held it to his ear.

I looked at J.T. and tried to stand. Was this true? We were too late? And eating fricassee dinners and reading humors while Grandpa faced the gallows?

A hot flash came over me. "J.T. What is he saying… Is Grandpa… When did–"

"Calm down, Jeremiah."

J.T. turned to the man. "Let's take this into the library, sir. The boy–"

The man looked offended. He tinkered with the gold watch. "The lad's got to grow up some day, Martin. It's no concern of–"

"Let's just take it into the next room, please. I have questions."

J.T. led the man into the next room, but I could still hear. They quickly fell into heated argument loud enough for anyone in the house to hear, but I could not control my sobbing which ruined it. My eyes and nose ran so freely that the words could not penetrate. I pressed an ear to the wall.

"Like I said," the man said. "He's got to…" Muddled voices. Garbled words and fists. Angry words.

"Aw, be a man, will you?" More hostility and rising voices. "Juvenile ploy... can't you have some decency? This is a man's life..."

Tears and sobbing competed for attention, but I got a little more, and soon realized J.T. was bleaching the man's hair.

"...get off your high horse... what kind of cold-blooded..."

"...might just as well be guilty... he's like all the rest... go home and forget him..."

J.T. finally raised his voice loud enough for every word to penetrate the clapboard wall. "We'll be at that prison tomorrow, buster. I'll settle up with you later. You best learn some manners in the meantime. You hear me?"

J.T. burst back into the parlor with a red face and tightened fists. His cravat and collar hung down across an opened white shirt. He could not focus for more than a second, clenching his fists, swinging and kicking. He finally lifted a parlor chair and slammed it into the washtub cart, sending it crashing to the floor. The remaining guests fled as the house mother flew into the room for an explanation.

"I am sorry ma'am," J.T. said, seeing her alarm. "I'll clean this up, and if there is any damage you may put it on my account. It was just an argument, no threat to life."

"See that you do, son. And if such an outburst occurs again you and your comrade will be put out of the house. Is that perfectly clear? Out into the street, you will. And I'll have the constable out here with a writ. I don't tolerate—"

"Yes, ma'am. I apologize. This will all be cleaned up."

J.T. turned to me. "That's the type. Right there." He pointed into the other room. "I'll take ten carpetbaggers over that hyena."

"So, Grandpa's—"

"He's perfectly fine. Don't believe a word he said. He was just riling your nerves, putting you in your place before this thing gets underway. Understand? It's a maneuver. A lawyer's tactic to put you off balance. Hiram is fine."

I searched J.T's eyes for more. "Okay... I guess. But how do you know? Maybe he's—"

"I just do. Trust me. Are you ready for tomorrow?" he asked.

"Maybe we'll see Hiram or maybe not. But I want you to be strong and composed. Your grandfather will need that. He's got enough to worry about."

"Yes, I'm ready. If you'll come with me." I smiled, slowly brightening up. "Otherwise, I'll just yell through the knothole again."

He growled and grabbed my hair for a good shaking.

Chapter Ten

WHEN I FINALLY SAW GRANDPA again, a whole week had passed and he was knee-deep in a canal of black sludge. Him and eleven other prisoners with gum waders and hoes over their shoulders. A rush of slurry flowed past them carrying articles of every possible description: shoes, books, Bibles, shirts, underdrawers, hats, spectacles, fifty squealing rats, and a million hungry flies.

It stunk so bad I could taste it.

Nothing in Randalls Flats ever smelled that bad.

"Keep it moving," the boss growled. "Dredge this channel and keep it moving. We've got three more sinks to flush before sundown. You don't flush, you don't eat."

A canal of fresh river water had been opened into the prison sinks and was washing the refuse back out into the mighty Missouri. Thousands of gallons flooded through the black waste. It flowed into one end crystal clean, and out the other thick as bread pudding. Dark cakes of debris broke apart, releasing all manner of foul odors. Men waited at the door to the sinks to do their business, and could not enter until the job was done.

Or maybe just to watch.

The prison guard who had brought me in pointed. "Your grandfather is busy at the moment. Hiram Cantrell, right? He'll be free

85

in a half hour, maybe less. They'll take a little break and start the next sink soon after. We've got ten sinks here. They'll flush five today. Five tomorrow. Each one can accommodate twenty men doing their morning… ahh.. you know. Ten sinks times twenty is two-hundred men. This is pretty big, and we got ta do it every three months, just like this."

"The smell is so bad," I covered my nose with my shirt.

"I'm a corporal. See? Two stripes is a corporal." He pointed to another man in uniform, toting a double-barreled shotgun in the crook of his arm. "Three stripes is a sergeant."

"Okay, Corporal. But that smell."

"Yes, the bad air — that's what makes folks ill. Disease and all manner of sickness come from it. The odor coming off these sinks is what does it. Typhoid, consumption, and influenza. It all comes from bad air, you see." He waved his hand over the whole putrid area as if the source of every ailment arose out of it. "We learned that in the War of 1861."

"Do you mean the War of Northern Aggression?"

He looked at me sideways. "Uhh, folks have different names for it."

He turned back to the canals. "We flush these ten sinks every three months, and that keeps the whole fort down to about four cases of typhoid a year, maybe six." We stood there at the edge of the canal as the rushing water washed out everything that wasn't bolted down.

"Dredge it up good, boys. Get 'em hoes moving," the boss-man hollered — also a corporal, judging by his two stripes. "Work it all out. I want this ditch flowing clean or you'll be filling your canteens with it. Want a dipper of that, Cantrell? Keep dredging or you'll get it for breakfast tomorrow." The corporal paced back and forth at the edge of the rapids, still barking out orders and insults. A shotgun also lay over his shoulder.

Over the course of a half hour the river water became cleaner and carried fewer articles with it. The men began to lay down in the canal and rinse their clothing and hair. Most of the stink had passed and the cool water even looked inviting to me, standing there in the hot sun.

But not that inviting.

"You'll get some time with your grandfather now that this sink is done. See how they're closing the gates?" the corporal said. "They'll open the next set and start the whole process over again." He pointed to the row of buildings. "All five get flushed today."

Grandpa and the other exhausted men climbed out of the trickling canal and laid in the warm sun. Some men drained canteens of fresh water over their heads. Others stripped off and laid in their underdrawers, soaking up the warmth. They all smelled a little rotten, but tolerable.

Grandpa trotted over and grabbed my shoulders with a flourish. "Boy! I'll need to strap Noah Webster's dictionary on top 'o your head," he said. "Keep you from sprouting!" He wrapped his arms around me, drew back and eyeballed my height.

"Guess I grew a little over the summer."

"A handbreadth! How is your Ma holding up? And your Uncle Olin?"

"Ma's okay. Uncle Olin is here to see you. But not 'til later. He's scouting for a druggist. It was a bad trip. Uncle Olin's wife ran off with a boot peddler or something like that, like she always does. Then it took six days to cross three counties into Kansas. And we had trouble. Busted an axle and bent a tire. Lost a king pin into a ravine. And the water barrel slipped off the wagon without nobody seeing it. I saw a lot of stuff, like a riverboat in the middle of a corn field. Mostly I just wanted to fetch you back home. We miss you real bad, Grandpa. But all the folks are saying you might get…"

I could not fight back the tears.

"You might get—"

"Oh, let's not fret just yet. I'm just glad you're here. Let's lay out in the grass a while and forget all that."

The boss-corporal tossed hardtack bread to the men out of a box labeled 1865. "Finish these up quick. When they're gone we start that next sink. Y'all loving this yet?" he teased with a big rotten grin. The men nibbled their crackers slowly.

"Here, take this Jeremiah," Grandpa said, handing me the palm-sized hard-bread. "Have you et? They fill us with so much grub here that

I can't hardly stomach it all. You go on and take it."

"J.T. and I ate at the rooming house."

Grandpa's eyes raised a little. "J.T?"

"He drove up here with us. With Uncle Olin, Buford, and me." I didn't want to tell Grandpa the whole story. He might get mad. 'Specially if I told him that Ma had sat up all night and baked cookies for one of the men who had brought him in. And that Ma smiled every time he talked, and that she giggled and twirled on one foot. Grandpa might thrash me just for telling the story.

"A friend of Uncle Olin's, then?"

"Sort of. They talk about the war a lot. But mostly they argue on just about every topic: whether the South had the right to secede, and whether the occupation soldiers should git out and let us be, and if the darkies should vote and hold office, all that dumb stuff." But I didn't really want to talk about those things.

I looked down at the green patch of grass because I could not look Grandpa in the eye. "Grandpa?" I asked. "Are you here on account of them notches? On your old musket lock?"

"Alright, men. On your feet," the yard-boss hollered before Grandpa could answer. "Let's get this next sink started. I got men lined up to use them. Form up over here." He pointed to an imaginary line along the second canal which was already flowing black from under the next sink. The stench brought water to my eyes.

Grandpa nodded at the line. "We'll talk. Can you stay long?"

"We're staying in town. Uncle Olin, Cousin Buford, J.T, and me. Ma couldn't travel. She gets poorly from time to time."

I didn't mention the bankers and carpetbaggers. Or how Mrs. Branson shot me on accident when she put the very scoundrels to flight. Or how Sheriff Cletus got bushwhacked and kilt on his way into Fort Smith.

Within minutes the men had grabbed up their hoes and plunged into the dark slurry.

Grandpa didn't hesitate. He jumped right in with them. "We'll talk," he yelled, attacking the muck with all his effort. "We'll talk soon!"

"I'll take you back to the office," the corporal said as I turned away. "I hope you had a good visit with your grandfather. General Blunt wants to see you and the other gentleman in his office. That's the new stone building. Number 468."

We walked the full length of the yard and past six more buildings, past the shoe and harness shop, broom factory, masonry building, and then through two wooden gates, over a bridge with waterwheels and levers, and then up three flights of stairs. I was lost. J.T. already sat waiting outside the office door. Large block letters read "GENERAL ASA BLUNT, COMMANDANT, UNITED STATES MILITARY PRISON." A sergeant led us in.

A heavy man rose from behind his desk after stowing a roll of papers. "My name's General Asa Blunt. I am the commandant here. The warden, you might say. But we use a different title because this is a military prison."

Two stuffed eagles, an owl, and a red-tailed hawk hung from the walls with wings outstretched. A stuffed turkey perched on his roll-top desk. Fancy wallpaper covered the walls. Brass lamps. Fittings. Machines. It was real pretty-like, as if he had ornamented it just for himself to sit and muse upon. Another Yankee pastime, I guessed.

The man eyed us and pondered. "Now you are J.T. Martin, correct? And Jeremiah Clark? I understand you are here for Hiram Cantrell. Is that right? Mr. Clark, he is your father, I am to understand?"

"Grandfather, sir." I touched my hat and looked at my boots.

J.T. extended his hand. "I'm John T. Martin, sir." He looked around the office and said, "Quite a sportsman. Nice trophies. I like that red-tailed hawk!"

General Blunt smiled proudly.

J.T. whispered to me, "Shake the man's hand, Jeremiah. And quit looking down."

"I understand you helped bring Cantrell in, Mr. Martin. Thank you for that." The general pulled out a wanted poster and handed it to J.T. "You'll be handsomely rewarded."

J.T. nodded and grimaced.

"Marshal Upham is looking for you. Have you talked?"

"No, we just arrived from Missouri. Do you know what it's

concerning?"

"Just some work he had for you. Not quite sure. You'll have to see him. Upham's quite proud of you. I guess you know that."

The warden struck up a cigar and offered one to J.T. He puffed vigorously until a small cloud of white smoke arose. "Gentlemen, have you had the opportunity to tour my facilities? This is the most modern institution of its kind." He walked to a large drawing board with layers of thin papers. "I am here to make the United States Military Prison one step better. Take a look!" He bent over the plans, eyeing every detail with pride, shuffling through them and pointing out features of interest.

"You see, each cellhouse has three tiers. We stack them for efficiency, one row on top of another, three high. And we don't even have to open the padlocks to feed prisoners; there's a little slot to slide food through. That's innovation. It lets us house over forty prisoners per building! All we need is one guard with a riot gun on his perch." The general let out a long satisfying sigh.

"Very nice," J.T. said. "But we're here to—"

"You have heard the term: United States Disciplinary Barracks? USDB?"

"Uhhh, well—"

"Through an act of Congress no less, I alone have devised the finest new military prison system in the West. They'll talk about this institution for a hundred years." He traced his fingers over the detailed diagrams on the large papers. "Six million bricks," he said, tapping on two large diagrams with diagonal wings protruding from them. "These will be the new inmate cell blocks when my plan is fully implemented. I call it 'The Castle' or 'The DB'. Eight stories sitting on twelve acres of prime land overlooking the river. Hope to have it finished in twenty years. Or thirty if we get greedy."

"Anxious to get started then?" J.T. asked.

"There are some who think the whole plan should wait. Maybe until the start of the new century, they say. Or later. It's an ambitious plan, I admit."

The general leaned over the plans and traced his finger over the lines.

"We'll be completely self-sufficient. Look here." He pointed to the edge of the paper. "We'll make our own soap. And have fruit and vegetable farms. Potatoes, apples, even oats and wheat. Look at this turkey farm! And we'll bake a thousand loaves a day in this new bakery. Brooms are already for sale in Leavenworth City. All the factories are prisoner staffed. Just like one of those old-time castles back in England."

His aide smiled. "The stone wall around this thing will be twenty feet tall. We've got a twenty percent escape rate now, but this new wall will fix that. Takes a lot of men to raise a castle!"

The warden glared. "Thank you, sergeant. You are dismissed."

"Lot of labor, then?" J.T. asked. "Need quite a few prisoners for such a job."

The warden cocked an eye at J.T. "It just so happens there is a fresh new supply coming out of Arkansas, Tennessee, and Missouri. We're getting them, now that Fort Smith is overrun. Bloody Bill Anderson's old crew, mostly. And Quantrill. James and Younger gangs. You know the type. Mutinous characters, every one. They'll all hang eventually. But until then—"

He looked back at the plans with a twinkle.

"I know the type," J.T. said, sniffing a little. "Never quite got their fill of killing during the war, did they?" The warden smiled as J.T. elaborated. "Burning Lawrence wasn't enough. Sacking Fort Leavenworth and bushwhacking half the state of Kansas. Massacres all over Fayette County, Missouri. So, you bring 'em up here and let 'em bust rocks on the castle. Takes the fight right out of 'em, don't it?"

Both J.T. and the warden smiled. "Mr. Martin, I believe you understand exactly how this new era of reconstruction works! You are an intuitive individual; I can see that. Do you like this open territory we've got? You're a Northern man, I could tell right off. But I wonder if you might consider the open plains of the West as a settling place. A place for a challenging new career in the Department of Corrections. Care to work at the DB?" He beamed and puffed the stogie even more vigorously, letting out a new smile every so often and patting J.T. on the back with each glance.

J.T. stiffened. "Warden, I am here to see after the welfare of

Hiram Cantrell. And unless you have hard evidence, I am here to fetch him back to Missouri. I am sorry, but he is not your slave labor."

The warden's smile fell and wrinkles formed over his eyes. "Mr. Martin, I think you have the wrong idea. I am Cantrell's jailer. Pure and simple. Not his judge or jury." He paused confidently to examine the cigar tip. "And he is here on very serious allegations."

"What are the charges?" J.T. asked.

"That's the darnest thing," the warden said, lifting his nose. "There are none. Not as yet." He laid the cigar on a glass tray where it smoldered. "No charges whatsoever. Not that I've seen."

"Then you've got no right to hold him."

"Hold 'm as long as I like," the warden said, retrieving his cigar. "As long as he's under investigation, that is. And you know that could take months." He stooped over and eyed the plans again, and then looked back up at J.T. "Yep, takes a lot of men to raise a castle. Now you leave Hiram Cantrell to me, or one of these days he may just turn up guilty. Take my meaning?"

Chapter Eleven

WIDE CORRIDORS, REDBRICK FLOORS, tiny cells with flatiron doors and brass padlocks – row after row of tidy little spaces. Each with a bunk rack, a night jar and candle, and one chair, all exactly alike. Each corridor with seven cells, a potbelly stove for every two, and an open ditch for dumping night jars.

A truly modern cell block in every way.

That's what we found inside Fort Leavenworth prison the day we were finally permitted in. I cannot say it was dark and gloomy, but my skin prickled as we passed each iron-clad cell housing lonely and broken men. Every click of shoe leather, every tin cup on iron bars, and every lonely whistle reminded me of the reason for this awful place.

"We insist upon near silence here," the guard informed. He wore an indigo-blue federal frock coat just like the sergeants in the yard, a leather waist belt and cartridge box belt over the left shoulder, and stiff blue cap. "You may speak to one prisoner," he added. "But only one at a time. And your voice may not carry into the next cell. Boisterous and unruly visitors will be ejected from the institution."

The guard's heel plates clicked down the corridor at a measured pace. Uncle Olin, Buford, and me followed four or five paces back. J.T. stayed back to look some things up about some guy named Raines that Uncle Olin and him argued about. Plus, we weren't exactly sure what

Grandpa would say when he saw him. Cousin Buford received a blow across the hand whenever he insisted upon touching and counting each flatiron bar. Tap, tap, tap they went across the bars until a swift whack ended the obsessive behavior.

The guard turned to speak without breaking pace – twenty-eight inches per step from heel to heel at a rate of sixty steps per minute. Each heel landed precisely at the edge of every seventh brick, without looking.

"You are not to touch the cell doors or peer into them. You may not speak to prisoners you are not registered to visit, or offer them anything or receive anything from them. Do not make eye contact or attempt to signal prisoners or guards. Do not converse amongst yourselves, express amusement, interest, or alarm. No crying. No laughter. No coughing or sneezing. Do not emit bodily noises or crack your fingers. The consequence for such infractions will be ejection from the institution."

I whispered to Uncle Olin, "Mother would not like this place."

The soldier remarked, "Women are not permitted in the institution."

Click… click… click… the heel plates continued. Seven bricks per step.

Even Uncle Olin minded his manners.

We came up on a leather-covered sawhorse between cells. Four iron rings with leather thongs hung from each corner. Bloodstains splattered the contraption and a fair amount of brick under it.

"This is the old gray mare," the guard said, tapping his baton on its splattered covering. "Do not look at it or touch it. Do not discuss it with prisoners – its location, size, or color. You may not verbally describe the layout of the institution, cell blocks, routes or passages. You may not gossip or complain against the institution. The results of such activities will be ejection from the premises." He turned his attention from the old gray mare and continued down the brick corridor. Click, click, click.

A weapon cocked overhead. A guard appeared on a little wooden perch above us with a shotgun in hand. He glared down, and twisted the barrel just once for notice.

"That man is watching you," the guard reminded, glancing

upward. "He has orders to shoot first and sort out the details later. He has no superior and no other duties except to protect this single hallway. He cannot be charged with wrongful death while executing his duties."

The guard stopped in front of a cell door but remained facing down the corridor. He spun a quarter-turn on his left heel and proceeded six paces toward the door. A key clicked in the brass padlock and the three-foot wide flatiron door creaked open.

Grandpa looked up from the lower bunk.

"I will remain in this corridor for the duration of your half-hour visit. You will have one such visit per week – Saturday's only. During that time, only one member of your party may enter the cell at a time. The others will remain in front of me but no closer than six feet from the door. The cell door will remain locked while you are inside." He signaled one of us to enter.

Uncle Olin tapped me on the shoulder. "Go on, Jay. I'll watch Buford fer a spell. If he gets itchy I'll make him sit down and count bricks."

Cousin Buford sat down right off. "Count bricks," he said, looking down the long corridor. "Count bricks and don't get itchy. 11,657 bricks. Don't get itchy."

I poked my head inside. "Grandpa?"

"Have a seat, boy!" Grandpa said, smiling. Suddenly the world seemed right again; I felt I could stay here in this little brick cell forever. Grandpa was here, and that's all that mattered.

But that didn't last.

Heavy iron doors crashed in behind me. And then the tiny six-by-eight cell suddenly became a smothering tomb. I could not breathe. Two heavy iron bunks blocked movement to the left, leaving only a sliver of space next to a cold brick wall. Even the six-foot ceiling hung just inches overhead. I decided to sit but the little wooden stool had to be positioned parallel to the bunks for legroom, soon straining my neck to speak.

"I'm sorry; we don't spend a lot of time in here," Grandpa said, leaning on one elbow to face me. "It's mostly just for bunking." A weathered negro peered over the edge from the top bunk, but soon disappeared from view. He said nothing.

"I don't care, Grandpa. I just want to see you. Can you come home soon? Did they tell you when?" The black man sniffed loudly and settled in his bunk. A fine haze of dust filtered down over Grandpa's face as the negro found his position.

"When can I leave? Aw, tell me about your mother instead. Did you say she was poorly? How about the twins? Let's talk about back home, not this place."

"Yes, Mother is poorly. But the girls are fine. They don't know when to shut up sometimes so I smack them around a fair amount. Uncle Olin comes over almost every night for vittles, and he cuffs them up some too. But they still don't keep shut. Ma says they're getting shoes for Christmas, but I don't believe her. She's in a bad way and it's got so that Doc Dieter won't charge her no more. He just mumbles the same old Dutchy talk and bangs the door on his way out. 'Schmutzige Kinder don' t-sogar Versuch zum Säubern,' he says, or something like that. But I don't know what that means. Something about the kids, Ma says."

"It means the children aren't washing," Grandpa said. "That means Ma is real bad off. What's her ailment? Did the doc say?"

"Tired heart, he said. But it's only after the bankers and carpetbaggers come calling. It wears her plumb out and then she sleeps for a week. But then she's better, so I guess it's nothing."

"Now y'all know how da black man on dem plantation live," the negro said, without invitation. "Chillin's got no shoes. Dirty rags an rotten teeff. And can't so much as vote, even affa da law been passed. Sound like you all white folk ain't no betta off dem us. De devil's in da po house."

"Shut up, Thomas, you old woman. We got a private conversation down here."

"Humph." The black man rolled over and another cloud of dust filtered down.

"Hello, Thomas," I shouted upwards, and waved when the black man reappeared. "My name's Jeremiah Clark. Nice to meet you, sir."

"Sho iz a pleasure, likewise," the man said. He winked down at me. "Yessaw."

"Grandpa? Are you going to be hung, like they say?"

Grandpa laughed. "That's all a bunch of bellering. Jeremiah, some fellers like to stamp around like an old bull in the pasture. He's the biggest hunk o' beef on four hoofs, and every cow in the pasture knows it, and every other he-cow within bellering distance. It ain't nothin' but a big show. He paws the dirt and kicks up dust. And makes a spectacle. But that's jes his way. You've got to learn that about some fellers. They don't act much different than brutes. Figure that out, and you'll be better off."

I looked around the dank cell. "Yeah, but it's so bad in–"

"Jeremiah, the worst I've got here is missing my euchre night with the boys. I get hardtack and coffee every day, and mule steaks on the sabbath, and fine companionship with old Thomas up there. Sure, the hardtack gets a little weevil ridden, and the chicory grounds are used a dozen times but I'm used to that. Do you think old Braxton Bragg fed us any better? Sometimes during the war we only got rations every three days, and ate them in one day. Half the men were starving and deserted in the thousands. So this is high living, being fed every day!"

"But I still don't understand what you did." I leaned in and whispered, "Are you a Klansman, Grandpa?"

No answer.

"Because that's what they are saying. You rode with Nathan Bedford Forrest down in Pulaski, Tennessee after the war. And some other place in Arkansas."

"Son," Grandpa paused and rubbed his chin. "That's more than I want to get into just yet." He looked away. "It was chaos after the war. You have to understand that."

"Well, they say you're a killer. A night rider, and murderer of women and children. How am I supposed to understand that?"

Grandpa's hand shook. "Jeremiah, that's all just..." He sighed.

As I studied Grandpa, my eyes turned red. I could not stop the anger and hate and sadness and meanness – all mixed together in one big mess. Grandpa had not told me anything, and would not answer the questions. Everyone was saying he was a killer, and even he wouldn't deny it. It just made me so mad I wanted to yell.

"You know Sheriff Cletus was killt on account of you. When Uncle Olin and him went down to Fort Smith looking for you. Killed by a mess of bushwhackers."

"Oh, Jeremiah… I did not know that. I'm so sorry."

"Well, he was. All cuz they went looking for you. Down where you did them night rides. That's what they all said, anyways. You was a Klansman and a killer. And now they can't even find his bones. He's just dead."

My eyes burned as the hot words spilled out. "They say you killed so many men you had to come up here."

Grandpa placed his hand on mine. "Tain't true, son."

"Are you a Klansman, like they say?"

Thomas leaned over his bunk and peered down at Grandpa. He waited a minute. In that space of time not a sound could be heard. Not even Buford, who had been slapping bricks and sliding back and forth on his bottom.

Grandpa finally spoke. "Jeremiah, yer going to hear a lot of things if you stay. And when you hear them jes remember who I am – your granddaddy who loves you. The one who raised you. And fed you. And read scripture over you, and prayed for you. You'll understand everything else in time."

Grandpa tried to reach out, but could not. He just breathed a ragged sigh and peered into the wool bed sack above him.

Thomas shifted from Grandpa to me. I looked up and saw that he wanted to speak. To explain everything Grandpa could not. And calm every fear that raged within me. But he kept his tongue. His big dark eyes did not condemn me. They did not condemn Grandpa. He just nodded and rolled over.

"Okay, Grandpa," I said. And sniffed and wiped my eyes. And shook my head.

"Have you been reading your verses?" Grandpa finally asked.

"No, Grandpa. I've been gettin' up here. As fast as I could."

"Don't use that. Serving The Almighty only when He's giving you something isn't really serving at all, is it? Now I don't fault you, son. It just takes discipline, is all. But don't leave off your scripture readings on account of me."

"Time's up," the guard said, inserting a key into the lock. He opened the door and tugged my shirtsleeve. "Time's up, son. You can come back next week. One half hour a week. That's the rules."

Uncle Olin stepped up to the door. "But what about–"

"Step back into the corridor, sir," the guard growled and raised his firearm. "It's a half-hour visit, and the boy took up the whole time."

Uncle Olin cocked his head and set his jaw.

"I'll see you soon," Grandpa said, grasping my hand. "Read your scriptures and pray. That's your duty now. Everything in due time."

We headed back down the corridor, again at sixty paces a minute. Click... click... click... and I cried.

Chapter Twelve

"RECKON I'LL NEED A JUG of corn liquor and a month's leisure to warsh that memory out: worshipping at the altar of God with a Yankee devil," Uncle Olin announced.

Gleeful worshippers in fancy stitching and pressed suits spilled out into the churchyard along with us. Hats blew off and women shielded themselves against a hard northern wind. Winter would be on its heels. We all tightened down our coats. Uncle Olin shook out his long hair as he strode across the yard. Folks eyed him like a chicken-coop rat.

"Yankee devil?" J.T. asked, smiling and looking around. "Who would that be?"

Uncle Olin stared at him, and then went back to settling out his tangled mane. Week-old flakes of straw bedding flew into the wind as he rubbed deeply into the scalp. Nearby ladies fled the raunchy cloud and gentlemen leaned back to avoid contact.

"Straw? Don't you sleep in a bed?" I asked.

"Livery, some nights, when I come in late." He answered. "Like last night."

I shook my head.

"Hope my pards never get word o' this," Uncle Olin remarked. "Jay, you let slip one word back home, and I'll wrangle yer neck raw. Reckon I'm ruint for religion from here on out."

"Ruint for religion," Buford repeated. "Reckon I'm ruint for religion too. And I hates the Yankee Nation, and everything they does." He shook his hair like Uncle Olin. "I hates the Glorious Union, a drippin' with our blood."

"Will you shut up, Buford." I smacked the back of his head.

"Indeed, it was an experience I will write Father about," J.T. said, sidling up to Uncle Olin with a broad grin. "Worshipping alongside Johnny Reb. Yes, the nation's healed and all the rebels reconstructed, I'll report!" J.T. laughed and tried to put his arm around Uncle Olin like an old chum. But Uncle Olin shoved him in the chest. "We ain't that healed; now git that baggage wagon up here. I want some o' that grub Mother Thayer fixed up."

J.T. blinked. "But that's for your father, Olin. Up at the—"

"Don't care. I'm powerful hungry, right now. The Word of God does that. I'll eat a basket of that chicken myself. Hope she put in a few hoe cakes and some collard greens."

J.T. drew the wagon up into the street in front of the church yard. He put it on the opposite side, so the invalid and crippled could get to theirs. At least a tenth had pegged legs or wheeled chairs, or had lost an arm or an eye. Many carried ear trumpets. But they all seemed genuinely happy in life even if the war had taken a little from them. I soon realized it was not just southern men who had suffered for the cause.

But the nation was not healed.

With the wagon loaded, we headed for the prison. There was no visitation on the Sabbath but we still had baskets for Grandpa and Thomas which the guards would deliver for us. I noticed Uncle Olin raiding the chicken basket. I guess he needed it pretty bad, but I wondered if there would be any left for Grandpa. I pulled the baskets closer to me.

Uncle Olin yelled out from the back, in between bites, "You sweet on my sister, Yankee devil?"

J.T. didn't answer. He just tilted his head and gazed out at the blowing trees and smiled. I knew he was, because he always looked that way when her name came up in conversation. And he sometimes brought it up himself. But Mother wouldn't take up with no Yankee devil.

I was sure of that. Even if she had twirled on one foot and laughed and baked cookies.

But I had not seen her so happy in a good while.

The streets were almost empty except for folks heading home from church along the dusty avenue. A few bells rang for special occasions or late services. All the store windows read "CLOSED." Some signs dangling half-cockeyed, others prim and straight – the wind flicking them against dark windows. I guess it was right to honor God one day a week. But I wondered if He even knew or cared about me, or Grandpa sitting in that rotten little cell. Did Jesus know anything of pain? How could He, I thought. A million miles away in Heaven. But somehow that didn't seem right either. My old schoolmarm had read from the scriptures, "If I take the wings of the morning and dwell in the uttermost parts of the sea; even there shall thy hand lead me and thy right hand shall hold me." So I guess it don't matter how far away you are.

The old wagon bumped up the lonely avenue. Clunk, clunk, clunk went that back wheel.

Uncle Olin licked his fingers and studied my angry face.

"Jay… you miserable mutt. A boy yer age ought not have a care in the world. What's got into you?"

I just shrugged.

"I got just the treatment for a sour mug like that. Hot Jackets!" Uncle Olin announced, heartily. He had gotten enough of Grandpa's chicken and biscuits to brighten his eyes. And now I guess he wanted a little fun. "A game of Hot Jackets, just fer you, Jay!"

J.T. cocked his head. "What's that, Olin? Hot Jackets?"

"Pull the wagon off next to that little stand of brush, J.T. You'll like this!" The idea did sound enjoyable, something to run off the thoughts of prison, and Grandpa in that little brick cell, and Jesus not caring a lick about us, being a million miles away and all.

J.T. pulled Rosebud and Black Jack over and we all got out. Even Buford and I got a little excited at the idea, but J.T evidently had no notion of what he was in for. Didn't they play Hot Jackets up north? Uncle Olin pulled his Bowie knife from his boot and jumped into the brush like a wild Injun.

"What's he after?" J.T. asked. "Buried treasure?"

I smiled. "You'll see."

"You'll see," Buford repeated loudly. "Ooh, ooh! Hot Jackets! You'll see. Ruint for religion! You'll see!" he howled in delight, stamping and jumping up and down. Folks on the avenue turned to look at the shrieking boy.

Uncle Olin emerged from the thicket with four long green switches. Stout, but supple enough for a good game. We each took one.

"Hot Jackets! Hot Jackets! I'm ruint fer religion, nowww!" Buford shrieked, drawing more attention from passersby. Some stopped and stared.

"I don't understand," J.T. said, wrinkling up his nose. "What do we do?"

"Stand like this," Uncle Olin said, positioning J.T's back towards us. We all stood in a circle with our switches in hand, all facing in, except J.T. who faced out. "Just like that, Yankee devil. I'll learn you the game of Hot Jackets right off." Uncle Olin grinned like a rabid coon. "Yeah, just like that, Yankee devil."

J.T. lifted his hands in confusion. "Like this? With my back to you?"

"Yessir. Now take off your coat." As soon as he did, Uncle Olin hauled back and buried the switch into J.T's lower back, right in the fat above the buttocks.

"Ooow!" J.T. practically doubled backwards to absorb the blow.

Buford could hold himself back no longer and landed a switch on Uncle Olin's backside, just about the same place. Right in the tender fat. It landed just about the same time as mine. Uncle Olin went down and rolled for safety, but Buford and I landed three more stinging blows each – on his arms and legs. He howled in pain and delight.

J.T. finally got the idea and tried to get in on the fun but was not quick enough. Uncle Olin leaped up narrowly avoiding his switch. Whiff, whiff. Uncle Olin beat J.T's legs like a willful mule which sent him down again wailing in pain. "Ooow!" He yelped again.

That was five hits for Uncle Olin, and none for J.T.

"Not quick enough, Yankee devil!"

By this time, I had gotten six good licks into Cousin Buford. His aim was not always dead-on and his reactions a little slower than mine. Uncle Olin and I beat him mercilessly. But he got a few licks in. Beating a retard cousin offers a degree of satisfaction city-bred folk don't normally get. It was easy work and I liked it.

It took J.T. awhile, but he finally got it. He slashed and whipped me and Uncle Olin, and even landed six or eight lashes over Buford's back when it was turned. I saw the same satisfaction on his face.

Beating a retard boy is a rare pleasure.

Soon, we were all tangled up in a brawling cat-fight, every man for himself. Bloody switches fell on legs, backs, fingers, ears, necks – any exposed skin where a welt might form, or skin would break and get some blood flowing. That was the game. Pure and simple. Buford finally stood fixed, whipping over and over again in the same axe-swinging motion. He might have been slow, but his lashes ripped the skin just the same.

Zip, slash, whack, Buford's switch dug into arms and ears. "Ouch, gaah," J.T. cried out, laughing and crying at the same time. "Aaah! Buford, you die now!" he yelled, landing a brutal blow across his neck.

Buford didn't even turn.

Within five minutes, Uncle Olin fell to the ground exhausted. J.T. landed on top of him, their arms and legs tangled up, laughing and howling together, still the victim of Buford's brutal blows. Two former enemies, their blood and sweat now mingled together as they hooted and hollered with what little energy their guts allowed. I was next to fall from a slash to the face. Buford alone stood victorious, still flailing wildly and yelling "Hot Jackets! Hot Jackets! Ruint for religion, now!" at the top of his lungs. He finally stopped and looked down at the squirming heap under his frazzled switch. Bloody welts had already formed on my arms, neck, and ears.

I'd be marked for a month.

The game was over, and J.T. staggered up first. He lent a hand to me and Uncle Olin. We dusted ourselves off and soon learned of a crowd of churchgoers standing in disbelief around us. Ladies lifted white gloves to their mouths. Men and boys laughed and cheered. Old folks stamped off with disapproving words trailing skyward.

"Bravo!" a man shouted. "One man left standing! Bravo, lad!" He bowed to Buford and lifted his hand in victory. He walked him in front of the crowd, hands high.

Uncle Olin staggered up to the citizens with his best bushwhacker look, grasping his Bowie knife in one hand and the switch in the other. His face ran freely with blood and his eyes opened wide as a hoot owl's. A vicious backwoods look came over him as the curved blade came up next to his bloody ear. Then he became still as a dead man, peered deeply and slowly into the eyes of the single ladies, and then suddenly threw his other hand out. "Boo!" he shouted, and the ladies fell back with a start. Uncle Olin staggered back to us with a big laugh.

"Bravo! Bravo!" the man said again, and the crowd applauded. He held out some water. We all drank from the same canteen.

When J.T. and I finally quit laughing we started the wagon up the road again. I knew exactly where it led, but no longer feared it like before. Uncle Olin had cleared that up. We only needed to hand the baskets to the sergeant of the guard and head back to the hotel we now lived at. No need to wait. But it had been a task I could not bear until now.

I looked back and smiled at Uncle Olin.

He was my best friend.

The hotel was only a mile from the prison, and after delivery we parked in front. Uncle Olin jumped out before we set the brake.

"J.T, git these animals combed and stabled," he said. "I need some powders and a nap before I go out tonight. These mules need awful good care. Make sure you attend to them."

J.T. rolled his eyes and shook his head. "Anything for you, Olin. Enjoy your nap."

The hotel clerk in the lobby faced his key boxes stuffing mail into various slots, dashing from one to another, emptying a small letter box. Evidently the mail had come in yesterday and he hadn't gotten to all his tasks yet. No mail came on the Sabbath. It was a day of rest but not for this poor fellow. He raced back and forth from box to wooden box as quick as possible and then caught me out of the corner of his eye.

The clerk swung around with an armful of envelopes, dropping most across the desk. "Urgent telegram for you, Mister Clark. Looks like Randalls Flats. Got kin thereabouts? Ain't never been that far south, myself. Rebel territory, I heard. Ruffians and bushwhackers. Cut your throat just for lookin', they say."

Uncle Olin walked past bristling with revolvers and Bowie knives. The clerk eyed him and suddenly shut up about bushwhackers and such.

J.T. and I had been laughing about the game. I turned to the clerk. "Mail? Uh, yes. My mother and sisters live in Randalls Flats." Feeling lighthearted, I tried Uncle Olin's bushwhacker look on the clerk. "We're all border ruffians so don't mess with us."

"Official telegram," he stuttered, handing it over with a trembling hand. "Looks urgent."

"Open it up," J.T. said.

I slashed it open. "It's from Mother. She must have come into some money."

The neatly typed Wells Fargo letter read:

Carpetbaggers and scalawags. Stop.
Papers filed. Stop.
Farm lost. Stop.
Come when practicable. Stop.

My knees sunk.

"Oh, Jeremiah," J.T. said. "What are you going to do?"

"What are you going to do?" Buford repeated. "I'll beat you again, like I did. Remember? Remember how I beat you all?" But even Buford's smile turned to a frown.

I fell onto the circular upholstery. All the air went out of me, and the room paled.

"I… I know these men," I said. "Northern bankers and carpetbaggers. Taking everything in their sight. I hate them. They want Ma's farm real bad. Now that Grandpa's gone they figure they can get it."

The telegram fell to the floor. J.T. picked it up. "What can I—"

I turned my fierceness on J.T. "These are your people. Northern scum. Come to starve us out. Burn us out. Drive us out. Anything to get our possessions and heap them upon your own lusts. Can't you just leave us be? Don't you have property of your own? Do you need ours too to feel happy at night? I hate you all. You are cowards and thieves. You caused this," I screamed. The hotel clerk ran off. "I hate you, J.T. Get out before I kill you!"

"Ahem." A voice came from the corner of the room.

J.T. raised his hands. "Jeremiah, we've discussed this–"

"Shut up. I hate you. I'll kill every last one of you leaches."

"I know you're heartsick, right now. You've been through a lot. But–"

"Ahem." The voice sounded again.

We both turned to a table in the corner of the parlor. It was U.S. Marshal, Daniel P. Upham sitting right there with a big shotgun over his lap and a leg tossed up on a table. A mug of coffee steamed in his hands. His eyes looked as amicable toward J.T. as anyone could. He set down his coffee, and those same eyes steeled up for business.

"Kick that stray dog off your leg, J.T," he said, standing up. "I need you."

J.T. tilted an angry eye toward me. And then he turned to Upham. "I'm a might busy right now, Daniel. Is it important?"

Upham headed for the open door. "Come on, J.T. I've got a job for you."

Chapter Thirteen

Christmas, 1877

J.T. NEVER CAME BACK. And I cried almost every night afterward.

Mostly, I cried for Mother, and the trouble I knew she was in. But also because J.T. didn't come back and for what I had said to him. Maybe he just went back to work for Marshal Upham and would never come back. Especially after those awful things. Uncle Olin left for Randalls Flats, but only after a big fight to convince him to look in on Ma and find out what that telegram was about. He said he would, but I had to look after Buford because he wasn't taking the kid along. But I didn't want Buford tagging along everywhere I went either. He was getting into trouble and making people mad. I felt like smashing something.

The hotel had kicked us out on account of Uncle Olin coming in at all hours. That was not the type of behavior they wanted to be known for. So we were back at the rooming house.

On top of that, Buford and I had to share a bed, and he patted me on the head every night before we went to sleep. I wanted to push him out of bed. Every night, he fussed with his nightcap and refused to go to sleep without Uncle Olin. When is he coming back, he asked? Every night. And then when we finally settled in, he commenced to patting me on the head and saying, "Maybe you can get a cat, Jay. A big hairy cat that catches rats. Some don't catch rats, you know; they just lay next to the fire and sleep. But I like the ones that catch rats."

Will you just shut up and go to sleep!

Cousin Buford was a year older so I suppose he knew more about cats than me. But as far as I knew, they all chased rats. At least the ones on our farm. And the more rats they caught, the more cats there were. Grandpa just bagged up a passel of cats and whacked them on the head with a two-pound hammer when they got too numerous. On one occasion, a feral cat bit me right through the thumbnail. I knocked it on the head with a mallet and it quit biting real quick.

I didn't care much for cats; I just wanted to go see Grandpa and tell him what happened to Ma and about J.T. Maybe he'd know what to do. A half-hour a week was just not enough.

I prayed to Jesus. Maybe He'd know what to do, if He wasn't a million miles away.

Jesus said to play with them little girls at the rooming house. You like that little one with the button nose. Play with her; it'll take your mind off things. So I did. She liked to play.

My half-hour visit finally came up and I was glad to go alone. The house mother reluctantly took Buford into town for a haircut but said I had to pay the five cents. She said he probably needed a bath too, and that would be another five. She took Rosebud and the wagon. Uncle Olin had Black Jack, so I had to walk up the hill to the United States Military Prison – the disciplinary barracks or "The DB" as General Asa Blunt liked to call it. He sure wanted the Army to take on the new name. Plus, he liked his big plans and all the prisoners working for him.

After signing my name, a guard escorted me up the long corridor like a mechanical soldier. He stopped before the iron-laced cell door just like before.

"Cantrell," he said coldly. "Visitor. Out of your bunk right now. Front and center."

Grandpa stood up and smiled. "Merry Christmas, Jeremiah!"

Christmas in jail? How was that merry? But I answered the best I could. "Merry Christmas, Grandpa."

"Where's your entourage, son? You're all alone today. Important man like you."

He smiled again, but I just growled under my breath. "Where's your Uncle Olin and Cousin Buford?" he asked. "Leaving all the important business to you today?" I stepped into the cell with a frown. "How about your friend, J.T?" Grandpa asked.

I wondered if Grandpa even knew who J.T. was.

"He's gone." I looked around the tiny cell. It had shrunk since the last visit. "Two-hundred-and-sixteen bricks," I remembered Buford saying. "Twelve this way and eighteen that a-way." He was right; the floor of the tiny cell contained only two-hundred-and-sixteen lonely bricks. And every one scrubbed clean twice a week, plus the walls and ceiling.

Thomas lay in his bunk a foot below the ceiling, reading his Bible. From the Old Testament, I judged from his position in the tattered pages. Half were falling out and the others half-crooked.

I wondered how he had learned to read.

But I think I learned more Bible verses from Thomas than any of my old schoolmarms or church parsons. He liked to challenge me every time I visited. "Which book of the Bible does it say, I shall make you fishers of men?" he'd ask. And I'd have to tell him, or he acted all put out. It was kind-of fun, and Thomas and me became good friends.

But I was in no mood today.

"J.T. gone to town today?" Grandpa asked. "Helping you out?"

"No, he's gone for good," I said. "Gone. Already told you that. Don't you listen?"

Grandpa said nothing and there was a long pause.

"I don't know where he is," I finally said. "Marshal Upham came into the hotel last week and J.T. went off with him. I guess to catch more rebels. And hang them, like you." I glared at Grandpa.

"Aw, son—"

"Well, he did." My voice rose up. "What did you do anyways?" My eyes misted up again and my voice trembled with every word I hurled at him. "You don't tell me nothin'. Uncle Olin don't tell me nothin'. J.T. don't tell me nothin'. First he's here to look in on you, and then he just up and leaves with that marshal. Everybody's gone but me." I cried and wiped my face. Words began flying out before I had time to think.

"I even had to leave Ma and the twins. Nobody cares about her. Nobody cares about you but me, and I'm all alone in this terrible place. Grandpa, what did you do to get in here? Tell me right now or I'm leaving."

I could not stop the tears and messy nose, all coming at once like a mudslide.

"Now, son—"

"No. No more of that. Tell me straight. What did you do? Why are you in here?"

Thomas leaned over the top bunk. "Dat's no way ta talk. The Good Book sez, 'Honor thy fadda and thy mutta: that thy days may be long upon da land which da LORD THY GOD giveth thee.'"

"Well, I don't have a fadda, now do I, Thomas?" I said, throwing my hatred upward.

"You know what I means, boy."

Grandpa raised a finger. "It's alright, Thomas," He said. "He's got a right to know. I am not a sinless man. In here for a reason, I reckon."

"J.T. said you did those night rides down in Arkansas. Is that true?"

"Yes, that is true. But not like—"

"What about shooting them Yankee officers in the head?"

"Yes, but that was—"

"Are you a murderer of women and children, too?"

"Jeremiah…"

Guilt poured over me for abusing Grandpa. But that didn't make me stop. Waves of meanness and spite washed over me. I didn't even tell him about Mother's wire, and how she lost the farm and needed me back; I just wanted to see him suffer. And maybe I did want to see him hang. Maybe I wanted to hear that one wicked crime he had committed and make him pay for it. After all, if he wasn't up here Mother wouldn't be in the trouble she was in, and Uncle Olin wouldn't have to look in on her, and J.T. wouldn't have left me all alone, and I wouldn't have to look after Buford every hour of every day and put him to bed every night and listen to stories about cats and mice and such. Why couldn't everything just go back to normal?

It all just piled up like slab wood, and I could not get out from under it.

Hang… you guilty old man, I thought – accusing Grandpa a hundred times in my mind. And practically bawling it out with meanness.

"Did you terrorize negros and block polling places so they couldn't vote? Start one those good-old-boy rifle clubs? Law-and-order league, they talk about. Wear a white hood and cow horns?" The arrows just kept coming, but it didn't satisfy my rage.

"No. None of that. If you'll just simmer down, I'll tell you about Arkansas. It's not something I'm proud of, but it had to be done. There was no one else to do it."

"You tell 'm about them hearings?" Thomas asked.

"Well, that's another thang, Jeremiah. I've got a hearing coming up. Don't worry; it is not a trial, just some meetings with the judge. No hanging, just talk. But Marshal Upham will be there. And he'll be pitching his case and trying to convince the judge to try it. If he convinces the court there's enough evidence, they will proceed with a trial. I'll warn you, Jeremiah; even though it's just a hearing, it will be ugly. But I want you and Olin to be there. And you best have a layer of ox hide on. All your questions will be answered there."

"I don't know… Ma needs me."

Grandpa slumped. "I need you too."

"Okay. I guess I'll come."

"I doubt I'll have time for too much of Arkansas today. We only get a half hour. But what Upham said about Arkansas and Missoura is somewhat true. Like I said, there was work to do and precious few with the constitution for it. I'll explain later but right now I thought you should know about those night rides. Are you ready?" He leaned forward to wipe my face. "I love you, son. Are you sure you want to hear this?"

"I can manage, Grandpa. But you better not lie."

"Awright then." He smiled up at me. "Your uncle and I fought for the Confederacy. You know what that was, right? The Confederacy seceded from the Union and fought the Northerners for States Rights. And mostly because they invaded us without cause."

"Rights to do what?" Thomas asked, peering down over the iron rail.

"What?"

"You fought for rights to do what, Mr. Hiram?"

"Be quiet, Thomas. You know well-enough what. But you also know I'm no slaver, so be quiet up there, you old woman. Jeremiah, that's why they call us rebels and secesh. You heard them words?"

"Yes. They call me that too, and I wasn't even born until the last year of the war."

"Yes, well, after the war the slaves were legally freed. The Radicals in Washington did that. Republicans. You've heard of the thirteenth amendment to the Constitution? That's what did it."

"Do tell," Thomas said.

"Shut up, Thomas. The boy needs to know." Grandpa looked at me again. "That was all good and proper. Problem is, those same radicals wanted to try us Confederates as war criminals. Because of the rebellion and all the damage. Some wanted us hung as traitors. Others said land should be confiscated and given to freed slaves. And still others said the vote should be taken away until the matter was cleared up, or maybe forever. Nobody quite knew what to do with the rebels back then. You know... after the war was over. Hang 'em, punish them, or just let them go. Nobody knew. Of course, we all had to pledge allegiance to the Union, and not just once – every time a Union soldier crossed our path. We were outlaws, and they never let us forget it. So we swallowed the dog."

"I think we still are," I said. "Criminals and outlaws, that is."

Grandpa nodded. "Maybe... Rebel flags were gathered up and burned. Uniforms and weapons burned. Government men dragged out of office, and carpetbaggers and scalawags put in their places. All the governments were reconstructed with Northern men."

Grandpa looked at me. "Okay, so you got this?"

"Time's up," the guard hollered in.

"Silas, I ain't even just started. You goin' to be a hard-nose?"

"You know the rules."

"Yes, corporal. But as one high private to another, I'm asking for a few extra minutes with my grandson."

"Make it quick, Cantrell. I got a captain to report to. You know that."

Grandpa turned to me. "Jeremiah, the problem came with them land confiscations. Not ours, but the fellas I served with. And not just one or two land confiscations, a lot of them. Some of the radicals felt blacks should be repaid for their years of slavery with Southern land, and they set their sights on the planter class and anyone with property. But mostly slaveholders and politicians. The old Southern Cavaliers."

"You mean they took your land and gave it to the slaves?"

"Yes, to ex-slaves, that's right. It happened a lot under Johnson, even though the federal government never made such a law. Johnson hated Southern aristocrats and wanted them to pay. He even made them come to Washington for personal pardons so he could watch them beg. Thousands of them. And when things like this happened, he turned a blind eye. Rebels really paid for their sins under Johnson."

"I still don't understand. Did something bad happen in Arkansas? Uncle Olin mentioned Woodruff County. Did you do something?"

Grandpa looked up and breathed deeply. "Jeremiah, there wuz one bad night. First off, there were danged few of us rebels left after the war. But there were thousands of federals. And we weren't trying to fight 'em all, jes save a few of our neighbor's farms from illegal confiscation. That's why we rode at night, when they was half-asleep on guard mount, picketing farms they had taken."

"Which farm? Do I know it?"

"No, no. This was just over the border in Arkansas. Owned by a colonel yer uncle and me served under. You heard the name Raines? He was like my boss in the war. A colonel in the Confederate army."

Grandpa turned to the guard outside the cell. "Silas, you best keep shut of this, you understand?" The guard just wagged his head and nodded.

"Six or eight of us ragged rebels slipped in past them lazy federal pickets one night. A thousand acres is pretty hard to patrol, ya know."

"This was during the war?"

"No, no. This was a few years after. 1867, maybe? '68?"

"But you said Raines was your boss in the war."

114

"This was just his property. This was after the war."

"Oh."

"So we got by the pickets and close up to a cabin next to the main plantation house. It was lit, and we could see movement inside. Inside that cabin, that is."

Grandpa tried to remember. "We could see federals inside, and some of the boys got itchy to let loose the artillery."

"Soldiers inside the Raines cabin?"

Grandpa continued, "Yes… One of boys whispered to me, 'Shoot 'im Cantrell,'. 'Plug that Yankee invader right in the bread box. He ain't got no right on Raines' place. Plug 'im, 'for I do.' The shadows just keep moving from room to room, and I couldn't see a dern thing. 'Hit 'm. Hit 'm now,' the fella kept whispering in my ear. 'For ya lose the shot.'"

"Did you hit him?"

Grandpa ground his teeth and looked up with a quiver. "I did." He looked away.

"Good!" I said. "Whoever he was, he got what he—"

"No," Grandpa said.

"But he—"

"Next morning…" Grandpa's lip shook. "Next morning, it turned out to be the colonel's niece. She was—"

"Ohhh."

"Young girl, only fourteen years of age… Your age, Jeremiah. And it was me that done it." Grandpa sat quiet for a long time. Nobody moved, not even Thomas. He just lay there like a dead man. No pages flipped, no breathing, even the air stopped moving.

"I'm telling you this," Grandpa continued. "So you know that vigilantism is the devil's work. At first, you go off all self-righteous and then you wake up a man-killer. That practically ruint them night rides fer me. I'm a guilty man, Jeremiah. And whatever Upham's got cooked up, he's justified in bringing it."

"Did you get arrested? On account of that?"

"We was too quick. After that, Olin went home to Randalls Flats. I stayed in Arkansas. Us renegades stayed about two steps ahead of

Upham. Like jackrabbits in a thicket. But he hunted us vigorously through all of Tennessee and Arkansas. We recovered a quite few farms, illegally stolen from rebels Johnson wanted to punish. I guess that was the only recompense of the whole affair."

Grandpa sobbed and hung his head. "But that little girl…"

Chapter Fourteen

January, 1878

"MR. CLARK... SON, YOU'LL sit right there," a sergeant said, guiding me to a row of wooden benches near the front of the courtroom. "It's the closest you're allowed to be, and you'll see and hear everything. Your grandfather will come through that door in just a few minutes. Some other men will arrive and then you'll see the judge come through that other door. That's when you'll know the hearing is about to commence. Any questions?"

Of course; I had a thousand questions. Why did we have to be here? Couldn't the Yankees just leave us be? Was Grandpa a bad man? What would Mother do if he was hung? Was Uncle Olin looking in on her or drinking barleycorn whiskey with his pals? Did my sisters get shoes for Christmas? Did Ma have enough food? Did she really lose the farm like the telegram said?

Did Patricia remember me? Or did she find another beau to sit under the oak trees with? Would she cook prairie hens and rice for him? Did he have rotten teeth or good ones like me? Was it okay to play games with the little rooming house girl and not tell Patricia?

And a hundred more. And a hundred more after that.

I looked up at the sergeant. "Do you think Grandpa will come home today? After he sees the judge? Should I fetch the mules up?"

"Ahh, no. This is a hearing to learn more about the alleged crime, and decide if a trial is to be set, and when that trial might occur. And this is just the first. There will be others. If there is insufficient evidence to warrant a trial then your grandfather will be free."

"So, maybe next week?"

"No..." The sergeant looked up. "This will take time. Figure next year some time. Judge Pennypacker is thorough."

The breath went out of me right then. Next year? It was only January.

I could not see straight. I forgot to breathe and it caught in my chest. Every sound from the busy room crashed in on me with pitiless disregard. I could not even sit up straight.

Next year? How could that be?

The sergeant bent down and took my hand. "It's going to be okay. If you want, I'll sit with you. My captain won't mind." He patted my hand. But that didn't help. It shook and I wanted to hit something, anything, so he rubbed my hand and smiled. "Yeah, I'll be right here. We'll watch together."

Tears started down my cheeks and would not stop.

Out the window a gristmill squeaked as it turned, and a big clunk came from each turn of the millstone. I stared at it and tried to breathe. The sergeant laid an arm over my shoulder and rubbed it.

Clunk. Clunk. Clunk went the millstone.

And then everything happened so fast I couldn't get it all. Just like the sergeant said, Grandpa came in followed by the U.S. Marshal, a few others and then finally the judge. His gavel slammed down and he immediately spoke. No one but me and the sergeant sat on the benches. No J.T. No Uncle Olin or Buford. A few minutes of legal talk passed, but I didn't get any of it.

The judge finally turned to U.S. Marshal Upham. "I understand you have a case for me. Mr. Hiram Cantrell, a former sergeant of the Confederate States of America, uhh... if such an organization ever legally existed in these United States. And you allege the crime of murder?"

"Yes, Your Honor. If you'll just cast one good look at the accused—"

"Yes, yes. I am certain I can deduce your entire case with just a few good looks. But unfortunately for you, I'll require proof of everything you allege today." The judge peeked over his papers at Marshal Upham. "Evidence, Mr. Upham. All we want today is evidence and witnesses. You do have evidence, Mr. Upham?"

"Oh, yes, Your Honor." Upham lifted a stack of paper from his table. "In these documents, you'll find enough—"

"Yes, okay." He flicked his finger and the papers fell.

Upham grimaced. "We're calling for the sentence of hanging for these heinous crimes, Your Honor."

"Mr. Upham, I'll be invoking the presence of The Almighty at these meetings. If He has no objection to hanging this man then I will have nothing further to say. But if He does object, I doubt you'll find a judge in the whole county capable to the task."

Upham rolled his eyes and rubbed his mouth. "Judge Parker never…"

The judge looked askance. "Something further to add, Marshal?"

"Nothing, Your Honor." He just wrinkled his nose.

The judge prayed. His voice calmly invoked the God of Heaven to direct the councils of men and execute justice. He then lifted his eyes and turned to the men at his side.

After another spell of legal talk, Marshal Upham spent an hour telling how Grandpa had traveled up and down the Kansas border during the war ambushing this captain, and that colonel, and such-and-such man on a horse at such-and-such distances. Or sneaking into federal camps dressed as a sutler and dispatching the ranking officer with a belly gun and then skedaddling out like a coward. It seemed like Grandpa was the only one shooting anybody during the war. In every town from Dan to Beersheba, Grandpa had shot or stabbed someone of notability. And all out of the meanness of his evil heart.

Brevet Major Dunstan at five hundred yards with a sharpshooter's rifle.

Colonel Billings in the heart with a butcher knife.

Lieutenant Colonel Rangoon with a boot pistol.

Colonel Thomas Ashton while eating breakfast with five shots from a revolver.

Captain, Major, Colonel, Lieutenant... It all ran together, each with its own short stack of paper passed from one side of the desk to the other. And each followed by a nod from the judge, and a little flick of the finger. Clunk after clunk of the gristmill, and grandpa didn't even open his mouth. He just let the marshal accuse him. Did he know how bad that looked?

"Okay, okay, Mr. Upham. I think I take your point. You certainly have your paperwork. That's an impressive stack." The judge leaned over for a drink of water. "For now, let's focus on your best case. I'd like to get into the details and see where you're headed. Remember, I need to justify a trial. No evidence, no trial."

The marshal shuffled his papers again. He set aside two documents and pushed the rest into his satchel. "This one," Upham said. "Kansas. The Baxter Springs Massacre of 1863, just outside the old earthen Fort Blair. Some call it the Fort Baxter Massacre. It's one-in-the-same. An act of butchery and mayhem."

"A war-time murder? Umm... I'm not keen on–"

The marshal pointed to the courtroom door. "May I call a witness, Your Honor?"

"By all means."

The marshal whispered, and one of his aides headed for the door. A new man returned. The man leaned on a cane, working to get his wooden leg around the chairs and furniture. One arm hung limp. He was about Grandpa's age. With some work, he took a seat next to Marshal Upham, detached the wooden implement with his good arm and laid it on the table next to him.

It clunked like the millstone.

The marshal turned to the man. "Sir, would you please tell the court your name."

"Jesse Smith."

"Mr. Smith, you were a private in the Union army in 1863, correct?"

"Yessir."

"And did you witness atrocities at Fort Blair at that time?"

"I did." The man tried not to look at Grandpa, but he couldn't stop. With every side-look, his shaking head and batting eyes gave him up. It was the look of bitterness – anger stored up for a good long time I guessed. I could tell he was going to say something bad. And Marshal Upham wanted him to. This man was like a weapon in Upham's hands. Like a boot pistol or revolver. And that weapon was about to go off in Grandpa's direction.

"I understand you were discharged after your service at Fort Blair, in 1863."

"On account of my injuries," the man said, stealing another sideways glance at Grandpa.

"What were those injuries?" Upham prompted.

The man breathed deeply and hung his head. "I was shot five times and suffered four broken ribs. Lost my…" He sniffled, hung his head again and then followed the ceiling line while wiping his eyes. "Lost my leg on account of that shooting. They… they took it off." He tried to clear his eyes again. "Took it off to stop gangrene from–"

Judge Pennypacker sighed, "I'm sorry to hear that, Mr. Smith. That is a tragedy, indeed. It was the misfortune of so many during the war. But…" He turned to Marshal Upham. "But how does your story relate to this case? We're here to gather testimony and evidence to warrant a trial for the charge of murder."

"Understood," Upham nodded.

"But this man is not dead."

Upham turned to the man. "Mr. Smith, please tell the Court what you saw on October 6, 1863 just outside of Fort Blair on the morning of your injuries."

The man wiped his face and spoke. But just before, he took one good look at Grandpa. It was a bad one. "I was in a small detachment of soldiers escorting General James Blunt to Fort Smith, Arkansas. We were just out of Fort Blair, Kansas at the time. There must have been about a hundred soldiers – half of them white, the other half negroid, and a little brass band with a half-dozen drummer boys and fifers. Those boys couldn't have been over twelve or fourteen. They played cadence on the march, you know."

"And Quantrill's guerillas attacked," Upham interrupted. "Is that right?"

"That's right. But I didn't know that at the time. I just knew we were over-matched maybe by as much as two to one. Regular army? Infantry? No, there must have been two-hundred partisans on horseback. Every one with a half-dozen pistols in their belts and screaming like wild Injuns."

"What did you do?" Upham asked.

"We gave up. There were just too many. Plus, the general told us that if we surrendered without a fight we'd be paroled and sent home because the rebels couldn't take no prisoners. They didn't have the men to guard us like the armies of the North."

"So you surrendered?"

"Yes." The man's chin began to quake. "We surrendered."

"Were you paroled and sent home like the general promised? Or taken prisoner?"

"Neither. Quantrill screamed like a madman, riding up and down the column and swearing every vile oath he could recite. His horse rammed into men, knocking them to the ground. Other men in his crew did the same."

The man looked over at Grandpa again, this time like he wanted to grab him by the hair. "The guerillas taunted and molested our men, especially the negro soldiers. But I never saw a soldier quail. So they taunted and called them invaders, man-killers, and scalpers. 'We're going to hang you all,' Quantrill screamed. 'And shoot you in the back when we're done. And then hang you again. You're all killers and condemned to die,' he screamed, brandishing his revolver and galloping up and down the column. Then I saw men loose themselves. Some bawled. Some begged for their lives. But not a man warranted the actions that came next."

"What came next?" Upham asked. He seemed to work this man like a fanciful machine. He'd pull a lever and out came a ration of pent-up anger. Pull another lever and produce a whole new batch. It was like Upham planned it this way.

"What came next?" Upham urged again, forcefully.

122

"I don't even know if I can say it. I don't regularly speak of this," the man said. He sat quiet for a minute and then opened his mouth. "They just started shooting. From their horses, mostly. Every man…" He cleared his nose. "Every man got a bullet in the back of the head while they stood there with their hands up. Every man. Me included."

"But you're not dead," the judge insisted, confused and impatient.

"I never lost consciousness. Don't know why, but I didn't. I could feel the bullet slam into the back of my head, but it didn't kill me. Felt like a horse kick but no worse. I've had those before. I just fell down and I saw the whole affair from where I lay."

I whispered to the sergeant, asking him if that was possible, and if he thought the man was lying.

"It all depends on how the ball hits," the sergeant whispered back. "The angle, that is. It could glance off. Or it could follow the scalp around to the other side of the head and come out there. Under the skin, that is. But if it doesn't smash the skull bone, you'll probably live. I've heard of that. Bullets don't always go straight in. Sometimes they just skip off at an angle."

Marshal Upham pointed over at Grandpa. "Think hard, Mr. Smith. Did you remember this man during the incident?"

"I don't have to think hard," he said, glaring at Grandpa. "I know exactly what he did. But I don't want to say…" The corners of the man's mouth turned down, and he stared up at the ceiling, not offering a word. He was about to cry.

"Don't be embarrassed," the judge said. "We need your full testimony."

The judge addressed Upham with a frown. "Although, I sure wish I knew where this line of questioning was leading."

The man thought for a while and shifted in his seat, and then grunted. "Like I said, Your Honor, I don't often speak of this." He paused. "The rebels got down off their horses after they had shot the men. Some men were still twitching in their death struggles but most were dead. But the rebels didn't stop there. They put five or six more shots into every man. Some got two or more in the head. Even those twelve-year-old drummer boys. The first ball hit me in the back of the head, like I said. And the next four went into my neck, chest, leg, and hand." He twisted his head around to reveal a wound in his neck.

"The shots came from this man?" Marshal Upham said, pointing at Grandpa. "The ones that hit you came from him?"

"He has to be lying now, right?" I whispered. "Nobody can get shot five times and still live, right?"

The sergeant shrugged. "I don't know. But I think you can. Again, it just depends on where and how the bullets hit you. If they don't hit a lung or heart or an artery, then maybe... But look at his eyes." The sergeant nodded at the man. "I think he's telling the truth."

The man glared at Grandpa. "Yes, the shots came from him. All five. But there's more." The man breathed deeply. "I was pretty bad off. Blood was running down my ear. It also ran out my leg from another wound and collected in my boot. My right hand was completely shattered, and I couldn't move at all. That's when this man," He pointed at Grandpa. "Turned my body over with his boot heal and smashed my face into the dirt."

"Wait, wait, wait," the judge said. "You were lying on the ground on your back, and he flipped you over onto your stomach?"

"Yes. He didn't know I was still alive. After stomping on the back of my head, he jumped up onto my back and laughed. When he did, all the other rebels laughed and mocked. Some of them did the same. Then this man danced... danced a jig on my back while the other rebels hooted and shot off their guns and burned and scalped the dead soldiers."

The judge looked ill.

The man tried to say more but he cried too hard and got too embarrassed to even sit there. He kept throwing his head around like he wanted to leave the room and not have everyone look at him anymore. Nobody spoke.

The judge finally collected his wits and nodded at Grandpa.
"Is this true, Mr. Cantrell? A jig?"
Grandpa breathed deeply. "Wall, Your Honor. It's true, but—"
"No buts. Just the truth."
"I know this ain't going to sound right, yer Honor," Grandpa

continued with his forehead wrinkled in thought. "But we jes gave like they gave us. It wuz all back and forth, up and down the border with Kansas. You know them Kansas Red Legs was just as bad. Done the same things. It was an eye for an eye all during the war. They didn't take no prisoners neither – shot rebels in the back or hung 'em. And then scalped and left them on the roadside for citizens to see. Back then, there weren't no quarter – not for Yankees or bushwhackers, leastwise not in Missoura. It was the black flag for everybody. We wuz different than back East. You got to know that."

"I do know, Mr. Cantrell. But still… You danced on a dead man's back?"

The judge looked like he could vomit. But he turned to Upham and cleared his craw. "I'm sorry, but we can't try every rebel that committed atrocities against the Union."

"They tried Henry Wirz," Upham retorted. "The Butcher of Andersonville. A Confederate officer. Thirteen thousand men passed into eternity in his filthy prison. Tried him right there in Washington D.C. after the war. Just like this one sitting here before us."

"Yes, I know. But I'm sorry, Mr. Upham. We're not trying ex-Confederates in this courtroom. I'm sorry; no war-crimes."

Upham shrugged.

Judge Pennypacker shook his head. "The most I see is a hardened border ruffian with a penchant for blood-thirstiness. A little cold for my liking but just doing his duty for the Southern cause."

Upham smiled. "Good. That's all I was aiming for."

"Huh?" The judge leaned in. "I fail to see your—"

"Your Honor, do you now freely admit that this man is a natural killer? A talented one at that? Did you detect a single ounce of remorse in his statements? One ounce of fear and trembling to the Almighty God before whom he sits so arrogantly? No sir, you did not. He says federals did the same to rebels, but that's not remorse. It's an excuse. He listened to the whole story without a tear, without so much as a blink. Your Honor, that's the sure sign of a killer. And you witnessed it right here in your own courtroom. Do you not admit as much?"

The judge turned hot. "Do you take me for a fool, Mr. Upham?

Of course I saw it. But I won't convict a man on cold emotion alone. I'll grant you, his former occupation runs a little icy for my tastes, but to hang the man on that alone? For what happened during a terrible war where atrocities where committed on both sides? I will not."

"Not asking you to. It took me a long time to catch this man, and I just wanted you to know the sort he is. That's all."

"Well that has to be the weakest case I have ever heard," the judge shouted. He threw up his hands.

"That's not my case. Baxter Springs don't matter one bit. Toss it all out. That is not the case at all."

The judge shook his head. "Well then what have we been doing for the last two hours? Playing mumblety-peg with this man's life? You're trying my patience, Mr. Upham. Get to the point or get out!"

"Okay, here it is. When I bring a man to Judge Parker down in Fort Smith, he just looks him over real good. Real, real good. Looks him in the eye. Watches his actions and movements. Asks a few hard questions, and then he knows… knows the man is a born-killer. Takes about twenty minutes. A month later the man is hung. Next case."

"Yes? And your point, for Heaven's sake?"

"Today, we just took a little longer getting there."

Chapter Fifteen

UNCLE OLIN BUSTED INTO the rooming house parlor where J.T. and I were talking. J.T. had come back and wanted to explain things. He hadn't joined back up with Upham like I thought. Sure, he had a job to do, but it wasn't what I thought. And now he was back. But he didn't get much of a chance to explain because Uncle Olin came in hollering like a mountain man, riling everybody up.

"Bears!" he hollered, shaking men by the shoulders and racing from man to man, pointing out the windows. "A pack of wild bears out of the mountains! They're a comin' up the street right now. Already mauled and killt a mess a school kids and the ugliest, humpbacked schoolmarm I ever opened eyelids to. Git yer guns, boys! Pistols, rifles, knives, whatever you got. Let's git out thar and kill 'em off!"

Men rose to their feet and pressed against the windows for a skeptical look. Sure enough, a knot of citizens ran past. Women shrieked and gathered up their younguns. J.T. grabbed his pistol from his knapsack and started for the door.

Uncle Olin snatched him by the collar. "Hang on there, Yankee Doodle." Uncle Olin hummed a little Dixie and waited for the men to leave. Then he busted out laughing and staggered around, knocking over chairs and pitchers of flowers. After a good belly-laugh he cleared his tears and pointed up at J.T.

"There ain't no bears, you fool. Put yer little girl gun away 'for ya hurt yerself. But I still want a little talk with you. So don't run off."

By now, all the men, women, and children had gone down the street and the parlor was empty and quiet. Uncle Olin staggered over and flopped down across from me and grinned as wide as any jaw bone allowed. "Glad to see yer ol' Uncle Olin, Jay? Figured you'd a missed me terrible bad." He laughed and settled into the upholstery, adjusting his hat and sliding off his boots. Two pistols and a dried snake skin fell out. He didn't wear socks, and his feet were practically as black as a pair of dead lizards.

"So, there's no bears?" I asked, dumbfounded at the alarm he had just raised.

J.T. shook his head. "What makes you do such things, Olin?"

Uncle Olin looked confused. "Rye whiskey?"

"What do you suppose those men are going to say when they come back?"

Uncle Olin puzzled for a spell. "Reckon if I got to make another trip up here to Yankeedom, I'll just as well brang a little excitement in with me."

"That doesn't make any sense at all, Olin. Just what do you—"

He snickered and glanced around with his neck bowed up. "I emptied a bushel of hair clippings and hog's blood down at the end of Front Street 'for I rode in. Them fellers'll be in such a state of vexation, they'll be out all night with pitchforks and lanterns. By that time, I'll be down at the Red Lion Inn doing some awful drankin' and sparkin' the wrought-up females." He slapped a knee and rolled off the upholstery.

J.T. shook his head. "So that's your family tree, Jeremiah?"

Uncle Olin stood up and grabbed J.T. by the neck. "Aw, don't be so stiff, Yankee Doodle. Come down to the pub with me tonight and I'll learn ya some fun. Maybe a little bare-knuckle fisticuffs?"

J.T rolled his eyes.

"Heard some stuff about you when I was down in Randalls Flats," Uncle Olin said. "Me and the boys done some checkin' up on you. Let's go on down to the pub and talk her over. Leave Jay here."

"Sorry, Olin. We've got other matters to discuss."

Uncle Olin's eyes floated upward and his tongue fell out over his lip. Then he shook his head like a retard and said, "Okay, Okay. What's so all-fired superior than a night of marauding bears and fisticuffs?"

"How's Ma?" I asked, because I knew Uncle Olin was just trying to get on J.T.'s nerves, and danged-near succeeding at it. "Did you straighten everything out with them bankers? Her telegram—"

"She'll be along, Jay. Coming up the road from Randalls Flats, as we speak."

"Randalls Flats? But what about the—"

"Yep, her and two varmintty brats. Comin' in by the wagon-load. Be here 'for that clock ticks twelve." He nodded upward without turning his head. "And..." He smiled and batted his eyes like a burlesque dancer, "She's got another little 'ol gal in that wagon with her. And I ain't talking about no axe-swingin' Mrs. Branson neither. You know exactly what I'm talkin' about, Jay, you rascally little polecat." He shoved me in the shoulder and batted his big green eyes again.

My face turned so hot I had to get up and look out the window for bears. Otherwise Uncle Olin would lay it on even thicker, and I wasn't in the mood.

But J.T. brightened up at the news. "It'll be good for Mrs. Clark to see her father," he said, rubbing his hands together. "I'll escort her over there myself, this afternoon. That is, if she has the constitution to enter a place like the U.S. Military Prison."

The last I heard, they didn't allow women.

It wasn't five minutes later that Mother and the twins came through that hotel door toting a thick molasses pie. With Patricia following hard after, in a little yellow cotton dress.

"Ma!" I yelled out, running over to fall on her neck. "Oh, Mother, I missed you real bad. I've been here all by myself."

The twins ran up. "Look! Jeremiah's a dandy in fancy duds!" They were referring to a new shirt, cravat, and derby hat J.T. told me to buy.

The girls skipped around and sang, "Hoity-toity, dandy-doity. Hoity-toity, dandy-doity." That is, until I turned them upside down and shook the devil out of them.

I only bought the derby because J.T. said a person can tell everything he needs to know about a man from his headgear. Uncle Olin's old slouch hat looked like a dried-out cow stomach stretched over a burlap sack, so maybe J.T. was right. Heck, the whole outfit came to only $2.32, which hardly set me apart as a dandy, but the girls sure giggled at it. I still had the same old brown and gray jean-cloth trousers, such as they were, but the girls seemed to miss those and focused on the blocked hat and factory-made shirt. Even Mother examined the machine stitching which her tight hand-stitches still could not compare to. She just clucked and flicked it away. But still, I wasn't no dandy.

Patricia jumped up and pressed against us, hugging and scooting around. "Jeremiah, I'm fourteen now! Isn't it grand?" She lifted her hands and danced around, and then looked at Ma. "Now that I'm full-grown, Mama says maybe Jeremiah and me can—"

Ma grabbed me by the shoulder and walked me straight to the upholstery. "We got some awful happnen's down home, Jeremiah. Don't mean to fret you, but it's all coming apart at the seams." J.T. sat next to her. Uncle Olin, Patricia, and the twins gathered around.

Mother spent the next hour in a perfect state of aggravation while Patricia dished up molasses pie and fetched drinking cups and a canteen, and some rags to lay over our laps. All eyes fixed on Mother with her news from home. Even the house mother's little girls edged in for news. The little one took my hand and giggled. She didn't know about Patricia.

Mrs. Branson had been arrested for firing off her eight-gauge at them county commissioners and that dutchy politician from up North. They wasn't even dead, but she still had to spend thirty days in lockup because she didn't have bail. Then the newspaper took the part of the bankers and slandered Mrs. Branson as a gun-totin' yahoo. That made it even harder for her to plead her case before the judge. But he finally sided with her and dropped the charges after Mrs. Branson railroaded him for treatin' those southern soldier boys the way he did. The little shooting affair probably saved us from debtor's prison on account of the new sheriff being afraid to come around. But still, she had been in jail for thirty days and that made things hard for Patricia. But she managed by praying and reciting her scriptures every afternoon.

Mother took breath, and continued.

Five more farms had gone under on account of back taxes. Ever since the carpetbaggers came in to speculate on land, the taxes went to the moon. More speculators came in to top them, and soon the whole county was up for auction. And of course, folks didn't take kindly to that – but it mostly put off the good ol' boys of Uncle Olin's type who spent their days lingering about the mercantiles and their nights terrorizing northerners from whence this whole trouble had originated. 'Course there weren't no law against that, she said. But still, Ma also said there were a fair number of mysterious new crimes in Jackson County, and that she had a pretty good idea who the perpetrators were. But she wasn't about to help the likes of them carpetbaggers and scalawags who was running her off her great-granddaddy's homestead neither. You had to back yer kin.

Uncle Olin nodded and put in, "It's a regular slaughterhouse down there. Just about as bad as '68. Not so much as a safe corner to sit in. So I come back up here for some peace and quiet." He looked at Ma. "Got practically run out of my own house."

Mother edged in and took the conversation right back.

Men with lanterns had been skulking about and rifling through the farmhouse. She and the twins had to stay with Uncle Olin in Randalls Flats. Grandpa's old three-band rifle from the war was missing. All his rebel flags and uniforms, gone. His letters and diary, and some old letters from after the war, gone. His steamer truck was practically empty – everything of value carried off. And it wasn't on account of no rats, neither. Or maybe it was rats, but not the scrawny four-legged type, Ma said.

"What would they want with that old stuff from Grandpa's trunk?" I asked.

Mother shrugged, but J.T. spoke up. "They're reinforcing their case against Hiram. D.P. Upham, I calculate… Collecting information they can use against him. That was one of the things I wanted to talk to you about." He paused. "Before Olin's bears came through."

"Bears?" Ma asked.

J.T. rolled his eyes. "I'll explain later." He reached down and touched her hand, earning him a smile and squeeze. "We could stroll the avenue later. Do you have a parasol?"

Then his eyes narrowed. "But I think we'll see some new information at those hearings."

Mother took on a shiver. J.T. removed his frock and laid it over her shoulders and smiled.

"Like what?" Ma asked, smiling again at him. "I know what the folks back home are a sayin' about Pa – and it ain't pretty. They're all talking. Like that he rode with some Raines fellow, and was involved in a shooting down in Woodruff County, Arkansas back in '67 or '68. I don't hold stock in any of that talk. That is, if I know my own Pa. I remember him bein' down there but I never heard a peep of what happened or what he even went down there fer. That was three-hundred miles from our house, down near Little Rock. We just didn't ask no questions."

J.T. waved it off. "Probably didn't have much to do with this case anyhow. I don't believe Upham will even go into that incident. I think he's got other plans, which is what I wanted to discuss with Jeremiah."

"I know what happened in Woodruff County," Uncle Olin spoke up, with one eye pinned on J.T. But at least he had put his boots back on so his feet didn't stink so much. "I was there with Pa. We rode with Colonel Raines during the war. And…"

Uncle Olin stopped and stared at J.T. again. "Turns out, you know old Colonel Raines after all, now ain't that right, J.T.? I learnt that when I was back in Jackson County lookin' in on Mary. Me and the boys, we checked up on—"¬¬

J.T. edged in closer. "You're in the weeds, Olin. Forget Raines. Forget Woodruff County altogether. I think your Pa would rather see his daughter and grandchildren while they're here. Maybe we should go up to the prison instead." He nodded and motioned for the door.

"That's a guilty look, Yankee Doodle." Uncle Olin said, still eying J.T. "Yeah, I reckon you do know the ol' colonel. Rainesy, Dainesy. Yessir. Seems you and Upham struck a deal with the rebel Eli Raines.

Leastwise, that's how I heard it around the pickle barrel."

J.T. didn't answer.

"Who's Eli Raines?" I asked. "Grandpa mentioned him."

Uncle Olin turned to me and then nudged J.T. in the ribs. "Old Eli Raines hated D.P. Upham real bad, didn't he, Yankee Doodle? 'Course that was back when D.P. riled up them militia wars agin the good ol' rebel boys who was protecting their homes and right to vote. All riled up. Got them Klansmen stalking ol' D.P.'s house every night – killing pigs in his yard, burning crosses, chucking rocks and bottles through windows… all that."

Uncle Olin wagged his head and snickered. His eyes lifted back up to J.T., who said nothing.

"You know this story, don't ya, J.T?"

"You're in the weeds, Olin."

"Weeds? Nah! Turns out, Upham had a thousand troops and he wouldn't abide ruffians and night riders in his county. They say Upham slit the throats of two ol' Klan boys right there in his own dooryard. He is one rough character, I know that. But they say–"

"Olin, I just think you need to let Raines go before you open up some wrong doors. You're going to get your Pa into more trouble than he's already in."

"Now how could that happen? He's already in jail for the worst crime they got. They're going to find out what they find out. But you know somethin', don't ya Yankee Doodle?"

J.T. shook his head uneasily. "I'm trying to help Hiram. Can't you see that?"

"Was ya going to tell us about the Raines deal? Or just slide it up under the carpeting?" Uncle Olin tip-toed over to the edge of the carpet and lifted it with his thumb and finger. He peeked under for effect. And then back at us. His eyes popped back and forth between J.T and that carpet corner. "In fact, it seems there's a little more to the story, or so I heard."

Uncle Olin and J.T. argued about Eli Raines for two hours, so we never did get to see Grandpa. Patricia and I got tired of it and went outside to hold hands. At least we didn't have to listen to Uncle Olin. It wasn't that I didn't care about Grandpa or Eli Raines or D.P. Upham or Woodruff County. It was just that my mind was too mixed up to care. And I wanted another peek at Patricia's yellow dress without Ma glaring at me. Plus, she was fourteen now, and that made a big difference.

We sat outside by a flower box and talked. And held hands.

Miss Patricia handed me an envelope.

"Have you read this?" I asked.

"No, it's from my ma. To you only."

I opened the note and read silently. "Any further than her wrist, and you'll be looking down a breech-loader when I ketch up with you."

"What does it say?" Patricia asked with interest, bouncing on the bench seat. "I like secret notes!"

I smiled. "She says I'm her favorite, and we should hold hands all day." I slipped the note into my pocket and eyed the dress again.

All them same cravings came back, from when we laid up under the oak trees and Miss Patricia played with my eyebrows and fingers, and said my muscles were like strapling oaks. It made me want to touch that fine-spun yellow dress, right off. I imagined it soft and smooth, like a basket of peaches you couldn't have until your chores was done. Soft peaches. But then I wasn't keen on looking down the end of a breech-loader neither. So I had a fair bit of conflict right there.

But then a big steam traction engine rounded the corner at the end of the street dragging a load of sawed lumber, puffing and lurching under the heavy load. That was enough to clear my mind of Woodruff County, and Eli Raines, and breech-loaders.

What a machine!

Black smoke poured out one end, and blasts of steam from the other. Rocks broke under the big iron wheels, which left a deep mark in the dirt street.

I wondered what those big iron wheels would do to a cat. Or a possum, because they aren't as fast as cats. But still, a cat squashed under those massive iron wheels might be bully to watch.

Patricia turned her back to the monstrosity. "My cousin Zerelda gave me this here bottle of perfume." She produced a tiny vile of amber solution and dabbed a little on her cheeks. Then she leaned in. "Do you like it, Jeremiah? I got it for you, and today's the first time I tried it. Can you smell it?"

The toilet water and yellow dress took my mind straight off that machine, for at least a minute. Plus, Patricia was fourteen and definitely not the same little girl I had left. Things had changed.

Patricia breathed a nervous sigh. "My cousin Zerelda says folks ought to…" She turned back at the noisy machine and then to me. The loud machine irritated and flustered her. "…well, Zerelda says when two folks is to get hitched, they ought love each other first. That's the first step."

She got flustered and flipped her auburn hair back and tried to think.

"Well, they ought to love God first, and then each other next. That's what Zerelda says. She gives me extra advice on account of she's already got her man and a youngin' on the way, and she ain't yet fifteen years old. She also says… Are you listening, Jeremiah?"

I peeked over her shoulder at the machine just as she lifted her eyes. Bad move.

"Of course I'm listening. You were saying about Cousin Zerelda."

I noticed that the load of sawed logs behind that contraption could have been two tons. It made me wonder if a few plow shares hooked behind might work just as well, and if I could sit on top instead of walking behind like I do with Rosebud and Black Jack. I'd throw on about ten plowshares if the machine could tolerate it. Rosebud and Black Jack would flat give up the ghost under a load like that. The folks in Jackson County would stand by and watch me plow up the whole danged county, and say what a rich man I was to have it. We could use a contraption like this, they'd say. Unless they had cats running about.

I'd be the only one with it. Rich and admired.

Patricia tried not to notice. "Well, anyways, if what Zerelda says is true then we should make sure we do every step just right," she said. "That way everything will be perfect!" She stopped fiddling with her toilet water bottle and looked up again. "Do you know what I mean?"

"I reckon so," I said, sounding as interested as possible. But the chain-steering is what really got me. Big iron chains turned the machine whenever a wheel was yanked one way or the other. Just yank it left, and the machine went left. Or yank it right, and off it'd go in that direction instead. What an invention! I sure could plow a straight furrow with that contraption under me. Soon the big iron machine started around the next corner when the left chain went taut, not twenty feet from us.

"So, you do love God? Right? That's the first step."

"Yup. Sure do."

"Okay, good. Umm, well do you... umm... do you love... me then?"

"Ouch!" I said out loud. Ma's fat yellow cat came to mind when a thick pine board cracked under the iron wheel. Splinters flew into the air, and the big engine kept coming right up onto the plankway busting everything in its path.

Patricia's mouth flew open. "Ouch? I thought you were my beau. Don't you—"

I flew back to Patricia's searching eyes. "Of course I am. You know that. It's just... I don't know what to think these days. Grandpa and all. It's a lot to think about. I got to take one thang at a time."

"That's okay," she said, looking down and going back to messing with her handbag.

I put my hand on hers. "It's just... Well, Grandpa has another hearing in a week, and I got to go to that. And J.T. left me all alone here, but he's back now and I can't even ask him where he went. Uncle Olin is back too, but he picked a fight with J.T. And Ma can't even live at home on account of skulking robbers with lanterns. It's all just gettin' up on me like a big pile of rocks. I just need one thing at a time."

Patricia leaned in and laid her head on my shoulder. "I understand," she said. "We'll be here for two days, if you want to—"

The steam tractor turned wide and smashed ten more feet of the sidewalk planking and busted down a box of flowers, but continued up the avenue like it wasn't even there.

Bully!

Chapter Sixteen

THE MILLSTONE OUTSIDE THE courtroom window sat quiet this morning. Either there were no customers or the little brown donkey had gone back to Mexico. In either case, the clunk, clunk, clunk of the gristmill had ceased its racket and the courtroom was mostly just hot, stuffy, and quiet. No breeze came from the open windows. No clouds floated by. Secretaries and military men were setting up their stations at the head of the room, just like they had at the last hearing. Grandpa had survived that one, so maybe today would be the same.

J.T. and I sat waiting for the judge to appear through the little door in the back.

My wits had begun picking away at J.T's story. He made out like he was protecting Grandpa – had paid our way up to Leavenworth City and arranged everything all nice – but something still didn't sit right. So maybe Uncle Olin was right about J.T. There were certain things he wouldn't discuss, or skipped past as fast as he could, and I still didn't know his connection to Daniel P. Upham, the man who had made a ruinous affair of our lives. But now wasn't the time to fret over that.

J.T. smiled and patted my knee.

The judge finally came in and whispered to his aides. Upham shuffled and stacked papers like he loved to do. And Grandpa came in last – no cuffs or leg irons. He didn't sigh or wrinkle his forehead like I expected. He didn't weep or sniffle, or fidget or complain. Instead, his quiet motions reminded me of Christ as He went from Annas to Caiaphas when the cock crowed thrice, and then to Pontius Pilate to be beaten and crucified.

He never spoke a word. And neither did Grandpa.

That was the first time I really felt sure Grandpa could win. A power beyond his own bore him up, and I admired that.

J.T. finally whispered, "Don't worry; this is Upham's last run. Remember the last hearing? That was pretentious sham. Sloppy and weak. Upham probably expected this judge to pronounce on looks alone. Pennypacker won't put up with that again." J.T. nodded confidently.

That's exactly what I expected from J.T. Exactly what vexed me so. He didn't even tell me why Upham's case was weak or explain the Raines affair, and didn't tell what really happened down in Arkansas. It was as if he just expected the whole trial to just slide off into the Missouri River when they flushed the sinks. That didn't sound like what was really going to happen.

But still, I didn't actually believe Grandpa deserved to hang, so maybe J.T. was right.

"Yeah, let's just think along those lines," he said, pinning up a half-smile.

"Marshal Upham," the judge began, beckoning Grandpa's accuser to the bench. He pursed his lips, furrowed his brow and glared. "I am not one bit pleased with your... your antics in the last hearing. Do not play me for a fool. Evidence, Mr. Upham. May I remind you again that we're seeking sufficient evidence to warrant the trial of Hiram Cantrell." He glanced at Grandpa and then back. "Don't feed me a stack of sweet cakes. Or I'll set the man free today."

J.T. nudged. "See what I mean," he said. He tried to look confident.

"But, Your Honor—"

"Don't argue with me, Marshal Upham." The judge proceeded to upbraid him and then finally let Upham speak.

"But, Your Honor, was I wrong about the Baxter Springs massacre? This man danced on a dead man's back. Or what he believed to be a dead man. And do you not have his own admission of the act?"

The judge nodded reluctantly.

"In like manner, I will show that Hiram Cantrell and other such cowards cloaked in the darkness of night are the sole cause of the late tribulations in Missouri, Tennessee, and Arkansas. And that Hiram Cantrell did himself end the lives of fourteen honest citizens of Woodruff County in the summer of 1868. Just like he tried with the God-fearing Private Jesse Smith so many years ago in Baxter Springs. These are not wartime atrocities; they all occurred ten years ago or less. After the war had ended."

The judge frowned and waved Upham onward. "Produce it forthwith."

Upham continued. "But please remember that it is this cold and craven nature for which we have already established a firm foundation that you must view these crimes through."

"No. I don't need to view these crimes any way than what the evidence demands. Please produce your case with alacrity, Mr. Upham. I'm growing weary."

"Fair enough," Upham said, lifting his hand. "Politics," he said next. "I'd like to lay a little groundwork in southern politics, if I may. And then I will present the evidence for fourteen murders in and about Woodruff County in the summer of 1868, just ten years ago."

"Do you have any objections to this line of reasoning, Mr. Cantrell?" The judge gestured to Grandpa, who said nothing. The judge turned to Marshal Upham. "You may do so, but keep the politics on a leash. I probably already know it."

According to Daniel P. Upham's account, a whopping two-hundred murders had led up to the '68 elections in Arkansas – all politically motivated – and Grandpa was in on nearly every one, in one way or another. And according to Upham, ever since the southern governments had been reconstructed with northern republicans, the night gangs sought to redeem them. I guessed that meant put in their own men. Violence was their chief tool. It had all been a full-fledged effort to stop reconstructed governments from reelecting republicans and blacks: intimidation at polling places, night raids on freedmen and their political allies, murders of elected officials and those hoping for election, armed robbery, train robberies, bombings, and the like.

A second Civil War.

But this war waged at night under the cloak of flour sacks and cow horns.

Upham raised his hand. "Your Honor, out of the two-hundred-and-twenty murders in eastern Arkansas in the autumn of 1868, we have Hiram Cantrell on fourteen of them. Fourteen is the number I wish you to keep in mind as I proceed. I will lay out each with its own particulars, documents, and what-nots. Fourteen murders, and fourteen indisputable collections of facts. That should be ample certification to warrant the execution of Hiram Cantrell. We'll have one less murdering mudsill in the area, Your Honor."

Judge Pennypacker scolded the marshal for his choice of words.

Upham shrugged. "This is no chicken thief. Although I would not put the very act beneath him. You'll see."

Upham said that Grandpa and his night gangs, and the likes of Frank and Jesse James and his low-down cousins the Youngers, had led the Ku Klux Klan into violence against the reconstructed governments – acts a savage would blush to own. The Klan had been just a lighthearted cluster of drinking buddies until they imbibed the cold elixir brewed up by men like Hiram Cantrell and Jesse James.

And William Clarke Quantrill would have gladly led the gang, if he were not moldering in a Kentucky grave.

"I'll begin here," Upham said, holding up a page, satisfied with his choice. "The savage murder of The Honorable Andrew Balkin, a federal judge in Cotton Plant, Arkansas, just a shade tree up the road from Little Rock, into Woodruff County." He scanned the paper with his finger. "Let's see… Yes, this one's Klan."

"Why do you say that?" Judge Pennypacker asked.

Upham looked up over the papers. "Cotton Plant is seventy-percent black. Only thirty-percent white. Clearly an attack on the colored population."

"And what race was the judge?" Pennypacker asked. "Black?"

"No, he was white."

"Any ambrotypes?"

"No photographs, just verbal affidavits. The judge was white, age forty-eight. Massachusetts born. Moderate constitution. No facial hair." Upham scanned for more information. "Some gruesome work here – punctured through the stomach with bayonet. These ten pages were pinned to the ground with him."

Upham held up the bloody sheets, each with bayonet cuts through them.

The judge retrieved the papers and read, "HOMESTEAD TESTIMONY OF CLAIMANT."

He peered over his spectacles at the pages. "Humm. It's an 1802 homesteader's deed."

The judge asked, "Do you ascribe any significance to a land title bayonetted to a judge?"

Upham nodded. "That's an old Bloody Bill Anderson maneuver – clearly the work of an ex-bushwhacker or partisan ranger. Pinning documents to their victims, that is. It's some sort of message. We're all supposed to sit up and listen."

Upham mocked, "But who listens to the ravings of a lunatic murderer?"

He continued reading his notes. "Boston birth. Married. Two–"

"Wait, wait," the judge called out. "You said Boston birth. What's a Bostonian judge doing in Cotton Plant, Arkansas, Mr. Upham?"

"He was a Freedman Bureau judge – looking after the affairs of freed blacks – appointed by President Johnson. Evidently down south to see to the distribution of abandoned lands held by ex-Confederates."

"Was the homesteader dead? Is that why his lands were considered abandoned?"

Upham shrugged. "Who knows…"

"Why Cotton Plant?"

"There was a battle in '62 – two-hundred Confederates dead. By '68, their lands were considered vacant or abandoned so the federal government was to take them. Anyway, this judge was on a one-year assignment from '66 to '67, when the bureau was to be disbanded."

The judge glanced back at the bloody papers and nodded.

"Okay… abandoned lands. Left over from the war, and now government owned. But then pinned through the gut of a federal judge. Strange. What else have you got, Marshal? This case looks to be in order."

Upham's next twelve accusations passed in a blur, with Grandpa gunning down three freedmen in a back alleyway, an investor from New York while dining next to an open window, and eight more Freedmen Bureau officials from distances of three to six-hundred yards with a heavy target rifle – one of those Berdan sharpshooter models with telescopic sights. Upham claimed to have the rifle nearby along with the spent balls that had killed the government men from distances most men could not so much as focus an eye upon.

Each and every man was a political enemy according to Upham. Northerners, so-called scalawags, freedmen, bureau men, and reconstruction officials installed by President Johnson and a radical congress for the singular purpose of punishing the South for their rebellion. He reminded the judge that this was the same South that prevented anyone without a voting granddaddy to vote himself. And that this was the same South that invented 'croppers and the tax conundrums to keep them where they belonged. And a virtual web of unnavigable Jim Crow laws aimed squarely at newly freed slaves. This was the selfsame Confederacy that Hiram Cantrell had fought so hard to preserve in the Late Unpleasantness. He meant the Civil War, but I didn't figure that out for another fifteen minutes.

So, in Marshal Upham's view, it was all politics. And Grandpa was the centerpiece of a big conspiracy to redeem the South from the northern occupation. And to keep the war going.

"So, you can see that Mr. Hiram Cantrell's motives are clear. I'm not wide of the truth when I say he's no bastion of negro enfranchisement. Yes, it is true that our physical evidence for these incidents is scant at the present," Upham allowed. "But we will produce enough to convict by the time the trial is called up. We'll get that heavy target rifle for sure. And probably a good deal of those spent Minnie balls. Until then, our eyewitness account should be sufficient to warrant the trial, at least."

That didn't please the judge.

Upham then trotted out a fair number of deputies who had helped hunt the unreconstructed rebels. Every one attesting to the low moral character in Grandpa and his cohorts, as witnessed during the manhunts in Arkansas and Missouri. To their mind, even William T. Anderson, AKA: Bloody Bill had not shown so great a disregard for human life when he murdered those unarmed soldiers in Centralia, Missouri – shot, scalped, and mutilated, such as they were. Nor William Quantrill's band who had murdered two hundred civilians in Lawrence, Kansas.

One of the deputies even tried to assign Grandpa the title of "Bloody Cantrell," on account of the Cantrell's being fifth cousins to the Anderson's in Kentucky. And the Cantrell clan being so infamously murderous. "Every Missoura cur is cousin to some other," the deputy said. "They're all kin." But that didn't work, and the judge just waved him off.

He wanted evidence, and got rhetoric instead.

Another deputy gave testimonial of one particularly bad individual by the name of Olin Cantrell, the son of the accused, who had been man-hunted for some time, but who had turned around and bushwhacked every bounty hunter on his trail. Nobody wanted another try at him since the bounty was so low and the risk high. This younger Cantrell – Olin – was evidently too intelligent to be tracked by anyone but the Pinkertons, who never sleep. And his cunning and intellect may have even exceeded that agency's resources. Nevertheless, it was well-known that the Cantrell's were no men to fuss with, and that they had ruined no small number of good men.

"Bad blood runs in Little Dixie like mud through a millrace," the deputy testified. "It has been that way ever since the border wars with Bleeding Kansas. And it will be that way until the Second Coming. Every offspring of this man's loins is cursed to treachery."

I guess that meant me.

"So, we're definitely going in with these thirteen murders you've heard testimony of," Upham summarized. "As you can see, Your Honor, we've got enough right here to charge the man several times over. A dismal reckoning. I've been chasing midnight assassins ever since we ran the Klan out of Arkansas in '69. Of course, the rats fled into Tennessee and Missouri, but we're rounding them up one at a time. And this one's no different."

The judge squinted. "Are you asserting Hiram Cantrell's connection with the Klan?"

"No doubt of that. I know the behavior. They live merely to obliterate the landmarks of justice and bear us onward to anarchy and destruction."

"Fair enough Mr. Upham, but you said you had fourteen charges," the judge reminded him. "But you just said thirteen a moment ago."

"Yes, this last one is especially heinous. I've saved it for last. It involves the death of a child just east of Little Rock. Pulaski County. Rough characters in that part of the country after the war, and still are. But this one murdered a child." Upham nodded at Grandpa.

The court gasped.

Marshal Upham leafed through papers. "A farm… near Augusta, I believe… Yes, here it is." He held up the papers. "Just outside Little Rock. Involved a certain colonel in the rebel Confederacy."

On that very word, J.T. flinched. His straight-back chair squeaked on the floor.

"I've got a deputy here today as a witness. Wait 'til you hear what he has to say." Upham waved J.T. over, calling him to give testimony to the crimes Grandpa had perpetrated.

And he did – got up and stepped forward, that is.

Upham read from his notes, "On the night of October 31, 1868, we have Hiram Cantrell caught red-handed in a gully with the manifest evidence of slaughter on his face – temporarily caught I'll admit – two-hundred yards outside a farmhouse owned by a rebel colonel. Cantrell had performed the bloody act of murder by sniper-shot when a detachment of federal soldiers fell on him unawares. In those short moments an innocent girl passed into eternity from her wounds. Of course, this coward later slipped the officer's bonds with the aid of the aforementioned Olin Cantrell and had not been apprehended until just months ago. It is for that blameless little girl that we are principally here today."

Upham lifted his hand and spun around like a circus showman.

"I ask you all, what can a man give in exchange for his soul? It's one thing to run a man through with a bayonet, but defenseless women and children?"

Grandpa sighed deeply and his lip began quaking.

Upham returned to his stack. "The little girl in question was…" He squinted into the papers. "Lydia Ellen Raines. Age fourteen at the time of death. Niece to Colonel Eli Raines of the late Confederate States of America. Killed by gunshot to the face."

The courtroom stilled.

The showman waved again. "I ask you all. What ammunition so damaging to the forces of evil does a child possess that she must be shot in the face at long distance? By a sharpshooter of the skill known only to exist in Hiram Cantrell?"

His arms fell with some drama. And his hopefulness for all mankind seemed to fall with them.

"She was found slumped under a kitchen table in the home of Colonel Eli Raines of Augusta, Arkansas approximately four days ride northeast of Little Rock." Upham looked up from the paper and grimaced. "And in her little white hands were found a collection of wildflowers and a newly baked apple pie, now awash in the blood of her own body."

Grandpa's head fell back as if to beseech the heavens for relief – just like on the porch with his Bible under the maple tree. Tears flowed and hands shook.

"The back of her skull lay three feet to the rear by the wall."

The whole courtroom seemed to turn their moral temperament upon Grandpa. Their eyes burned in their sockets while evil-surmising heated their brains. I knew exactly what those people thought – when they looked like that.

But it all seemed like a big lie. Did Grandpa really do this? He was a good man, nothing like Upham trussed him up to be. Did Upham even know him like I did? Like Ma and Uncle Olin knew him?

Grandpa just sat there weeping while the whole world looked on. I felt so bad for yelling at him.

Even Marshal Upham gave Grandpa time to get his wits back. But then he started right in again.

"I'm told it took six days to clean up the mess."

J.T. leaned over to Marshal Upham. "Are you sure you want to carve this Christmas goose, friend? I recollect a few details of my own." J.T. glanced at Grandpa, still in a state of undoing, then back to Marshal Upham. "You were there too, remember?"

Upham jerked.

He immediately dismissed J.T. and reached for a long leather bag on the desk before him. But his shocked countenance had already drained back into the former devilish ambition, and he was at it again. Out of the bag came an old shoulder arm, thoroughly beaten and weather-worn. I immediately recognized the lock plate I had tinkered with many months ago.

Upham held the weapon before Grandpa. "Recognize this, sir?"

Grandpa brightened up. "Wall, it's mine... but I ain't sure what it's doin' in this courtroom. I, for sure, didn't brang it. Where'd y'all get it?"

Upham ignored the question.

He asked an aide to examine the weapon. "Please unscrew the lock plate from this musket and tell the court what you find."

The aide called for a corporal's tool set and soon had the cover off the right side of the rifle. He shrugged. "Seems like just a plain ol' mainspring, tumbler, and seerspring to me. Nothing uncommon for a rifle of this vintage. Pretty clean. No rust or mistreatment. In good serviceable order, I'd say."

"Anything else?"

"Some knife marks," the aide said. "Notches, I'd guess."

"Notches. Hmmm..."

The showman returned. "Folks, how many murders did I ask the court to keep in mind? What was that number?"

"Fourteen," the aide recalled.

Upham turned to the aide. "Please hand the musket to the judge and ask him to count the notches in the wood behind that lock plate!"

Chapter Seventeen

June, 1878

"BUT HOW WILL YOU get to know your neighbors when nobody trades like they used to?" I asked. "Ma says I probably know more neighbors than she does on account of Grandpa and me working their fields. She only knows 'em up to about ten miles out from trading eggs and coffee and flour and such. But Grandpa plowed a lot of fields."

We knew a lot of folks.

I don't think J.T. even understood what I was saying. He just kept pointing out items in the modernized mercantile and telling how times were changing and trade is not what it used to be. He bent over a new washing contraption and claimed mothers would use that instead of Cottonwood Creek where they all go to catch up on the gossip. But that only seemed to prove my point. And then he said they would no longer grind their own coffee and wheat and barley; it would all be available up and down these isles in little cloth bags. Yet the grocer didn't even carry Lowcountry corn grits, which you could trade for anywhere back home. Of course while J.T. waxed eloquent I toted the numerous sacks and packages he piled on. And they were starting to slip.

"Uncle Olin says you're sweet on my Ma on account of her and you walking the avenue under a new parasol. And you calling her oatcakes whenever you saw her. Is that true?"

J.T. drew breath. "I wouldn't object to another visit," he said.

"Your ma and I shared some pleasant words on her last trip. There's just one more thing I'm thinking of asking her." And then he noticed movement out the window.

"Umm… stay here, Jeremiah. I've got to talk to some folks right quick."

He laid another paper bundle onto my stack and went for the door. I couldn't exactly see outside, and didn't know how long he'd be out there. More stuff started slipping so I began looking for a place to set it all down. The big bolts of cloth looked like a handy place.

"Are you coming back for this?" the storekeep complained as I shucked bundles onto a stack of worsted wool fabrics. "You can't just leave it; it doesn't go there. You got to put it back on the shelves where it belongs. Everything has its place." He raised his hands and shook his head. Outside an argument had started between J.T. and some men. I decided I could either stack groceries or go out and see what the fuss was about.

"I'll be back! Hold them right there for me." The storekeep muttered, "Young folks…" as I bolted for the door.

It was a nice spring day; winter was finally over. J.T. was in mid-argument.

"Alright then… where's the evidence?" J.T. asked in a huff. Judge Pennypacker, General Asa Blunt, and three aides circled him. They didn't look happy with J.T's questions right there on the public street. "He wasted your time twice and where's the evidence he promised? Hiram Cantrell is growing weaker every day he spends in that hole. Men are going to the gallows around him. Don't you think we're at the point where you need to–"

"I'm sorry, Mr. Martin," General Blunt interrupted. "But this isn't the forum for such a line of questioning." He looked around in a scolding way. Mothers with baby buggies and gentlemen passed by. The commandant didn't look comfortable talking with so many strangers about. "May I remind you that we have a perfectly suitable courtroom for such discussions? And as for the timing of this investigation, we will be the judge of that."

"Asa, I can tolerate a little discussion on the matter," the judge said, turning toward the warden. He faced J.T. with a squint. "But something smells green to me. Marshal Upham may have difficulty producing the evidence but I get the feeling he's got enough to start proceedings."

"Already scheduled for next month," the warden said. "Reckon it's over for that rebel. Plus, I did some checking myself. There are some awful stories about Hiram Cantrell down south."

"Like?" J.T. said, challenging the warden.

"Like the Christmas Eve massacre. Russellville, Arkansas, 1872, just six years back."

J.T. waved him off. "Rumors. Flat rumors. Hiram Cantrell was living in Jackson County, Missouri by the time the Pope County and Brooks Baxter Wars started in '72. Remember, I tracked him. Upham and me."

"Not the way this story goes," the commandant said. "The way I heard it, Cantrell donned a blue federal uniform, walked into a plantation house in Russellville and demanded that all the occupants step outside. Of course they did, wanting to satisfy the demands of law. Arkansas was still under occupation until two years ago. Cantrell's band made them all lay down on their bellies and then shot them one by one. A month later, the previous owner, an ex-Confederate captain retook the house and claimed the dead family had usurped it from him. He was elected a Pope County judge a year later!"

J.T. practically laughed. "I rode with Upham for twelve years after the war and I never heard that one! There are a hundred rumors like that still circulating Pope County. Got any witnesses?"

"Of course not! They were all shot."

"Then how do you know it happened?"

The commandant shrugged. "These are just the type of stories I ran across when I looked into the man. That was not the only one."

"So, because of a few dubious stories, you believe everything Upham hands you?"

The judge shook his head and raised his hands. "We won't be using that one in the trial."

"But still," the warden said. "Those are the type of—"

"What if I had some new information?" J.T. asked. "Information that throws Upham's whole case down the well?"

The warden and judge looked at each other. "It's already been scheduled," the warden said. "And I doubt—"

"But wouldn't new information be worth a postponement?"

"I suppose it would all come out in the trial, anyway," the warden said, lifting his hands.

"We are scheduled…" the judge added, apologetically.

J.T. threw up his hands and turned to me. "Have you got the groceries? Well, you best git 'em. I can tell this crew just needs some good men to build their precious disciplinary barracks. That is, until they're done with them, and then they hang 'em and get some new ones."

The warden stepped up with fire in his eyes.

The judge blocked his advance, which looked like it would have landed J.T. in jail himself. "Mr. Martin, Mr. Martin, I sense your frustration. Please let me assure you I am a fair man. If Hiram Cantrell is innocent, he will go free. But try to see things through my eyes. We've got fourteen well-documented incidents, and notches on a musket to match them. Are they all false? Could be, but I doubt that. I've had a few years on the bench myself, mind you."

"My apologies," J.T. said.

The warden backed off.

"For instance," the judge said. "The most damaging is this incident with the girl at the farm. What was that all about? I certainly have questions. Unanswered ones, but I suppose they'll be resolved in the trial. Is there anything more we can learn from another hearing? Maybe, but I'm not sure right now."

Pennypacker edged in. "Now, Mr. Martin… Upham said you were there at the farm. If you want to get your man off, enlighten me." He raised his hands. "I'm open to new information. Tell me about this fellow, Eli Raines."

J.T. broke eye contact and looked down the street. "That's going into areas I don't feel—"

The warden stepped in. "You said you had new information. Here's your chance to keep Cantrell from the hangman's knot. Let's hear it."

J.T. glowered.

"What do you get out of all this?" the warden asked. "Are you here just to harass the court or do you have a personal stake in this man? Aren't you from New York? The son of a millionaire? Cantrell hates northern usurpers."

"I've had a change of heart since New York, and Hiram knows that."

"I still don't know what you get out of this," General Blunt said.

"That's a fair question." J.T. looked back at Blunt. "After the war, I was sold on the notion of southern reconstruction. That we could simply apply Christian principles and the American experiment to southern governments and that alone would miraculously bring the colored man into equality with whites. All he needed was a hand up – after all, the negro didn't have the legal right to the clothes on his back after emancipation. And furthermore, that we could just round up those who violently opposed his equality and punish them. Slavery would be finished. So I joined Upham's crew. I fought with him during the war, and figured he would do a fine job reconstructing Arkansas. And largely, he's done that. I commend him. But–"

"But in this case, he's wrong?" the judge asked.

"An innocent man is worth saving – no matter what color his skin is – even if it's white. That's all I'm going to say. I don't want to talk about Colonel Raines."

"Alright then," the judge said, shaking his head. "If I can't gather anything new then Hiram Cantrell is going to trial. And if you've got nothing else to say about that Raines incident, I'm going to proceed next month. And I'm not ignorant about how it's going to turn out."

J.T. kicked the hitching post.

The grocer stepped onto the plankway. He dusted a little flour off his apron and stared at me, hands raised. I guess that meant I had to go back in and take care of things. But I wanted this judge to have a piece of my mind first.

"I don't care what y'all think. My granddaddy is not a killer. We are honest folks right down to the floor cloth. And I don't know how you got his gun but you better put it back."

The judge and warden just looked down and kicked the dirt a while. I think they knew where the gun came from. So did Mother.

I followed the grocer back in and paid the bill. He put everything into a big burlap sack which made it a lot easier to carry. It reeked of rutabagas which I thoroughly despised, but I was glad for the use of it and I thanked him.

"Bring it back when yer shed of it," he reminded. "Waste not, want not."

J.T. argued outside with the judge. I was glad for that too because Grandpa didn't have nobody else to argue for him. Thomas didn't have nobody neither.

They were still fighting when I went out.

"So you're saying there was no deal between Upham and Eli Raines?" the warden asked. "But the way some say–"

J.T. drummed his fingers. "Yes, there was a deal," J.T. reluctantly admitted.

"Well, let's hear it," the warden demanded. He brightened up.

J.T. balked, but finally gave in. "Upham wanted a certain group of night riders who had looted and harassed republican offices, and held up blacks as they approached the voter registration bar. Most of those men rode with Colonel Raines during the war."

"And Cantrell was one of them?" the judge asked. "One of the night riders?"

"Yes. No… No… Not like you think. Anyway, Upham wanted those men because they were wrecking the '68 Republican campaign. Nobody in their right mind would go within a hundred yards of a GOP stump speech let alone vote. And Upham was tasked to secure the voting areas. Remember how bad the '56 elections were in Kansas? Pro-slavery men polluting the vote and harassing the citizenry? It was ten times as bad in Missouri, Arkansas, and Tennessee after the war. You could be killed just for voting the wrong way."

"True," the warden agreed.

"So Upham guaranteed Colonel Raines' pardon in exchange for those men – heads on a pike or run out on a rail, every last one. In other words, you hand over your gunmen, and your rebel days are over."

"Including Cantrell and his son, Olin?"

"That's right. But like I said, Cantrell wasn't–"

I stepped up to J.T.

"J.T, I don't understand what he needed a pardon for," I said. "Was the Colonel a night rider? Did he lynch negros? Or block them from voting? Was he a Klansman?"

"No, no, Raines needed a pardon for his part in the war," J.T. said. "For being a rebel to the Union. All the high-ranking officers did, or they couldn't hold office, or vote, or even conduct business like we do today. It makes it pretty hard to survive when you're labeled a criminal. After all, he raised his sword to the almighty federal government."

"And led a regiment of rebels against it," the warden added.

J.T. nodded in partial agreement. "Well, after a while Raines just got tired of living in the wild. It was time to come in out of the rain and get his pardon."

"And Marshal Upham could give that," I asked.

"Not really. But he was appointed by the governor and could go straight to the President for the pardon. All the pardons came down from Johnson or Grant, and now from Hayes. And of course, Johnson had to be a pig's knuckle about the whole thing, and required the rebels to come to Washington and bow down before him. Physically. No pardons came through telegrams." J.T. grimaced. "I really hated that aspect of reconstruction. It seemed so petty to criminalize good men – patriots, I've started calling them. As if men like Raines were still rebels and criminals."

"They fought against the United States and were still leading groups of hooded thugs when it was over," the judge added. "Nathan Bedford Forrest, for one. That's where the Klan came from. Grand Wizard. You know that!"

J.T rocked in disagreement. "You make all these ex-Confederates out to be Klan. Okay, some... But not Raines. Or Cantrell for that matter. Raines didn't lead anyone after the war. He just lived off in the rough without much connection to civilization. None of those men reported to him any longer. So to say he led men in midnight raids and

153

terrorism is a complete fabrication. Where's the evidence for that?"

The warden stepped in. "But he could have given up the night riders pretty easily. They were criminals, if not Raines himself."

"No, not all were guilty. But yes, he could have given up the rotten apples," J.T. conceded. "And that's where Raines stepped awry of Upham's demands. He evidently concluded that loyalty and justice trumped personal gain." J.T. threw up his head as if the whole idea of loyalty were completely preposterous in these modern times. "Upham flew into a rage over the soured deal, and called Raines a lousy secesh and stomped off. But not before he threatened to take his farm as punishment. 'I'll chop it into forty-acre lots and give it to the freedmen,' he warned. 'And you'll be living out in this woodlot until you're ninety.' That cut Raines pretty deeply."

"Okay, okay, okay," the judge interrupted. "I get all that – makes perfect sense. But where's the connection to Cantrell? He was a night rider, true?"

"Well, I'll tell you about Hiram Cantrell," J.T. said. "On the night of October 31, 1868 we were called in to confiscate the cabin that Raines was holed up in. He didn't do the deal, so Upham moved in." J.T. paused to think. He looked around a little. "You know, I don't actually believe Upham planned to follow through on the land confiscation. That was a little ridiculous. I think he just wanted to put some teeth to the threat. After all, he wanted those night riders, not the Raines farm. And I think in his heart, he just wanted the violence to stop. But he takes things too far sometimes. Upham–"

"So Grandpa tried to protect him?" I asked. "The Colonel? Grandpa tried to protect Eli Raines?"

"That's right, Jeremiah. And nothing more, as far as I can tell."

The commandant put in, "Yes, that's all good and fine, but a young girl was killed in the process. How did that happen?"

"Okay," J.T. responded with a wrinkled face. "You have to understand how things worked out that night. Upham's whole plan got mixed up. He wanted the night riders, so he threatened Raines to get them and ended up in a gun-battle he never expected."

J.T. extended a hand to me. "Your grandfather was just there for his colonel."

The judge waved J.T. on.

"First, you had Raines in the house with his family and niece – the little girl. Outside, you had Upham's men – me included, threatening to fire the house if he didn't give up the night riders or let us in. And next, you had twenty of Raines' men from his old regiment in the thickets about to sound the rebel yell. That's a bad recipe; I don't care where you come from. A half-hour later, we were inside the cabin about to throw Raines and the family out into the cold if he didn't follow through on the deal. Threats were made, and every voice was at top volume. Of course, outside, the night riders were setting torches and capping revolvers for action."

"Was that in Randalls Flats?" I asked. "Out near Ma's farm?"

"No. This was east of Pulaski County, near Little Rock – where all the murders had been going on. Little Rock is just south of the Missouri border."

My wondered if there was a road going down there. "I never been outside Jackson County."

The warden stopped J.T. "At least one of those men outside the cabin was a sharpshooter, or so Upham claims. Capable of putting a bullet through a window at a hundred yards in the dark. Upham says that's how the girl ended up shot – a cowardly sharpshooter in the brush."

The judge opened his hands to J.T. "I want to know straight up… honest and straight… understand?" He placed his hand under J.T's and the other over it. "In your opinion… was Hiram Cantrell the killer? Accidental or not, was he the man that pulled the trigger? Was he the sharpshooter who put the bullet through that cabin window?"

J.T. sighed.

He rubbed his face and looked away, but then turned back to the group of men. "No."

"Cantrell was not the shooter? Then who was?"

J.T. took breath. "Well, the cabin window was broken by a shot. That is true." He nodded to the judge as if to agree with that fact. "But a lot of other guns went off that night."

He grimaced and kicked dirt. "Including mine."

Chapter Eighteen

I WASN'T SURE IF J.T. had talked the judge and commandant into another hearing or not. They seemed interested in the Raines story J.T. finally spilled out in front of the mercantile. The two of them went away arguing but I never heard the final decision. But it seemed like Grandpa should get the chance to tell his side of the story. Or maybe that's what the trial was for.

In any case, it was Saturday. Visitor's day. And I was happy about that.

Corporal Silas led Uncle Olin and Cousin Buford and me to the cell – always a creepy walk past the stairs to the morgue, the surgeon's office, down the dark side of the cell house with candles in every cell, past the old gray mare and the six tiny cells to Grandpa's iron door on the left. As usual, I went in first, and Uncle Olin fought with Cousin Buford to sit and count bricks and stay out of the drainage ditch. Grandpa could see them if he stretched his neck around the iron bars. But there wasn't much room for that. Especially when I took up the space in front of the door. I wanted to ask if they all could come in, but was too afraid.

The door rattled shut behind me, and I sat down.

"My big ray of sunshine!" Grandpa spoke cheerfully, but not loud enough for a rebuke from the corporal. He half-sat up in the bunk to stroke my face, then lay back on the straw pillow. A single gray woolen blanket covered a blue mattress tick containing an inch of prairie hay, which was not allowed to fall onto the brick floor. Flogging was the penalty for such infractions, among other things like refusal to eat your daily rations, or failure to recite the prison regs upon demand, failure to shine buttons and shoes, rips in your black-and-whites, a missing cap, and a host of other violations. But none of this bothered Grandpa. He said he was used to it from his days in the army.

There was no movement from the bunk above.

"Grandpa! I'm glad to see you. J.T. talked to the judge for you." I leaned over and hugged him as best I could without bothering Thomas above. He must have sleeping because he wasn't stirring.

"Oh, really? What have you heard?"

"I think J.T. is trying to get another hearing and stop the trial. Something about Colonel Eli Raines?"

"Yes, I heard that. The judge is planning to bring the colonel in. Sent papers a few days ago. They'll have to fetch him out of the underbrush – backwoods Arkansas, I'm afraid. I guess they want to find out if he'll testify or knows anything about that shooting."

"That's good news!" I said, looking into Grandpa's eyes. The mere notion of a trial dragged Grandpa down a little. And I wanted to make him feel better.

"Could be good news," he allowed. "Raines has a story to tell, and his word could break up Upham's case. It's no wonder Upham never mentioned him in the first hearings."

The whole idea of a fresh new hearing with Raines sounded bully to me. I pictured the colonel in the courtroom with buckskin and tassels, and telling his story like Buffalo Bill and the Wild West Show, and him slapping Upham around with a leather quirt like a renegade Indian, and the judge trying to get a hit at him too with his gavel, and buckshot coming off Mrs. Branson's eight gauge right there in the courtroom with General Blunt. Upham would turn tail and skedaddle back to Little Rock while Mrs. Branson fired buckshot up his rear end. And then Grandpa would be let loose like he should be. It was satisfying imagery, but probably wouldn't happen exactly like that.

It was exciting enough to risk a scolding from Thomas for waking him.

"Bully news," I yelled up the other bunk. "Ain't it Thomas?"

No answer.

"Thomassss... I saaaaid... It's bully news, you old alligator!"

No answer, no movement.

"Where's Thomas?" I asked. "The old gray mare was empty, so he ain't there." I smiled at my little joke. Grandpa didn't.

"The old gray mare is empty," Buford repeated from out in the corridor. "The old gray mare is empty!" He sang out the words until Uncle Olin cuffed him in the ear. Then he coddled his head with manifest horror on his face.

I stood up to look in Thomas' bunk. It was cleanly made, but empty. No loose straw, no wrinkles, no Bible.

"Where's Thomas?" I asked again, trying not to demand too much from Grandpa. He didn't seem to want to talk about it.

He just looked down and drew breath. A sigh followed.

A hot terror came over me. I turned to the corporal outside the locked iron door. "Silas, where is Thomas, the old negro man who sleeps in this bunk?"

"Gone," the reply came.

"Gone where?"

"Where do you think, boy? Now finish your visit. You got nineteen minutes left and then I got to get you out. We got a rotation to keep."

I grabbed the iron doors and shook them, which was one of those violations that could send men to the flogging stool. "No! I'm not going anywhere until I know where Thomas the black negro is." The door shook violently. Uncle Olin and Cousin Buford stood up.

"Boy, you turn loose of that door," the corporal said, "or I'll have you beaten and dragged out of here. We don't tolerate–"

"Silas," Grandpa interrupted. "Let the boy know. He might just as well know now."

The jailer sighed. "Gone to the gallows, boy. Left an hour ago. Probably swingin' by now. Twitching and jangling and such." He smiled at his own humor. But I didn't think it was funny.

"I want to see him! Right now! Before he—"

The corporal shook his head. "No way under heaven, boy. Tain't goin' to happen."

I shook the iron door with all the strength in me. Each shove lifted the door up an inch on its pin, and then it slammed back down again on the iron frame. The racket rattled all the way down the corridor and back, and probably out to the muddy Missouri. Men from other cells joined the riotous act, and soon the whole block shook in unison.

"I WANT TO SEE THOMAS!"

"Sergeant of the Guard!" the corporal yelled out. "Riot on F block." He raised his musket to his chest with fixed bayonet and faced the end of the corridor for relief. "Sergeant of the Guard!" he yelled again with more force. He looked at me again. "You done it now, boy."

Twenty seconds later a sergeant arrived on the double-quick, also with his musket at Port Arms with bayonet fixed. He slid to a stop before Corporal Silas.

All the cell doors went quiet.

"What's the trouble here?" he demanded. "Do you need the Capt'n?"

"The boy's incited a riot on the block." He turned to me with an accusing eye. "Right here, First Sergeant. He wants to see Thomas, the old negro who was bunking in this cell. I told him—"

"Pull the prisoner from the cell," the first sergeant demanded. Then he pointed at me. "Thomas is gone."

The door swung open and the corporal grabbed Grandpa by the shirt and hauled him out, pushing me aside. The first sergeant grabbed him and walked him straight to the old gray mare. He forced Grandpa over the bloody leather apron and bound his hands and feet so that his head hung down the other side. "Prepare for corporal punishment, prisoner," he said.

Ten stripes with a heavy leather strap were enough to take most of the life out of any man. The flogging echoed up and down the brick corridor for all to hear. They knew exactly what was happening on that leather sawhorse outside their cells. No more doors rattled.

The preacher's voice came to mind: "He was wounded for our transgressions, He was bruised for our iniquities: the chastisement of our peace was upon Him; and with His stripes we are healed."

I felt awful.

Grandpa came back, hanging off two soldiers. He staggered into his cell alone, and the door slammed behind him. But instead of moaning from his punishment, Grandpa reappeared at the door with his hand though the bars.

"First Sergeant," he said weakly to the man who had just flogged him. "Take this. It will get you in."

The first sergeant reached out to take Grandpa's Bible. It practically came apart in his hands, and he had to scoop it together. Every page was loose and worn. Handwritten notes covered the thin brown pages. "What do you want me to do with this?" he asked, still breathing heavily from the exertion.

"It will get you in to see Thomas if you are questioned. Every man should have the Word of God in his time of trial."

"I ain't going nowhere. Now sit down before you get it again."

"Take it."

The first sergeant took the Holy Book, but contorted his face. "I can't take this from you, Cantrell. You won't survive a week in here without it. If it goes to Thomas, it will stay with Thomas. You know that. And if the Capt'n catches me, I'll be in here with you. You know how restricted those proceedings are."

"You can return it if you don't need it." Grandpa looked at me uneasily. "Take the boy. He needs to be a man. And he needs to say goodbye."

The first sergeant searched Grandpa's eyes. He pressed the Bible to his breast and sniffed the ragged pages as if to breathe in their meaning.

The man looked awful. I guess for the bad whipping he gave Grandpa.

He reached out and took Grandpa's hand. "Umm... awright... I'll try."

After leaving Uncle Olin and Buford at the prison entrance, the first sergeant took me behind the cell house and through a maze of

160

whitewashed buildings, spotless alleys and passageways inside other buildings. We passed men in their black-and-whites peeling apples. And others busting rocks, and three more digging a rainwater trench.

"We perform hangings in a particular place. It's not public, and it's not easy to find." We weaved through a half-dozen more doors and alleyways. "I've only been there once, and I'm not sure I'm going the right way. But we've got to go quick, so keep up. Thomas was taken out an hour ago. He's made his peace with God by now."

Two more right turns, and a left, and we landed in a small area between some buildings. It was not a courtyard, just a place where four buildings loosely came together at odd corners. A long strip of grass led to white gallows where Thomas stood facing a few dozen people. His hands were outstretched as another man probed his neck muscles with his thumb and index finger, the very picture of the negro slave wrought up from years of toil.

"Jeremiah," the first sergeant said, studying my eyes. "You can skip this, if you want." He laid his hand on mine. "This is going to be a horrific procedure. I'll take you straight back to Hiram. To your grandfather. And you can spend the whole afternoon with him. I promise."

The first sergeant had not yet needed Grandpa's Bible. It had been pressed tightly to his breast the whole time. But if questioned by an officer, he knew how to use it. The Bible was for the comfort and aid of the condemned. And the sergeant was just rushing it to Thomas in his hour of need. That was a black lie, but I went along with it.

"I'll stay and watch," I said. "Grandpa says I should be a man."

"Your grandfather isn't condemned. He hasn't even gone to trial. So you don't–"

"I know. But Thomas was my friend."

"Well, we'll stay back here in the corner behind everybody. You won't be able to talk to Thomas but at least you can be here with him in spirit. Hopefully we won't be noticed. If we are…" He held out the old leather Book I had seen many, many times out under the maple tree next to Cottonwood Creek. "I'll use this. Non-commissioned officers aren't allowed back here. But maybe with this…"

The procedure was nothing like I expected. Uncle Olin had told me all the particulars of a proper western hanging last summer. Western hangings are different than back East, he had explained. It's a public affair out here. Popped corn and goober peas. Musical calliopes and juggling acts. Preachers and defendants. Everyone comes out, and the merchants all get rich for a day.

"The Drop," he had said, was the principle key to a proper hanging. We had been piling loose hay in a farmer's hot mow that summer when he explained it all. The drop has to be ciphered just right for the condemned. Each man is different. A short man drops farther than a tall man. A skinny man weighs less than a fat man. Drop a man too far, and his skin rips off and bleeds, or Heaven forbid his head comes clean off and rolls out front for the children to see. But drop a man too short, and his neck doesn't break atall. The poor wretch writhes for fifteen minutes and then strangles to death while he fights the noose.

The man probing Thomas' neck muscles pulled a measuring chain from his front pocket. Each metal length was two inches. He held it from Thomas's head to his feet, then counted the segments and jotted the number into his notes. He tilted Thomas' head back and forth, and front to back, a second time – probing a little more and testing the muscles like an expert. Then he adjusted his big black top hat and checked his notes again. "Everything is in order," he said, but didn't sounded convincing. Seemed new at this. But then, he was fifty feet away and I didn't hear everything.

There must have been thirty people in the grassy area, but only a few public spectators like Uncle Olin talked about. Most wore blue federal frock coats with light blue piping and blocked felt hats – dignified and handsome with their right hands slid between brass buttons. Some had swords, others revolvers, muskets, and carbines. A small cluster of townsfolk stood near the scaffold, and one woman sobbed the whole time. Nobody else made a twitch.

Nothing like Uncle Olin's perfect western hanging.

That summer, Uncle Olin explained a lot. You got to soap them knots, he had pointed out vigorously, setting the hay rake down to improve his theatrics and let me do most of the work. Then a quick drop snaps the bone like a chicken's neck. Ever twist off a hen's head, he had asked as the hay mow grew thick with dust and chaff. Then you know the little snap it makes. Same with rebels and evildoers at the end of a good hemp rope. If it don't snap crisp, you got a strangler on yer hands. And that ain't no good fer nobody, not even the folks in the audience. Not one o' them good folks came out to see a pair of twitchin' boots for a quarter of an hour.

Of course, Uncle Olin had a remedy for evil-doers hoping to escape the hangman's knot. A broke rope. A broke rope was a sure sign of innocence, he had said. A man should go free if the rope breaks on account of it being a sign from Above. Of course he'd once seen an eager hangman trot a man right back up and try again. But it was a sure sign, nonetheless.

So maybe the rope might break because Thomas was so big. And then he'd be free.

Just as the hangman with the top hat waved Thomas up the thirteen steps to the platform, my skin turned cold and my stomach let loose. The morning eggs and grits came out in little splattery chunks all over the grass and onto the sergeant's boots. One man in his big felt hat turned around and frowned, but soon turned back to the scaffold. Thomas was half way up by the time I wiped the sergeant's boots with my sleeve.

I looked up. "I'm sorry. It's not what I thought."

"I know," The first sergeant said. "You can leave if you want. Maybe you've seen enough already."

I hadn't seen enough. If I was to be a man, I would need to see it all. Even if I threw up all my breakfasts for a week. I wanted to know what might happen to Grandpa if things didn't go right in the hearing. Because J.T. said if this thing goes to trial, Grandpa may have a hard go of it. Daniel P. Upham won't let loose when he gets the taste of blood in his mouth. J.T. had seen that before.

Thomas didn't stand on the platform long before they had a thick noose over his head. It had thirteen loops, just like the thirteen steps. The army chaplain said a few words and asked Thomas some questions. Thomas nodded each time, but had nothing else to say. Then the hangman handed him a single leather glove, and pulled a black bag over his head.

And that's when my stomach acted up again. Out it all came again and again.

Uncle Olin had said men sometimes throw up inside the black bag. Vomit comes running out the bottom and down their shirt like a slobbering lunatic, and their legs buckle and they cry. So they don't let 'em eat no breakfast on account of that. And if they do, it's dry toast. Thomas did not throw up, but I did. By now, it was just dry heaves. Sweat ran from my cold forehead and my stomach retched like a vice. The frowner in the black felt hat looked back at me again. I think he was a big bug because he had stars on his collar. But he did not ask what me and the first sergeant were doing there. He just frowned and turned back around. I'm glad the sergeant didn't have to lie.

But isn't it still a lie if you concoct it ahead of time? I wasn't sure.

Mostly, they don't hang sinners with their boots on, Uncle Olin had said. On account of them flying off and hitting somebody. 'Specially, if he don't get a good drop, or they don't soap them knots, and he twitches like a scarecrow. A boot'll fly off and hit a kid in the forehead, and nobody wants to see that at a hanging. Maybe back East, but not out here. We know better than ta let that happen. Dog-robbin' Easterners couldn't hang a man proper if they had him in a hemp mill.

I wondered if Uncle Olin really would have hung J.T. from the rafters if Ma hadn't stopped him. Probably would. And then where would Grandpa be now?

Thomas dropped the glove.

A quick jerk of a lever, and Thomas dropped only two or three feet through a trapdoor in the platform. The rope tangled and caught on the top beam above him. They hadn't tied his feet together, so both legs flung wildly for the platform. There was nothing to catch onto, so his legs kept flailing. Panicked shrieks came from under the black hood as Thomas twisted like a madman. Everybody on the scaffold scrambled to do something.

And then a boot came flying off, just like Uncle Olin said.

The hangman finally yanked the rope free of the beam, and

Thomas fell another two feet. But that wasn't enough to do the job either. His legs continued flailing until a man from below grabbed them and pulled down. That straightened the body out but did not finish the job.

I dry-heaved a third and fourth time.

The first sergeant peered into the grass with a disturbed look.

After fifteen minutes, the man at the bottom let go of Thomas' twitching legs. They were still. It had been a bad drop but at least the act was over. Thomas' body twisted a little in the breeze just like that hog we had slaughtered over a year ago. Everyone shook their heads and scowled.

"I want to go back now," I told the first sergeant, trembling.

"I understand," he said. "That was a scene I'll not soon forget. I'm sorry for that."

Ten minutes later we stood in front of Grandpa's dark cell. My stomach was empty but I didn't feel hungry, just shaken and jittery. I wiped my mouth again.

"Like I said," the first sergeant reminded me. "You can spend the whole afternoon here. I'll be outside this cell to make sure of that. I don't care what the Capt'n says." He handed me Grandpa's Bible and let me in.

I walked in with my head down. "Hello, Grandpa."

"Hello, son."

We didn't talk for ten minutes.

"Grandpa," I finally managed, with a scratchity voice from the vomiting and dry heaves. "What judge did Thomas have?"

Chapter Nineteen

October, 1878

"I'M TIRED OF WAITING," Judge Pennypacker said, drumming his fingers on the bench. He glared at the first sergeant. "I thought you said the witness would be here. This is the last hearing, and I want to tidy this up. You know we can't proceed without that man."

The sergeant shrugged his shoulders. "They sent a telegram but I never heard no answer." The sergeant wasn't sure what else to say. He just stood there nervous-like and waving his hands like it was somebody else's job.

"Send a runner into town, then!" the judge roared. "Is he even here in Leavenworth?"

The first sergeant detailed a corporal and a private soldier, and fled from the room with muskets across their chests.

Marshal Upham glanced up from his paper-stacking, adjusted his spectacles long enough to watch the men leave, and then returned to the numerous stacks before him. He loved his papers.

Then Upham smiled.

J.T. tapped me and Uncle Olin on the shoulders. "Come on, fellas. Eli Raines isn't coming."

J.T. rose to his feet and motioned to the judge. The judge beckoned him and they talked in whispers. The judge frowned and shook his head repeatedly, but finally nodded. He wasn't happy. J.T. had obviously talked him into something but I wasn't sure what. "Alright, let's go," J.T. said, heading for the door without so much as another look.

I waved and smiled at Grandpa. We didn't even get a minute to talk. I assumed the hearing would start like normal, and then Grandpa and I could talk about Thomas before he had to go back to the cell. The hanging was horrible and I wanted to ask Grandpa about it. He just returned the smile and waved as we headed through the door.

I didn't see him again for almost a month.

"Alright, Olin," J.T. said. "Get down to O'Shaughnessy's and pick out six of the best riding horses he has. I want long-distance animals with good wind." J.T. opened his wallet and peeled out two one-hundred-dollar bank notes. "That should do it. These are drawn against the Leavenworth City Bank. O'Shaughnessy had better not have a problem with that. Meet me in one hour. Get three saddles and tack, too. And Olin, that's not for knives and boot pistols. Good riding horses, understand?"

J.T. handed me another bank note, not quite as large. "Jeremiah, get some jerky, coffee, and bacon – nothing more. Oh, and we'll need some ammunition. .45 caliber, and some .36's for Olin's numerous amusements. You know the type. We'll meet up in an hour."

Uncle Olin and I headed off to make the purchases and meet back at the boarding house. But it was more like two hours when we finally got back.

"Where are we going?" I asked, but J.T was still wearing out shoe leather giving travel instructions.

He turned to Uncle Olin. "Ask the house mother if she can watch Buford for a few weeks. We can't take him with us. Black Jack and Rosebud should be fine at O'Shaughnessy's."

"A few weeks?" Uncle Olin said. "I give four-hundred dollars for these six ponies, saddles, and tack, J.T. You still owe him two-hundred. And he ain't happy 'bout that." He held all six horses by the reins. "If we run off without payin' they'll set a posse on us. I seen it before."

"Black Jack and Rosebud are worth a hundred dollars each," I reminded him. "They're a matched pair. O'Shaughnessy knows that.

He'll wait for the rest of the money, or take the mules as payment. But where the heck are we going?"

"Saddle up and I'll let you know. We're a day late already."

We rode south out of town, kicking up dust. Each pony had a trail horse tied to its saddle, and our meager rations sat on those.

I wondered about Grandpa. He was probably back in his cell by now, or on fatigue duty cleaning sinks or digging cistern trenches or laying brick on the new castle for General Blunt. I guessed Colonel Eli Raines was supposed to show up for the hearing but did not. My mind went over the crimes Grandpa had supposedly committed – over the fourteen murders Upham had accused him of, and the fourteen notches I'd seen on the musket. And over what little I knew of the Raines affair. J.T. knew more than me but didn't say a lot. He and Uncle Olin rode ahead, and looked back every so often to make sure I wasn't straggling. I didn't even know where I was going. That's how much J.T. told me.

I noticed a bunch of carvings in the wood railing as we crossed the Missouri River bridge, and slowed down to read them. The word: "FREDIM" caught my eye. Next to it were other such cuttings: "FREE" and "JESUS MAKES FREEDIM" and "YEAR OF JUBILEE," and the numbers "61, 62," and "63."

Curious words on an old wooden bridge.

J.T. slowed his horse back next to me. "Ten-thousand slaves crossed these bridges when the war started; there were over a hundred-thousand in Missouri back then. Called 'em contraband. Some crossed upstream when the river froze over, up near Atchison, and St. Joseph, Sumner, White Cloud, and Doniphan. Others downstream, near Westport and Sugar Creek – all along the frontier – crossing into Free Kansas and fleeing the slave catchers and bushwhackers. Mostly from Jayhawkers riling 'em up and telling them where to cross. They fled their Missouri masters by the hundreds, and looted their horses and wagons and all their tack. So when you hear folks say blacks loved their masters and that the masters loved them like children, remember this bridge."

"Grandpa never owned slaves. Are we still bad people?"

J.T. didn't answer. He just rode ahead scanning the dozens of crude messages in the bridge, carved fifteen years ago.

Uncle Olin fell back and flipped my hat off, "Ever sleep in the saddle, Jay?"

I had to stop and pick it up. "Of course. Whenever Grandpa and me worked out east, I'd sleep on Black Jack all the way back. Grandpa always led the way. I can sleep through anything."

"Well, good; we got four-hundred-and-fifty miles to cover," J.T. said, urging me on with a wave. "We're fetching Eli Raines back for a hearing. Let's git."

J.T drove us four hours before letting us stop and boil some coffee and fry a little bacon fat. I laid down in a creek and slept. Summer was over but this heat didn't end. Tree crickets buzzed and the summer sun beat down.

J.T and Uncle Olin didn't mind the distance. They squatted next to the fire and talked. I only heard about a quarter of what they said.

"Don't you clean your fry pan?" J.T. asked.

"I let the flies do that," Uncle Olin said. "Maybe later I'll lick it clean."

"Now about our route…" J.T said. "I say we go straight on through. It's shorter."

"No! I don't care if we're Jesus, Joseph, and Mary up out of Bethlehem," Uncle Olin complained. "You ain't goin' through them Sni Hills. Never in a hundred years. We got to go around. That's Bloody Bill's old hideout. It's infested with snakes, ticks, and fleas. I know the type what's still livin' out there still. We ain't going through, and that's all there is to it."

J.T. and Uncle Olin argued and I slept in the cool running water. The cicadas buzzed. And the heat beat down.

Soon, we were back on the trail again, this time on the remounts. J.T. said we'd swap horses every four hours, boil coffee, and get back on the trail again. He didn't want to dally. We wouldn't stop until we hit Woodruff County, four-hundred miles away. And that's just what we did – swapped horses and rode all day and all night until our bones jiggled like raspberry jam.

I woke the next morning, tied down to my saddle, stiff and annoyed. Still riding.

"It's your turn, Jay. Keep yer eyes skinned," Uncle Olin said, still half asleep. "I'm gettin' some derned shut-eye." We stopped and combed down the animals, and crushed some coffee beans and boiled then. This time, Uncle Olin and J.T. laid in a stream while I saddled up the reserves and cooked bacon in Uncle Olin's greasy frypan. They both grabbed a thick hunk of bacon and strapped themselves into the saddle and went to sleep as soon as they finished eating. I led the party south.

I soon noticed the trail leading into a dark ravine with high cliffs and fast running water – kind of nice country, but probably haunted. Huge moss-covered trees yawned over the thinning trail. The space between wagon tracks grew thick with weeds, and the road narrowed every hundred rods or so. I almost felt like sleeping too with the woods around us growing thicker and darker with tangled jungle brush. A few small unpainted shacks poked out of the woods from time to time, usually next to some running water or a mill pond, but otherwise there was not a living soul in this gloomy old place. The shacks didn't look any more inhabited than Uncle Olin's place back in Randalls Flats. So I guessed that folks might live there, but I didn't see smoke from the chimneys. So, maybe not.

As we passed one shack, a thin man stood next to the road with a double-barreled shotgun on his hip and a redbone hound by his side. He didn't say a word, just stood there in threadbare jean-cloth and a greasy skinning shirt. A pile of possum skins lay at his feet. Uncle Olin and J.T both snored in their saddles as I hailed the man – the only man I'd seen on my whole shift. "Howdy," I said, but he didn't reply – just spat out some black juice and admired the six ponies traveling down his road.

Funny thing was… he nodded at the horse. Not me.

His clothes were old-fashioned. I noticed them most.

I guess I had seen enough fashion in Leavenworth City to know it upon sight. J.T. insisted I replace my jean-cloth trousers and sack coat with black broadcloth. All the gentlemen wore it these days and it couldn't hurt Grandpa's defense to have a respectable grandson by his side. I wasn't quite sure how that helped, but I took J.T's word for it.

"You ain't wearing slave cloth at those hearings," He had said.

I was still wearing the same fine-spun wool coat from the hearing, which the man also eyed with some interest. He chewed on a weed and watched us pass, hefting his shotgun from hip to hip and fiddling with the two hammers with itchy fingers.

Not eight feet from me.

We rode out of that gulch and to the top of the next hill, and then started into another dark ravine. Gully after gully. Hill after hill. It seemed this whole country was nothing but deep defiles followed by high hills and sharp cliffs, all packed into dense brush and looming trees. Occasional strings of sunlight reminded me we were still heading south. But that's about all I knew. "Just head south," J.T. had said. "We'll make sure you stay clear of the Sni Hills when the time comes."

It seemed even the hoot owls and foxes stayed active in this dark place. Didn't they know it was daytime? A few yips and screeches broke the silence, and before long two more men appeared – one with a squirrel gun, the other an old three-band muzzleloader from the war. Both wore the same rotten wool trousers, greasy shirts, braces, and floppy black slouch hats – all cousins I guessed. They reminded me of Uncle Olin's friends that Ma hated so much. Mrs. Branson claimed none of them worked and never bathed. Mother said they were cutthroats and shiftless layabouts, and she didn't want me mingling with them, not even to pass the time of day.

And evidently, here stood two of their kin along this very road.

I put the ponies in a lope. They didn't look sociable. One drew a long drag off a dirty handmade pipe and the other spat forcefully, just like the first one I'd seen. Within ten minutes the owls and foxes sounded again, and three more men appeared.

This time I slapped the horse and leaned in for a run.

J.T. and Uncle Olin's ponies followed hard after. The six mounts flew under the dark canopy and over fallen trees. Ruts and washouts did not slow our stride. I rode for sunshine, wherever that might be, wishing I had a few of Uncle Olin's .36's under my belt.

More men scrambled from thickets and ramshackle houses. Each one let loose charges from their old shotguns, squirrel guns, flinters, muskets, revolvers or whatever they had. Even a few hatchets skinned by. I pushed the horses to their limits with hot lead whizzing overhead.

Pop, crack, zizzz… pop, zip… came shots from places I couldn't even see. I lashed the tired mount and slid in behind its flying mane. It felt like somebody had opened my veins, poured in a half pint of coal oil, and lit the fire.

"Don't kill the animals!" a man barked from a rooftop of an old barn.

"Let's scalp 'em alive!" another shrieked, with some enthusiasm. "And eat the ponies."

"I want their ears," his companion said, with a freakish laugh. "Fer me necklace!"

The horses coughed and fought the reins but I just lengthened their stride. I slapped leather and dug my spurs in harder. Bullets whistled over, and buckshot tore the brush on both sides of the crossfire. We flew into another gully and up the other side like a carnival ride at the county fair. But that didn't slow the rate of buck and balls flying thick and heavy across us. My horse had been already shot twice, and couldn't take much more of this. But I pushed him to his own demise.

"Keep ridin'!" Uncle Olin yelled from behind. They must have woken up awhile back.

Just as we dropped into another dark canyon, two slouch-hat hillbillies stepped right into the road ahead. They both lowered their muzzles and dropped the hammers. One ball tore through my hat, nicking my scalp. The other slammed straight into the pony's forehead. Blood and brains splashed over my face.

The pony dropped out from under me like dead weight and plowed right into the two hillbillies. I rolled over the horse's head and the two men, and bashed into the thick brush twenty feet away.

Both hillbillies were torn asunder.

"Get on, Jay!" Uncle Olin yelled. He threw out a hand and scooped me up. We rode hard for another hour, out of those hills and into a long meadow on the other side of the woods. Some cattle grazed next to a wide creek with a cabin nearby. All was quiet. We had escaped with our skins, but barely.

"You crazy bushwhackin' fool, Jay!" Uncle Olin yelled out as he let me off and jumped down. The ponies coughed and limped and snorted, all covered with blood and white foam. One of them stumbled and fell over. "You just rode straight through the Sni Hills, you danged ol' guerrilla bandit. With us two trailin' behind like a pair of ugly step-kids. You should see your bloody face. Oh, boy! Ain't it grand?" He slapped me on my wet chest and flopped down in the thick green meadow grass. "That is one story I am gonna love ta tell!"

J.T. cried out, "I'll give you this, Jeremiah: you sure got your bravery screwed on. That four-hour stretch saved us a day's ride. But I wouldn't care to repeat it anytime soon." He fell next to Uncle Olin and laughed until his belly hurt.

We crushed beans and boiled coffee, and laughed and retold the story ten times over. Uncle Olin acted out the bushwhacker parts, and J.T. and I laughed at how he spit tobacco and strutted around like we was invading Jerusalem with a squirrel gun. He pulled a Winchester from the scabbard and popped off a few rounds like a nasty hillbilly, still strutting around and looking as mean as he could. It was like a good minstrel show and we loved it.

After six cups of coffee each, we saddled up the hoof-sore ponies, minus one.

Uncle Olin tugged my shoulder and tried to look as serious as possible. "Where's your mount, Jay?" We all laughed again.

Four days later we dragged into Augusta, Arkansas – raw to the bone with bowed legs and saddle sores, almost as jaded as the mounts.

J.T. wanted to find his man. Real bad. But few in Augusta had even heard of Colonel Eli Raines.

"He lives up in those hills, I expect," one man said, but not quite convinced.

"You can try out that old road," another said, scratching his beard. "Raines ain't exactly a town bird, you know. He keeps to hisself, mostly."

The town sheriff looked at the man. "It's not that road atall, you old fool. Jes go up that there holler and turn right when you hit the saddle between those mountains." He pointed into an area that reminded me of the Sni Hills all over again. "Raines bunks in a little 'ol shack on the back side of that hill, right 'chair. They' ain't no road, but you'll see the trail. All this used to be his before the war." The sheriff pointed out a loop over a hundred-mile section of hemp, tobacco, and cotton fields. It stretched out to the horizon. "But as far as I know," the sheriff continued. "The land he lives on now ain't even his, and neither is that cabin he's holed up in. But you'll find him up thar, fer sure. Right up that draw, and behind that mountain, thar. Oh, and don't git ambushed on yer way in."

It took another half day to find the cabin.

Raines didn't exactly invite us in. At first only Uncle Olin could approach the cabin – on pain of death, if he was working for the federals. J.T. and me stayed back beyond shotgun range and let Uncle Olin parlay with the man. But soon Uncle Olin had him laughing and slapping knees. I couldn't hear a word he said; it was like a silent play. Uncle Olin pranced around, acting out some crazy scene up on the hill, and popping off revolvers and flinging his arms about. Raines doubled over and laughed and shoved Uncle Olin around a bit. The two of them jawed for fifteen minutes before remembering me and J.T. waiting down in the valley. They finally laughed and called us up.

The colonel looked at J.T. "Do I know you? You look familiar."

J.T. didn't answer.

The first thing I noticed about Raines's cabin was the complete lack of sitting space, or standing, or sleeping for that matter. Did the man use it strictly for his arms collection or did he actually live there? Ma kept our house so clean-swept I thought that's how all houses were. But not this one.

First off, a bunch of bullet holes had been shot into the cabin walls and ceiling – from the inside. A gunfight had, for sure, taken place here. Pretty spooky.

Four ragged rebel flags and every form of weapon, times three, hung from the walls – not just your rusty flinter over the mantle like most folks had. I saw four flintlocks, and four conversion muskets. Then there was eight of Grandpa's '61 Springfield's, and a few '53 Enfield's. Plus a few older Springfield's, carbines, two-banders, and one-offs from manufacturers I didn't recognize. Squeezed in-between the shoulder arms hung Colt revolvers, Remington pistols, Smith and Wesson's, .45 calibers, .36's, .32's, boot pistols, stock attachments, Henry repeaters, Sharps carbines, and every other firearm made for mankind.

"They're all loaded," the colonel said, offhandedly. "So don't lean up against 'em. Especially them old flinters. Could be touchy."

But it wasn't just the walls. Over every inch of floor space stood stacks of old Harpers Weekly's, hardtack boxes from 1863, '64, and '65, ammunition boxes – some opened, some sealed, friction primers, candles on bayonets, bear traps, man traps, varmint traps, ropes, tools, saws, saddles and tack, mining equipment, and a stack of wet-plate ambrotypes. And at the far corner next to the fireplace sat a big brass cannon, pointed straight at the door.

"That's a six-pound mountain howitzer. It's also loaded – double canister and a full pound of black powder – so don't trip the fuse." A lanyard stretched from the breach to a nail in the wall. "Touch that cord, and we all go to Kingdom Come," said the colonel, lifting it from the nail and pretending a little tug.

"Where do you sleep?" I asked, searching the floor for an empty spot.

"Mostly out back in a dog tent on a gum blanket." He pointed out beyond the mountain howitzer. "Couldn't no longer sleep in a bed after the war. Too shifty."

I didn't understand.

"Beds move," he clarified. "The ground don't." The colonel smiled back at Uncle Olin. "So, you brought your kin down to meet me!" He eyed me over a little. "That's a kind gesture to an old rebel like me. He looks just like you, when you and your pa rode with us and Quantrill. And you look jes like yer pa. But all growed up!"

Raines dug through a stack of ambrotypes and handed me a photograph of Grandpa and Uncle Olin from the war. Uncle Olin was scrawny like me with peach fuzz on his chin, maybe fourteen or fifteen. Grandpa looked like a wild-eyed bushwhacker, not no farmer. He wore a torn battle shirt with black powder stains down the front, a Colt pistol in each hand, and four more in his waist belt. His hair flew out like a dust devil but loosely held up by an ample supply of pomade. His eyes burned a hole straight back into mine.

His fierceness seemed to come right out of the ambrotype.

Someone had scratched the words, "The Archangel of Ambush" under Grandpa's image. All the men around him looked like dangerous fellows, not to be tangled with on any account, also bristling with revolvers and Bowie knives. Some had scalps hanging from their belts, and others a string of white things I could not identify. Maybe ears?

I laid the ambrotype back down and could not look at it again.

"Well, ya see…" Uncle Olin said, peering into the colonel's face. "That's what we come down here to talk to you about… Pa."

The colonel cocked his head.

"Pa's up in Leavenworth, right now. Got 'isself locked up. Guess his enemies caught up with 'm."

"Need me to bust him out?" the Colonel asked.

"Let's do!" Uncle Olin grinned. "I'd be like the old days again. I'll dynamite a hole in the wall."

"Remember Daniel P. Upham?" J.T. asked.

The mention of that name nearly sent the colonel for his weapons. His eyes steeled and his gut tightened.

He took another look at J.T. "I'm sure I know you."

J.T. still didn't say nothing.

The colonel said, "So… D.P finally caught up with ol' Hiram. Dang shame."

Me and J.T. and Uncle Olin spent that night explaining how Grandpa had been knocked out and chained in leg irons at the crossroads of Big Hollow and Randalls Flats, and how Uncle Olin rode all the way down to Fort Smith but could not find him there, but how J.T. came back to get us, and Uncle Olin bushwhacked him and tried to hang him from the rafters in the barn, but Ma saved him.

Uncle Olin chuckled and slapped J.T. on the back. "Dang near succeeded, pard!"

We told the colonel about the fourteen notches on Grandpa's army musket and the fourteen charges of murder Upham had on Grandpa. And how he liked to stack papers and look important.

The colonel's face turned hard at the mention of D.P. Upham.

"He is a brindle-tailed bull," the colonel remarked, staring at the opposite wall. "I fear I could not step foot into a room with the man. I would likely-as-not peel out a Bowie knife and do awful damage to his person, and not even remember the very act come morning. It would be so mechanical, I would just…"

He stared at the wall for good while, and tapped on his Bowie knife and ground his teeth.

I looked at the wall too. And besides the ample assemblage of weaponry I saw nothing that Marshal Upham ranted so much about: no cow horns or white hoods or burnt crosses, like he accused Grandpa and his kind of using. There were no signs of the Klan whatsoever, and I knew what to look for. As far as I could tell, Colonel Raines was nothing but a crazy old coot living out on the back side of some mountain. Upham's whole picture of unreconstructed rebels started to sound like a giant sham. But then… the Howitzer in the corner and loaded guns on the wall weren't exactly your happy home on the prairie neither.

The whole thing got all mixed up in my head. And then Grandpa's fiery eyes on the ambrotype came back into my mind.

"Archangel of Ambush."

I saw the same fire and fierceness in the colonel. He was no dirt farmer.

Uncle Olin worked a good deal on Raines. He wanted to bust Grandpa out, and said they could go west and rob Yankee banks and be outlaws again, like in the war. Jesse and Frank and Cole would welcome them in. And they could ride free again. And not be beholden to no carpetbagging federals. And maybe I could learn the trade like they did when they was young and free.

J.T. worked on Raines too. But instead, he wanted him to come up to Fort Leavenworth and testify on Grandpa's behalf. He explained how Upham had charged Grandpa with murdering the colonel's niece, Lydia Ellen, but that Judge Pennypacker still didn't have any idea what happened that night. All Raines had to do was tell the truth. Upham's story would be flushed down the sinks and Grandpa could come home. They wouldn't have to bust him out, and the colonel could keep his good name. Maybe Grandpa could even come down to visit his old pards from the war. And have a fandango.

The colonel just laughed. "Good name? I'm still a criminal, remember? Upham blocked my pardon when he couldn't get my men. I went to Washington and they threatened to prosecute. Never got it. And never went back. As far as I know, I'll die a citizen of the old Confederate States of America, nothing more – just a tired old reb. And I'll guarantee you," he said, looking around with a wary eye. "I take one step inside one of them military prisons, and they'll lock me up and swallow the key."

But J.T. and Uncle Olin kept working on him. Bust him out… or not. Either way.

Uncle Olin reminded the colonel of how I had risked my skin and rode straight through the Sni Hills and got shot at a hundred times, but it only creased my scalp, and that a horse was shot out from under me just like the great men in the war. He reminded the colonel of how many horses were shot out from under him. And Stonewall Jackson. And James Longstreet. And Joseph E. Johnson. But Uncle Olin didn't tell him how I was just stupid and took the wrong turn.

The Sni-A-Bar Hills impressed the colonel. "A horse shot out from under you, huh? Your first one? Up in them Hills? And you didn't surrender ta them bushwhackers?" he said, looking me over. "Reminds me of Hiram. You got his sand, kid. Grit and sand." He smiled and turned back to the guns on the wall. But I couldn't get out of my head that I was just stupid, and not brave at all. But the colonel didn't know that.

Colonel Raines stared into dead space. He tapped his shoes on the bare cabin floor, and tapped his Bowie knife. Then he scratched his beard and looked down.

Finally, he glanced up at J.T. and said reluctantly, "Alright then. You supply the coffee and I'll brang the hardtack."

He nodded back at the ancient cracker boxes along the wall. "We'll ride up there and see whose story wakes the dead. If that don't work, we'll bust him out."

The next morning we let out for Leavenworth, on nothing but hardtack and coffee.

Chapter Twenty

"DID YOU NOT RECEIVE our telegram? We expected you a month ago," Judge Pennypacker asked.

Colonel Raines lifted his eyes from his table in the courtroom, separated from Marshal Upham by two arm's lengths. "I'm not on the mail route, Your Honor."

Judge Pennypacker frowned. "Open loop system..." he muttered, scowling sideways at the first sergeant.

"Dern right, he ain't," Uncle Olin said louder than he ought.

The judge jerked up. "Remarks from the spectators?" Uncle Olin shut up and buried his head before the judge could identify him, but I think he knew who said it. "I will remind the spectators again that you are here by permission only and will stay your comments during this hearing or be removed from this courtroom forthwith."

The judge turned back to Colonel Raines. "I understand you were a U.S. Senator. From the State of Arkansas?"

The colonel's eyes widened in thought. "That... was a whole lifetime ago."

"A landowner and aristocrat, I presume." The colonel said nothing. "And I assume a slave-holder in that Southern agrarian culture."

I don't think the judge meant it but it sounded like an insult – like the colonel was less of a man than those northerners who had come down and conquered him.

The judge tried to make up for it. "In many ways, Colonel Raines, we are peers. But you... You have walked in the footsteps of our great framers, plumbing the finer depths of the constitution, and declaration, and the amendments, and those hallowed documents that guide our great nation today. I'm told you served in Congress in '58."

"That is true, Your Honor. Twenty years ago. Like I said, that was a whole lifetime ago. Everything was different; America was different back then; the whole world, in fact. But all that ended pretty quick-like, back in May of '61."

"When Arkansas seceded?"

"That's right, Your Honor. I found myself as a regimental commander in Ben McCulloch's ragtag army of rebels, but later joined up with some other infamous fellows. You might remember some: Joseph Shelby, William Quantrill, and Bill Anderson – also great men for the southern cause. Those partisan rangers took the fight into Missoura in a way McCulloch never could have, and Shelby is still a hero in all of Missouri. As I might say is the case with Hiram Cantrell, Frank James, Jesse James, Cole Younger, and his brothers. All Missoura heroes. But you got 'em in your books as criminals."

The colonel looked over at grandpa. He pursed his lips and nodded.

"Why fight in Missouri, Mr. Raines? You lived in Augusta, Arkansas."

"Two reasons, Your Honor: Missoura was where the action was, and it was a barrier between the northern hives. Fight 'em up there, and maybe keep 'em out of our territory. But it didn't exactly work."

"Fair enough."

"I commanded the little band of rebels that Hiram and Olin Cantrell fell in with, but we all rode for Quantrill and Anderson in the end. The Cantrell boys reported to me. And that is why I believe I am here today. Hiram's own grandson rode through the Sni-A-Bar Hills to find me. Risked his own hide." The colonel pointed me out with a smile. "I did not receive your telegram but this fine lad fetched me here to Hiram's aid. I respect a man with that much pluck." He smiled again and nodded.

The judge turned to me. In fact, the whole court turned to look at the crew who had ridden through the worst cutthroat alley of Missoura, just to fetch a witness for the court.

My face burned.

"And after the war?" the judge asked.

"All the southern governments were deposed after the war. Reconstructed, you call it. Abolitionists didn't trust them to ratify the slave amendments. But we would have, given some time... and a little respect for our losses. I went north and tried to see the President about that very prospect, but he would not see me, and because of my association with certain rebel guerrillas threatened to prosecute if I didn't skedaddle right back down to wherever I came from. But just before I left Washington, the President's men – that was Johnson back then – informed me that my plantation was needed for military training camps. 'Just temporarily,' they said. I had to clear out."

"So you lost your holdings?"

"That's right. When Arkansas was chopped up into military districts. Johnson refused my pardon; Washington would no longer seat me in Congress; and when I came home I found five-thousand Army tents in my dooryard, and I found that I could not so much as vote in any election. I was an outlaw. Of course, we rebels were still required to pay taxes on the property we 'owned,' but had no representation in Washington – except for a group of radicals that hated us. That's when the second civil war practically broke out."

The judge shook his head.

"Like I said, we would have signed those slave amendments."

"As I recall, that is precisely why we fought King George," the judge said. "No representation. It was no surprise to see it happen again. Men return to their oppressions every time."

"A goodly number of my men turned night riders after that, as did no small number in northern Arkansas. Governor Clayton declared martial law in ten counties, including Woodruff. The south was a wreck. We had to rebuild everything – railroads, bridges, courthouses..." The colonel looked around at the courtroom itself. "...government buildings, jails, homes, everything. And all that took money and oversight. But we had to do it at the point of a bayonet, under military occupation. And without the basic right to vote for our own representation."

The judge groaned.

"Men lost everything. Me included," the colonel continued. He paused to consider his words. "And I think, in part, that is precisely why we are here today." He looked straight at Grandpa who hadn't said a word yet. "This man stood in the gap for me. This man alone. He was there for me when the whole world stood against me. And he is imprisoned for going that extra mile."

"How so?"

"As you heard, judge, there was a little skirmish at my cabin."

"Where your niece was killed?" He peered into his papers. "Lydia Ellen Raines."

"That's right, Judge. But again, if it weren't for this man, Hiram Cantrell, I might not be sitting here today. He fought for me. I owe him everything."

Everyone turned to Grandpa.

Marshal Upham stood up. "Wonderful story, Your Honor." He clapped softly and put his hand over his heart. "Absolutely heart-warming, but also patently false. In fact, it was this man's crew, including Hiram Cantrell who was chiefly responsible for the '68 election bloodshed just ten years back. You remember it!"

The colonel shook his head.

Upham just kept right on. "A hundred unsolved murders a month in 1868 alone. You heard? It was these very men who terrorized blacks when voting, and in fact, when simply placing their own names on a ballot. To be a republican in the south was death to those freedmen. The old aristocracy – the big land owners – had their boots on their necks and these very men were the principle means of enforcing that control. Night rides, voter intimidation, and burning crosses. And yes, outright murder. Lynchings, stabbings, ambushings. I fought it for years. I led the Arkansas State Militia until they made me U.S. Marshal for the Western District Court under Isaac Parker in Fort Smith. Ever wonder why they called him the Hanging Judge? Because of all that hooded mayhem."

The colonel jumped up. "Upham, are you barking mad? Every word in your dictionary is Klan. Face it, your troopers were seizing farms and blocking ex-rebels from all commerce so you could build a kingdom in the south. Every low character with a carpetbag trundled down there to see what they could take from us, all claiming to be reconstruction officials under the unction of the federal government. All for the so-called good of the south. And all protected by the reconstruction puppets you represented. Our population doubled, just from northern vermin. What were we expected to do? Give it all away?"

"Okay, okay," the judge waved. "Let's just—"

"You heard the man himself," Upham complained, cutting off the judge. "He was a slave-holder on a big plantation for Heaven's sake. Where do you think his interests lay? He wants the old aristocracy back. And I guarantee you, they would never have ratified those amendments without—"

"Enough!" The judge slammed his fist down. "We are so far afield of the purpose for this hearing I don't know if we can ever recover. I know one thing about that whole mess," he said, eyeing both the warring parties. "The '68 elections were so convoluted it took months to discover who committed the greater fraud: republicans in their zeal to punish the south, or democrats to keep the black man in chains. So stop tearing open ten-year-old feuds or you'll find an enemy just as zealous in this very courtroom. Politics is not the purpose of this hearing and you both know that."

Upham threw up his hands. "You're not falling for this 'poor oppressed people' argument are you, Judge?" His hands waved wildly at the idea. "These men are bushwhacking killers. Klansmen. Notorious in their evil work."

"Oh, and you're the Blessed Savior?" Uncle Olin blurted out from behind the rail.

The judge's gavel slammed down. "I said stop! We will not rehash the past."

Both Upham and Raines huffed but sat down.

Both bared their teeth.

Sweat poured off the judge's brow. "May I remind you all of the purpose of this meeting? I have become aware of the death of a small girl, and Mr. Cantrell is charged with that death. We are here today for the facts and evidence surrounding that incident. Nothing more. Simply put, I wish to see the evidence you will present at the trial, should we proceed in that direction. Evidence, evidence, evidence. No politics, just facts."

The courtroom stilled.

"I'll start with you, Colonel Raines. Please stick to the facts of this incident. Your testimony counts as eyewitness evidence. That's all we're after here."

"Yessir, I will." He took another hard look at Upham but turned to address the judge. "This all started when Governor Clayton and U.S. Marshal Upham offered me a deal to turn over my men." He paused and looked at Grandpa. "That included Hiram Cantrell."

"And the substance of this deal?" Pennypacker asked.

"Turn over your men, and your pardon comes through. You might even get your farm back." He paused. "Let me be clear… Marshal Upham wished to arrest my former men on charges of voter intimidation, murder, theft, lynching, or any other millstone he could hang around their necks. In exchange for those men, my pardon would come through and my property would be restored."

Upham flipped his papers. "All night riders," he muttered under his breath.

"But I declined his offer. I value a man's life over a few tracts of land. Plus, I didn't actually believe the threat had merit. It's unconstitutional to seize land in America. After all, I was a U.S. Senator; I knew better. The whole 'forty acres and a mule' policy was an unconstitutional failure dreamed up by the most radical hordes in Washington."

"Back to the story," the judge reminded him. "No political commentary."

"I declined the deal so Upham and his men paid me a visit one night. I guess he wanted to apply a little pressure."

"Were you there, Mr. Cantrell? At this meeting?"

"I was outside with a few of the colonel's men. Not invited in."

"Hooded killers," Upham muttered again, which the judge reluctantly overlooked.

"An argument began inside the cabin," the colonel said. "Over this very issue. Turning over my men, that is. That lasted ten or fifteen minutes before some idiot cocked a revolver. Before long, all the weapons went off the half-cock."

"Did you witness this?" the judge asked Grandpa. "From outside?"

"Enough to git the idea. And that's when I raised my own musket, along with the other fellas in the ditch beside me."

"I can't even say who fired the first shot," the colonel said. "But the room was immediately filled with smoke, and my niece, who had just come over for apple pie lay dead under the table." The colonel pulled out his handkerchief. He wiped his nose and cleared his eyes.

"Did you see where the shot came from, Colonel?"

Raines finished clearing his eyes. "One of Upham's men. A young man, I believe."

"Can I speak, Your Honor?" Upham asked, impatiently. "This story is so full of fiction it makes my own eyes run." The judge waved him on, and Upham continued, "The part he left out was the broken window. There was a reason all the guns went off." He raised his hands in frustration. "People don't just start firing for no reason."

"Okay, let's hear about the broken window," the judge said.

Grandpa began sighing and sobbing, like before.

"Just before the guns went off, this coward..." Upham pointed at Grandpa. "This coward took a potshot through the window at the governor – Governor Powell Clayton. That's what started it all. At the time the governor stood roughly four feet from the girl. Evidently, Cantrell missed the target and hit the girl instead. But as soon as the window shattered, the girl went down, and everybody lost their minds. Ten revolvers went off nearly at once. I suppose everyone thought they had been fired upon, and reacted so as to immobilize their own supposed killers. But the only true killer lay outside in a filthy ditch like the coward that he is."

Grandpa could not stop the emotion. His sobbing turned into voice and he stood to speak. "I am not an innocent man, Your Honor."

"And why would you undertake to shoot the governor of the State of Arkansas?" the judge asked.

"The governor wasn't my target." Grandpa stopped to clear his eyes. "Clayton weren't no friend of the rebels, I'll admit that. But he was there to stop Upham from pushin' this deal. The deal was rotten and Clayton knew it. Jes like Raines said, you cain't take a man's land. It ain't in the constitution. But Upham couldn't be stopped. He gits like a madman when he wants somethin'."

"So who was the target?" the judge asked.

"One of Upham's deputies standing right behind Clayton with a boot pistol aimed at his head. But I guess I missed him and hit the girl, like the marshal said. But I still don't see how that's possible. I didn't often miss. Not at that range."

Grandpa looked at Raines. He sighed heavily. "I am so sorry, friend. But this has gnawed at me for ten years. I shoulda come straight out with it."

The courtroom went dead.

J.T. cleared his throat and stood up to speak. He was next to me. "That's close to what happened," he called out from the spectator's bench. He held up a mashed .58 caliber Minnie ball. "I dug this out of Colonel Raines cabin wall just weeks ago, adjacent to the window Hiram Cantrell fired through. This is the hard evidence you're looking for, Judge. Want to hear what I think?"

Chapter Twenty-One

December, 1878

"THIS MINNIE BALL HAS a story of its own, Daniel, and it wants telling," J.T. said, standing before Marshal Upham in the hallway, clutching the lead ball he had dug out of the Raines cabin wall. "I guess you'll just have to cinch up your braces when I tell it."

The judge had called a recess and Upham lit into J.T. about the Raines cabin and the shooting, and the Minnie ball he had dug out. All Upham's men joined in until there was almost a fistfight.

Upham peeled off his hat and threw his jaw out. "Then we might just as well count this case lost. All that tracking work, gone. Months and months. All those nights freezing in the rain, and spooning for warmth, and condemned pork and rancid coffee, and tracking this killer to the ends of the earth: all gone. You want that? Is that what you rode a thousand miles to see?"

J.T. shook his head. "You sound like you're hiding something. As if this single bullet could unravel your entire case."

"It well could."

"Alright then, let it be." J.T. paused. "Daniel, I'm just trying to find the truth for this man and his family. He deserves that much. He's had a raw deal. You have to admit that. And if your case hangs on a single bullet then you'd better dig up a little more evidence."

Upham shook his head. "Have you forgotten who this fellow is?

The acts he's committed? Let's just let this go to trial like it should. Then all the evidence will come out in due time." Upham lowered his voice and tried to reason with J.T. "John, okay, forget the bloody mayhem during the war. Cantrell was a murdering savage like those he rode with. But forget that for now. You know as well as I what he's done since."

I jumped in front of Marshal Upham. "Just what has he done since? Kept a roof over our heads with Yankee bankers at us every day?" I shouted, trying hard to get my courage up enough to challenge the lawman. I even threw out my chest and cocked my head back. I figured if I could ride through the heart of Confederate territory, I could stand up to a Yankee devil like Upham.

But I would've been better off facing down hillbillies.

The marshal stood a head taller than me. His face and neck were tight and hardened by years in the saddle. Razor-sharp eyes squinted like a hawk as he edged around and sized me up. And then all he had to do was put on that big felt hat and stare down at me. I soon learned it's harder than it sounds to face a man down. You either have the courage in your gut, or you keep shut. But I guessed he didn't really owe me an answer. I'd sat through the hearings. I knew exactly what Grandpa was up against. Fourteen murders for fourteen notches. And they weren't heroic ones like in the nickel books.

But maybe J.T. was right about this bullet.

The next thing that happened felt like a kick in the head. I found that the man wasn't so harsh, wasn't so monstrous. Upham's eyes were not as fierce as I thought they'd be face to face, but not piteous either. They searched for what courage I had in store, and what I secretly hoped to bring to bear.

I tried.

He just laid his hand on my shoulder and squeezed. "I'll look into that, son," he said. He could have been somebody's Pa.

But then the first sergeant threw open the courtroom with rough usage on his face. "Judge Pennypacker wants all y'all in there right now. He's not happy about how you spent the recess. The old man ain't deaf, you know."

Upham took J.T's arm and shook his hand as they headed into

the courtroom. "We're still pals, right?" He laughed and patted J.T. on the back and tried to get him to smile back. But it didn't work.

One of Upham's men tugged J.T's coat sleeve and whispered. "Did you know there's a captain's position in Fort Smith? Upham says you're a good soldier and could get it. But you'll need a good word from him, you know. He's not your enemy."

The judge called the hearing to order. "John T. Martin. I'd like to hear more about this lead ball you dug out of the Raines cabin. Your testimony may also serve as evidence in a trial, if it comes to that. When did you obtain this ball?"

J.T. held up the Minnie ball. "A month ago, when Hiram Cantrell's son and grandson fetched Eli Raines here to testify." He turned his hand toward Colonel Raines. "This bullet was lodged in his wall, just opposite of the broken window I mentioned earlier. The broken glass had been covered over with newsprint for ten years. I tore off layer after layer, and the window pane looked the same as it did ten years ago."

"Now you owe me a window glass," Raines said, smiling.

The judge lifted his hand. "Yes, yes." He thought for a minute. "Ahh—"

J.T. cut in. "Your Honor, in my opinion, Mr. Cantrell did not shoot Lydia Ellen Raines, the colonel's niece."

Marshal Upham slapped the desk and shifted in his seat. The judge glanced at him but didn't ask his opinion.

"And how did you arrive at this conclusion, Mr. Martin? There could have been two shots from outside the cabin. One that landed in the wall and one that hit the girl. Or, the ball that hit the girl could have lodged in the wall after exiting her body. Either way could explain a shot from Mr. Cantrell, as Marshal Upham alleges."

"Definitely not two shots. The window pane was still mostly intact. It had only one bullet hole. You see, there was a large broken area with cracks around. That was clearly from one ball. So that rules out two shots through the window."

Upham broke in. "If he's such a marksman, maybe the second shot went through the same hole."

"I'll concede that possibility," J.T. said. "But since there's no proof of that, it's just speculation. Maybe it did, maybe it didn't. But I'd guess not."

Judge Pennypacker asked, "And as for the possibility of the ball exiting the girl's body, and then lodging in the wall?"

"Too high. And too deep. Unless the Minnie ball glanced off a bone and ricochet up, it would never be found at such a high point on the wall. Again, it's a possibility, but unlikely. Especially how deeply it was embedded. This was no spent round glancing off bone."

"Please elaborate."

"A bullet glancing off bone loses energy. It can't go deeply into wood."

"A spent round. I see."

Colonel Raines said, "So, it happened like I remembered, then? The shot came through the window after the other shots went off? Not before?"

"I believe so," J.T. said, turning to Raines. "You didn't mention the broken window in your account of the incident because it happened after the shooting had started. When you were ducking for cover. Or, so I believe. Later, you probably assumed the window had been broken by bullets flying out from the room – from one of the revolvers fired from within the cabin. But I believe it came from without. And since it is a .58 caliber Minnie ball, it probably came from a sharpshooter's musket not one of the .45 caliber revolvers inside. Pistols don't fire this large bullet. And it's the only one stuck in your cabin walls. There are no others."

"No others? I thought all the guns went off," Pennypacker asked.

"All .45's or lower. This was the only .58."

"Did anyone think to extract the bullet from Lydia Raines's body?" the judge asked.

The whole room cringed.

The notion of digging bullets out of dead people didn't sit with anyone in the room. Everyone shook at the idea.

"Evidently, not," the judge said. "But if they'd had, we'd know the caliber of bullet that killed her. Don't you think that would help?"

A few eyebrows went up, but mostly everybody just shook the

creeping willies off.

J.T. picked up again. "I think the room was so full of smoke the sharpshooter did not know his target had moved. Which is why we found the bullet lodged in the cabin wall – where it might have hit a taller man. But it evidently hit no one."

J.T. held up both hands for effect.

"Picture this scene," he said. "Tensions in the cabin are rising. Arguments, words, and maybe a few threats are exchanged. Enemies and allies become clear. Then a few guns go to full-cock, then more, then one goes off, then another until you've got pandemonium... and then finally... after all those internal shots... the sharpshooter's Minnie ball comes through the window without notice whatsoever. It simply lodges in the wall opposite the window."

J.T. paused and looked at Grandpa.

"The shooter outside could not have known what was about to happen inside. He could not have heard the guns cocking, or known the tension in the room at the time. By the time he fires, the room is filled with smoke and his target has moved. That's what I believe happened."

"That would seem logical," Raines added. "I never put the two together. There are twelve slugs in my cabin walls, and I never once connected the broken window to any one of them. And never checked the caliber. Nobody in the room used a big .58 caliber bullet. They were all .45's or less. Mostly .36's in them little belly-guns, I'd guess."

J.T. continued, "Based on Hiram Cantrell's testimony, I believe the first man to cock his weapon would have been the man standing directly behind Governor Clayton. The one with the boot pistol. Like the assassin, John Wilkes Booth. This man's intentions were not honorable as I recall from Mr. Cantrell's testimony. If that were true, it would explain the shot through the window to immobilize him before he could carry out his intentions on the governor. But I have no proof of that. It just sounds logical."

Marshal Upham couldn't stand it any longer. He jumped up. "You're dern right you have no proof of that. All you've got is a mashed Minnie ball, and you're spinning yarns around it like an Easter egg."

Marshal Upham and J.T. fought over the Minnie ball theory for another half hour. Colonel Raines sided with J.T, and everyone else with Upham. Upham tried to say the shot came through the window first and hit the girl, and that's what started everybody shooting. J.T. and Raines didn't remember it that way. They thought the shooting started first, and made it impossible for Grandpa to see. That's why the bullet hit the wall instead of the man with the boot pistol behind the governor.

J.T. was getting the best of Upham.

But I just watched Grandpa's face through the whole thing. He almost smiled. And that's not something Grandpa often did. I hadn't seen him smile in a month. And never once when I was behind a pair of mules.

Judge Pennypacker had finally heard enough. "Mr. Cantrell… Can you shed any light on this mystery? It seems like we've got about three versions of the events. Frankly, I find it difficult to ferret out the truth of the matter. But I think I'm getting there."

Grandpa finally smiled widely. "Sons of thunder! When I squeezed off that shot, Yer Honor, thar was a puff a smoke inside that cabin, jes like young John said. But I had nary an idea of what was happening behind it. For ten years now, I thought the girl was killt by my own hand."

Grandpa could not speak after that. His eyes filled with tears and he shook his head over his lap and smiled, and then raised a hand to Heaven. "Glory to God," he finally muttered. "Glory be His Holy Name. I have not shed innocent blood in thy sight."

J.T. and Colonel Raines nodded. Upham scowled.

"Gentlemen," the judge called out. "I think this hearing has given us all we can learn from the incident. I'm going to call an end to the hearings. There is one thing I have learned from eyewitness testimony. It is notoriously poor, especially after ten years. Witnesses remember things differently. Words change; events change; even the participants change. We must take what we can from them, and attempt a fair rendition. That is all we can expect. Gentlemen, my decision to proceed with the trial, or not, will be forthcoming. Expect it within a month – certainly before the end of January for sure. I thank you all for your hard work, your patience, and the time you have spent here. It has been a hard eighteen months. But this matter will be resolved expeditiously. I will assure you of that."

The judge turned to Colonel Raines. "Colonel, when this matter is finally concluded, I plan to undertake the rectification of injustices done to you."

"Beg your pardon, sir?"

"That's exactly what I'm saying, Colonel. A pardon. I understand you have not yet received yours, and that is a crying shame. I also understand that your property in Woodruff County has not yet been restored to your ownership and practical use. I intend to rectify that as well if it is within my power to do so. I will make the trip to Washington and raise the matter before my superiors. I would enjoy your company on such a trip if you can spare the time away from your duties."

"I'm a rebel, Your Honor. I'd be arrested on sight anywhere above the Mason Dixon line."

"I doubt that. I think you've given enough for your country. And I think you're due an apology for the trials and tribulations you've suffered. I'd consider it an honor."

Chapter Twenty-Two

February, 1879

GRANDPA GOT A HALF day out of his cell on account of some dead president's birthday. He scoffed at the idea but I loved it. We walked out into the prison yard where all the other inmates were gathering. It was a big yard. Enough for three hundred-and-fifty men.

"Lincoln was no Moses in the wilderness," Grandpa said. He sat and plucked grass. Even though there was a little snow up against the new stone walls, the day was warm enough to lighten Grandpa's mood. He held his face to the sun and closed his eyes. That made him happy.

"Well, I'm glad..." he said, thinking. "I'm glad the negros got their independence. Lincoln did that for them, but at the expense of every comfort." Grandpa looked into the sky. "I've never admitted this, Jeremiah, but I do believe John Wilkes Booth shot the only friend the south ever had."

"What!" That was strange for Grandpa to say.

"Yup. I've been thinking. After Lincoln, Johnson came down on us rebels awful hard. And then everything busted loose all over again. If Lincoln were alive today things would be different. Raw deal all around, I reckon..."

Grandpa finally laid back on the grass and fell asleep.

I looked up at the new stone wall that replaced the old stockade fence and tried to remember the knothole I yelled through almost two years ago. The new wall was twenty feet high in places, running over rises and valleys. Stone gun towers on each corner had replaced the old wooden shacks on stilts, and armed men paced back and forth in them. The prisoners had laid a lot of stone in the last twenty-some months. This was the work of General Blunt with his grand dream to erect a castle. He had also staked out spots for all his buildings, but the work stopped several months back. Somebody said the generals in Washington wouldn't give him the money to finish his new disciplinary barracks – the USDB. The Indian wars were taking all available resources. So, all the perfect little white stakes started to turn brown and lean in. Most of the prisoners just worked on trenches and walls and such, and the general brooded up in his office about the progress of his dream prison.

"Couldn't we bust out of here? Up over that wall?" I asked.

Grandpa woke and shielded his eyes from the sun and scanned the wall. "Fine workmanship. Some of those stones are mine. Real fine work."

"But what if Uncle Olin and me was to lower a rope or something? Or cut a hole through that rock? Maybe we could–"

Just then J.T. walked up from the judge advocate's office. That was a whitewashed stone building near the prison entrance. Building 473, I think. He came right up to Grandpa with something on his mind. And he didn't look happy. I saw him come up but grandpa didn't seem to notice or care.

"Sure you could. If you wanted to be outlaws, like me," Grandpa said. "You want that?"

"I 'spect it's time you came home is all. Mother and me need you." I got up and paced around, uneasy and impatient. "Maybe if we…" I muttered, but couldn't come up with anything better than the rope idea. Cutting through stone and masonry stymied me.

It just seemed Grandpa didn't care what happened to him. I know if I was in here I'd bust out and go west. Uncle Olin said there was hundreds of outlaws out west. So what would a few more make? And I'd wallop every last one of them jailers on my way out too. Except maybe the first sergeant that took me to see Thomas' hanging. He was nice to us.

Grandpa looked into the sun. "I'll be home soon enough, son." He studied my impatient face, which by now had no shortness of fume and fury. "Bless them that curse you and pray for them that despitefully use you," he said, laying back.

That's the kind of stuff Ma always said. Or Sherriff Cletus, back before he was kilt.

"Hiram," J.T. whispered. He paced around impatiently. "We've got to—"

"But—" We both talked at once. J.T. stopped and let me finish.

"But Upham's got you on those fourteen murders," I said. "I even seen the notches under the lock plate, on your old musket."

"Sit down, Jeremiah. I've been meaning to speak to you about that." Grandpa leaned over to take my shoulder. "It's not what you think, son. I told you that from the beginning."

"But those papers... The Marshal don't seem like a liar."

"Listen to the boy, Hiram." J.T. said. "You've got to come up with something better or your case is definitely going to trial. We did what we could with that Raines affair but those other thirteen don't look good. I think the judge has already dismissed Eli Raines. He tried to come see you, but couldn't get in. Have you got anything else I can take to the judge?"

"Upham's papers are real," Grandpa said. "But them fourteen notches was fer somethin' entirely else." Grandpa stopped and drew breath. Then he looked deep into my eyes. "It's about time you knew what really happened down there."

"I don't care what happened," I said. "I jes want to jump this wall and go home."

"Cain't do that, son." He tightened his lips. "But at least you'll know."

Two sergeants with shotguns walked past. There were a dozen like them in the yard, as the men stretched out on the grass and soaked up the warm dry heat. I watched them and wondered if I could grab a shotgun off one of those sergeants and shoot our way out. Grandpa didn't even look at them.

"The fourteen notches are lands we took back from the

Freedman's Bureau," he finally said.

"From black folks?"

"No," J.T. said. "The Bureau of Refugees, Freedmen, and Abandoned Lands – in other words, the government. Folks called it the Freedman's Bureau because they just worked with freed blacks."

Grandpa nodded. "Them 'abandoned lands' is where we had our disagreements. Fourteen to be exact. That's what them notches is fer. One for every abandoned land we took back from them polecats in Washington."

"If they were abandoned, then nobody cared about them anymore. Right?" I asked.

"Problem is," Grandpa said. "They wadn't abandoned. That's jes what they called 'em so they had the legal right to take them, but they wadn't abandoned atall. You heard what Raines said. Some had darkie farms on 'em. Others occupied by a fat northern general and his army, or a carpetbagging bureaucrat and his family. But they all belonged to somebody at one time. And at least fourteen of 'em still belonged to my friends and acquaintances. Southern men of the Confederacy."

"Oh."

"Remember Eli Raines? The military men used his land for a training camp. More like a squatter camp, if you ask me. And they run him off, more or less. Look where he's living now. Happened more offen than you'd like ta think."

Grandpa eyed J.T. cautiously. "Northern vandals took whatever they could git away with. After the South was whooped. That's why Eli Raines is livin' out in that old shack, and not in the big house. Did you see it on your way in?"

"We saw it," J.T. said. "But not every northerner..." His words trailed off as Grandpa closed his lips and let his eyes return to the high wall. Grandpa didn't want an argument. He just wanted to explain.

"Go ahead, Hiram," J.T. said. "I'm sorry I interrupted."

Grandpa picked grass and let it fall it into the wind. "They was stolen lands as fer as I could tell. I ain't sayin' the Freedman's Bureau was a bad crew. They done good for the freedmen. And I never had no beef with colored folks. But the Freedman's Bureau wuz erected by the federal Government – white folks – northerner carpetbaggers and southern scalawags."

"But what happened, Grandpa? With those lands?"

Grandpa lifted his head. "What happened was that we took those lands back. And every time we done one, I nicked a little wood off that musket. Up under the lock plate, where you seen it. I ain't no killer, son."

J.T. bent down. "Did you go to Mexico with Shelby's gang after the war? He never surrendered. I just figured… maybe… if you were in Mexico at the time of those–"

"I did not," Grandpa said, looking into the sun, which occasionally peaked out from under the clouds and warmed us a little. It was still winter and we didn't even have coats.

"But yer right, Shelby never did hang out the white flag. And I reckon I didn't neither. Most a the boys did, but there wuz a fair number that kept right on raiding after the war. Train robbin' and such. Frank and Jesse, I reckon…" Granpda's voice quieted off as he named the men. "Cole and Jim and Bob… Sam Bass… The real men of the Confederacy, I expect. They never surrendered. Never reconstructed."

Grandpa looked up from his thinking with renewed passion. "But they never killed a man that didn't need killing. And they never robbed a train that didn't first earn the reputation of carting a horde of squatters onto our properties and stealing them out from under us. I don't blame them James boys a lick. And I don't believe Missoura does neither."

"But Grandpa, Jesse James was a night rider. That means he was a Klansman."

"No, he was not. Not all rebels was Klan. And Jesse James certainly was not. You got to understand that. The Klan was something else. Nathan Bedford Forrest got tangled up in it in Tennessee, but even he got out. Us bushwhackers ne'er joined it. Not Jesse, and not Frank."

"Did you ride with the James gang? Or the Youngers?" J.T. asked.

"Had the opportunity, but I had other work. Jesse and me wuz pals, ya know. Well, maybe Olin more than me. Olin wuz his age. Fourteen or fifteen when the war started. All the boys coon-hunted together back then. But I was an old man – thirty-something. So Frank and Cole and me wuz best pards."

"You said you had other work," J.T. asked. "What was that? Is this something we can approach the judge with? I've got to give him something."

"The other work I ain't particularly proud of."

J.T. picked his teeth with a stick. "But it wasn't murder. Not like Upham claims?"

Grandpa paused, and picked more grass.

"Ya know, I done what I had ta…"

"Did you help the Klan?" I asked.

"I did not. Had nothin' to do with them. Already told you that."

"Grandpa… does fighting for the Confederacy mean you are secesh?"

"Yes, it does. But that don't mean slavers, and it don't mean Klan. Secession from the government is something else. It's sayin' we ain't goin' along with yer nonsense. We weren't fighting for slavery, Jeremiah. Not a family in a hundred could afford slaves anyhow. We didn't care a lick for the 'peculiar institution', as they called it. I don't think you understand…"

"Abuse of power," J.T. said. "He's talking about the government overstepping its bounds and the rights of the states, and the rights of ordinary citizens. And protesting its abuse of power. That's why they seceded from the government."

"That's right. Abuse of power. Thank you, J.T. That's what we seceded from. Ain't no different than King George and the Boston Tea Party. We wuz fightin' for independence. Not slavery. For the right to control our own selves without some man in Washington sayin' what we can and cain't do. You got to get that through yer head."

Grandpa paused for his thoughts. "Remember, Jeremiah… They invaded us."

"After you seceded," J.T. added.

"No! Before! Lincoln invaded Missoura before we ever declared secession. A full five months before, dang it! The federal government is supposed to be limited. But they got the idea they didn't have to. And they could invade any state that didn't agree with them."

Grandpa raised his hands. "Can't ya see that?"

I nodded. "I guess so." But as far as I could tell states didn't have no power. It was all the federal government. So I didn't know exactly what Grandpa meant. The federal government was the ones that made all the rules. But I guess things was different back in Grandpa's day.

Grandpa tried to explain. "Does the President have the right to invade a state? Or set laws to control it? If so, what is freedom? Are we free or not?"

Nobody answered.

Grandpa continued. "And how about Nathanial Lyon invading Missoura with his Dutchies and Iowa gang? Wuz that right? Federal occupation in a sovereign state? Or McClellan invading Virginia? Missoura was neutral for dern sake, and we jes wanted to be left alone. But Lyon come bustin' right into Camp Jackson with ten thousand men. Somebody threw a bottle, and those Dutchy federals shot twenty-eight townsfolk. Now I ask you, was Lyon prosecuted? Or Lincoln impeached for invading his own people? I tell you... today people fear the federal government like they did King George. Just like in the Revolutionary War. I'll tell you another thing; I was a union supporter before the Camp Jackson affair. After that, everythang changed."

"All true," J.T. said, shaking his head. "But still—"

"Maybe that was the only way slavery could be stopped," I said. Then I stepped back because I wasn't sure if Grandpa might just haul off and snatch me baldheaded. He didn't tolerate backtalk. But I guess that didn't stop me. "They say power concedes nothing without a demand. How else could you stop slavers? You got to fight 'em."

Grandpa sighed.

"I am weary of this argument," he said. "The bottom is out of the tub."

"Let's go back to the other work you said you had," J.T. said. "Is there anything you can give me for the judge?"

"We just got them lands back, one by one. That's all. Jes like I said. We'd either smoke them federals out, or toss in one of them exploding shells, or run 'em off at night. Yes, sometimes it was negros that squatted on those lands but mostly it was northern men grabbin' 'em up and trying to get rich off another man's sweat. Ex-rebel lands. We burned and pillaged and done whatever until them northern usurpers cleared off. And that's just about all. Nothin' more. Every time we cleared another off, I marked it on the Springfield. And that's how I come to have dem notches."

Grandpa signed. "I jes wanted you to know."

Chapter Twenty-Three

"G RANDPA?" I WHISPERED, POKING my head between the bars of his cell door. "You awake?"

I had a pretty good feeling about today. And I was sure Grandpa would too. Almost two years of not knowing had passed. Months of crying and praying and waiting. Of visiting Grandpa and not knowing which day would be his last. And listening to Marshal Upham accuse him of every crime the Yankees had a law for. And seeing Thomas walk the thirteen steps to perdition for crimes I didn't even understand. Every day I woke to a start. Like falling down a well and not knowing when you'd hit bottom. But there was no bottom; you just kept falling.

But today we'd climb out.

For a good reason.

Colonel Raines had told me Grandpa should talk to a person he knew. Somebody that the colonel had in mind for Grandpa's very predicament, but that I probably hadn't met. Maybe he'd be worth having a talk with. And maybe there'd be a solution in it somewhere. It couldn't hurt. Back when we talked, Colonel Raines sent a wire for the man to come.

And he did!

"Grandpa, I brought somebody. I hope you don't mind." By now the first sergeant was letting any number of visitors into Grandpa's cell. That is, if they could all squeeze in. Sometimes it was Uncle Olin and me. Or Uncle Olin and Cousin Buford. Or maybe all three of us, but Buford got pretty fidgety when anybody got too close or touched him too much. He didn't like the cell at all. Sitting in the corridor counting bricks made him much happier. The count was always the same: 11,657. But he was not the least bit happy with a broken one next to the drainage ditch. He could not decide if that represented one brick or two. That single brick vexed him to no end. I asked to have it replaced but was ignored.

The first sergeant also started letting me see Grandpa more often. Sometimes three or four days a week. I'd show up on a Tuesday night or Friday morning, and he'd stand by the iron door and let the hours go by. Grandpa never got another beating on the old gray mare, never again got reduced rations, or punishments for talking too loud, or failing to sound off when his number was called. The sergeant just looked at him sad-like, like he was his grandpa too, and let me spend all the time I wanted. It took a little hog-trading but I finally convinced the sergeant to let this stranger in with me: the man Colonel Raines had sent.

I whispered in to Grandpa. "His name is Alexander Franklin. Colonel Raines said you might like to talk to him. He's just outside. Do you feel like talking?"

"Who?"

"Alexander Franklin. He just rode in last night. He says he knows you." I led the tall, slender man through the door. He had to step over the iron frame and duck his head at the same time. But he looked like he'd done it before.

Just like J.T, he wore a fashionable black broadcloth frock with silk cravat and round-top derby. Fine wool clothing, not cotton or linen like they wore back home. And machine stitching. Even his shoes were shined and his pant legs not frayed. He didn't look rich, just a well-heeled city gentleman. Maybe he was a lawman or a lawyer – something to do with the law, I thought.

Grandpa stood up to meet the man, and the three of us filled all the empty space next to the bunk. When Grandpa first laid eyes on the man, I thought he was going to fall over.

"Frank James!" he said, throwing his hands out and shaking his head in wild excitement. "Alexander Franklin James." Grandpa laughed and grabbed the man by both shoulders. Being a slender man, Grandpa shook him up a fair bit. He laughed and the man laughed too, and Grandpa shook him even more. The man tottered so bad he knocked his head on the iron door and had to coddle it for a good while.

"Yer going ta have me shook to death, Hiram!" the man said, and punched Grandpa in the shoulder and laughed some more. "What are you doing in here, pard?"

"Sit here, Frank, and I'll learn ya all there is ta know about prison life. You might need it someday at the rate yer going!"

"Oh, I know plenty!"

"Jeremiah, you stand by the door and let the man sit." The man sized me up but said nothing. He just smiled and removed his derby and cocked his head toward Grandpa who sat on the bunk. The two could not stop smiling and chuckling. Snapping their fingers and laughing.

Now I really felt good.

They spent the next half hour churning up old stories. Like all the trouble they had gotten into and how they got out of it just as easily. It was like the two had been schoolyard boys hiding behind a privy to evade a schoolmarm on the warpath. Stick in hand, the old bitty could not locate the two as they ran off to fish and swim in the creek and lay about in the sun. I never saw Grandpa so happy. Ever.

"Where's Jesse?" Grandpa finally asked. "That boy's a regular firebrand. Bravest kid that ever tore a cartridge."

"Oh you know, gallivanting like he does. He needs the adventure. Planning another job maybe. Or some new way to confound the likes of the Chicago and Rock Island Railroad, still carting in carpetbaggers from the penitentiaries and pest-holes of the northern states. They all want to see the devastated South and poor white trash in burned-out shanties, you know. It's a novelty up north. Like shaved ice."

Mr. James laughed. "As long as there's a wild-eyed rebel left, they'll come just for the sport. Yankees hunt Injuns the same way now. Can't let them be, neither."

"Yes, yes. So what brangs you in, Frank? I'm so glad ta see ya!"

"You won't believe it but I ran into another old friend. Remember Eli Raines? Our old colonel from the regiment? He stopped by my place."

Then Mr. James seemed like he wanted to change the subject. He squinted and tried to sound happy again, and talk about back home. "I'm living in that greasy little town of Nevada, Missoura now. Right on the border with them white-livered abolitionists. Cain't avoid 'em wherever I go. You knew about that, right?"

"I heard," Grandpa said. "Got a proper life now. I understand. But now... ah... back to old Eli Raines. He came to see you? That's a genuine curiosity cuz I seen him just a few months back, myself."

"Is that so," Mr. James marveled.

He sniffed and looked around the cell.

"Well, there ain't no dancing around this, Hiram," Mr. James said. He got serious right smart. "I know yer in a spot. Raines said your grandson needed some help, and thought I should drop in for a visit. Ta see what I could do."

Grandpa turned to me. The veins of his clenched jaw sprang up tight as piano wires. Not a good sign. But he didn't say a word. He just tilted his head and turned back to Mr. James.

"I don't need that kind of help, Frank," Grandpa said.

Mr. James jerked back. "No, no." He paused and lowered his voice. "Of course not. It's just that I did a bit of scouting on my way in last night. This place ain't exactly a fortress. Jesse, Cole, and me have hit banks with more rock. And I'm not altogether unfamiliar with fortresses neither. You know that. This place would pop like a grape." He leaned in and whispered. "They got low spots on the wall, dark areas under trees, spots a horse could practically jump over. Heck, they got wide open sluices to clean the sinks! A man could slip right down through and into the Missoura River. You seen 'em?"

"I've seen 'em."

"You could cut a skeleton key out of wood, or use a bent nail." He picked at the mortar with his fingernail. "Heck, you could loosen up these bricks and fill them in with oatmeal."

The first sergeant leaned in. "You boys best lower your speech.

Words travel in these brick corridors." He pulled his head back out and stood post like an obedient soldier. "Just sayin'…."

Grandpa looked a little confused. He looked at me again, grimly, and then back at Mr. James. "I ain't lookin' fer a way out. Already got that."

Mr. James looked relieved. "Oh! I didn't know you had that angle covered. My apologies, friend. But if you–"

"Don't plan to bust out, Frank. I've made my peace with God. I'm staying right here to take what punishment comes, or be let loose on legal grounds. What I done was justice, not murder. And like I said, I ain't lookin' for an easy escape. Jesus already done that fer me."

"Hiram, no man has touched my guns since '61. You know that. But I'm offering them to you now. Let's be realistic. You'll hang if you stay, just as sure as the cock crows. You and I know these thangs. Look around you! Yer in a Yankee prison, up on Yankee charges, tried by a pack of danged Yankee baby eaters. What do you think's going to happen?"

Grandpa just shrugged.

"I want to ask you just one thing, Hiram," Mr. James said. "And I want you to answer true."

"Go on. I'm listening."

"What have all them rebels done fer you? All Missoura's talking about you. And Arkansas, too. You rescued their lands from usurpers, right? Ten? Twelve properties?"

"Fourteen."

"Alright, fourteen properties, so where are the fourteen men now? Are they up here testifying for you? Standing up fer you? Busting you out of jail? Gittin' you free?"

Grandpa shrugged. "Don't rightly know. Eli Raines came."

"Well, that's the point, Hiram. They ain't up here helping you. 'Cept Raines. And the way I heard it, it wuz only on account of your grandson riding through them Sni Hills and getting a horse shot out from under him. That's what it took to fetch Raines up here. Yer taking all the blame, and not a single one's up here giving his life for you. So I say, bust out and go west. You don't owe them your life. And like you said, it was justice not murder. Every soul in Missoura knows that by now."

"I owe Jesus my life," Grandpa said. "And He's told me to sit patient for just a little while longer. But I take yer point, Frank."

"Hiram, Hiram. Listen. I'll brang in Jesse and some boys that are itching to lay down their skins for you after what you done for them in the war. Now… you know Cole is in prison and Sam Bass is dead, right? But still, I could have a dozen men here tomorrow. Hard men. Men willing to do what's necessary. I guarantee you, busting out of jail is no harder than bank robbing or train holdups." He laughed easily, like it was a small thing to stop a million tons of iron and rob all the citizens of their possessions. "We'll bust Cole out, and you can join us just like old times. Or heck, you could hide out to Colorado City, where the water flows out of the mountains so cool and clean, and there ain't no law. Whatever you want. Jesus won't have no objection to that."

Grandpa didn't respond so Mr. James turned to me. "Boy, is this sergeant a friend?" He looked out at the first sergeant, still standing post with fixed bayonet and an uncomfortable look. "Can you talk to him for me? Grease the skids a little?"

I knew Lucas had a cousin down near Dug Springs or Carthage, so he was half Missourian himself. But that didn't mean he'd just let Grandpa hop the wall. But maybe. I could ask.

"Heck, can you talk some sense into your grandfather?" Mr. James added.

"Leave the boy out of this. He's innocent, and I don't want him into that kind a life."

Mr. Frank looked red in the face. A few trickles of sweat came down his forehead, which wasn't uncommon in this place. He wiped them away and looked down. For some reason, Grandpa didn't like his plan, and I'm not sure why. Or maybe he did, but wasn't saying. Only a month ago I felt sure Uncle Olin and me could bust Grandpa out ourselves. And here was a genuine professional asking for the job. He'd be in and out before the guards even knew it. But Grandpa acted like he didn't need busting out. Like he and Jesus had talked it all out, and Grandpa was already free. Like he was living in another place and only slept here at night.

"I'm sorry," Mr. James said. "I'll leave the boy out of it, like you said." The man looked at me sadly, like he didn't know what else to say. And that he was sorry for exposing me to the workings of bank robbing and jailbreaks and such. But I was no longer a boy. I'd seen enough in the last two years to change that. None of this bothered me. But Mr. James didn't know that, and looked sorry. Terrible sorry.

"We sure had some times, didn't we Hiram?" the man said, trying to cheer Grandpa up. He laughed weakly. "Living off half rations and killing Yankees every day but Sunday. We sure did." But Grandpa didn't laugh.

"Frank... I've been redeemed," Grandpa finally said. "By the blood of the Lamb. Been forgiven of all that. All the killing and robbing and bushwhacking we done. Scalping, skinning, torture... You know it all. Can ya understand? I ain't the same man." Grandpa looked down and sniffed.

Mr. James also looked down and nodded a little. But then they both faced each other and sat quietly.

"Turns out, Cole is saying the same danged thing. Got religion, that is. He's got Jesus now, and there ain't no more bank jobs from here on out."

Grandpa nodded. "God has spoken clearly. He says—"

"Wait, wait, wait. God speaks to you? Now yer gettin' crazy on me, Hiram."

Grandpa held up the Bible. "Yes, He speaks."

Mr. James could not understand that. He got all agitated and stood up. "If God spoke to me in your condition, He'd say bust out of here and be free!"

"I am free," Grandpa said. "John 8:36. 'If the Son shall make you free, ye shall be free indeed.' I am forgiven, and I am free indeed."

"Well, forgiven don't git you off with them Yankee judges," Mr. James said. "Jump this wall with me, and you will be free indeed."

Chapter Twenty-Four

J UST AFTER THE MEETING with Mr. James strange men started coming
by Grandpa's cell and stopping in for a look. Men in suits. Men in
uniforms and shoulder boards. Men with clip pads. Judge Pennypacker
even walked by once, I think, but I'm not sure. He never had before.
They didn't talk to us, just stopped, wrote on their pads and continued
up the brick corridor. It was like they had a big conundrum they couldn't
cipher out and had to keep stopping by and looking in for more
information. I didn't know what information, though.

"Bunk space," Uncle Olin guessed. "And they're fixin' to do
something with Pa. You know what that means." He said he'd counted
the empty bunks on the block, and there was only two left. And that it
was probably the same on all the blocks in the whole prison. "Now that
it's springtime and prisoners can work outside, Blunt is moving the old
men out to make room fer young pups. This ain't nothin' to do with
justice," he said. "Jes slave labor and bunk space."

J.T. did want to believe it but thought he might be right, or that
something might be progressing with Grandpa's case. But he didn't
know and didn't want to speculate. And he hadn't heard anything from
Judge Pennypacker or General Blunt.

Lucas, the first sergeant said the general was always mad that he
couldn't have more manpower to finish his castle. He complained about

it at practically every staff formation. The prison was full and he couldn't imagine why Washington hadn't let him build more cell blocks, but that everyone would just have to get by with the resources they had. Maybe Washington would approve his plan, and everything would be better when the USDB rose up like his plans said. He'd started to get a little obsessive over it, Lucas said.

"Hot-bunk the prisoners," a colonel had suggested. "On twelve-hour shifts."

"Yeah, and what about the Sabbath when they're all off detail? No, I want this done right. If only Washington understood." General Blunt had said.

Lucas said the general carried plans around in long white rolls, and pulled them out to show people where new buildings should go or walls and roads should be erected. Even if they didn't ask; he showed them anyway. He pointed and drew lines with his fingers. But nobody did anything because the money hadn't been appropriated, and maybe never would. Everybody just said, "Uh-huh," and nodded. Some smiled. Some patted him on the shoulder. But mostly, just said "Uh-huh" and waved when they left him.

Word went around that the USDB was a just a big delusion in the general's head, and that maybe Congress didn't even know about it. Maybe it had never even been presented to the Army brass, and that crazy old Asa Blunt had just dreamed the whole thing up himself. Maybe no one knew about it but the soldiers stationed here, and maybe the whole plan was completely unfeasible. After all, Blunt's idea for Building 475 called for a rotunda eight stories tall. Most folks were quite sure that couldn't even be done. Or that it would fall down in the first good Kansas windstorm. You can't stack bricks that high. Lucas didn't know anything about stacking bricks; he just did his three-year contract out on the frontier and stayed away from Commandant Asa Blunt as much as practicable. Especially if he was crazy.

Another group stopped outside Grandpa's door. This time they talked a little longer and a little louder. Marshal Upham was with them, and I could hear most of what they said.

"Why don't you just go in and tell him," a man outside said.

Grandpa looked up.

"I don't think he's going to want to hear it from me," Upham said. "We're not on the best of speaking terms."

"Well, he's got to hear it sometime, and you're the best man to deliver the news. If he throws you out, let me know and I'll take care of it. After you're done, Marshal, you can be on your way. You've done a good service. And I'm sure you'll be happy to get back to Little Rock with your family. You've been a great aid to your government, and we appreciate you coming up here. I know it's out of your territory. But hopefully it's been a pleasant diversion from the wrangling mess in Arkansas."

The first sergeant unlocked the door and swung it open. What were they going to do now? Take Grandpa off like they had Thomas?

Grandpa stiffened.

"No!" I said. "You ain't coming in."

But D.P. Upham just laid his hand on my shoulder, and that was enough to make me step aside.

Upham knocked. "May I come in?" He poked his head in slowly. Sweat poured off his pale forehead. He didn't look comfortable. But I looked at Grandpa and he didn't look comfortable neither.

"Hello," he said again. "Can I come in?"

"'Tain't welcome. I'm spending my last days with my grandson. Whatever you got ta say, jes have the sergeant of the guard tell it. I ain't in no mood just now. Go away."

Marshal Upham didn't go away. Instead, he stepped right into the cell with Grandpa and me. He took off his hat and tried to apologize, but Grandpa didn't listen. I didn't realize it before, but the man was so tall he barely fit inside the tiny cell. Taller than Mr. James. His hair rubbed on the brick ceiling which made him hunch down every so often so he didn't bump his head.

And just like before, I didn't hate him. He wasn't a devil like Uncle Olin said. And I could see why J.T. had worked for him. He looked more like a good man who just had a bad job to do. But he also didn't look healthy. Sweat ran down his face and his left eye ran with some kind of gouk. He had to clear it every so often. And cough.

"My apologies, Mr. Cantrell." Upham waited for Grandpa to answer, but he didn't. So Upham tried to smile and repeat the rumors of the day. "Word is: you had a visit from Frank and Jesse James. Any truth to that?"

"Now that's about the dumbest dern question I heard in a long while. If I had, would I be yakking to you about it? Probably add it to yer list of crimes."

"Planning a breakout, are you?" Upham tried to smile again at the joke. But he looked awful terrible. "The whole prison is talking about it like it's going to happen tomorrow. Word's out that your son Olin is planning the whole thing down in Jackson County. They say he's got Frank and Jesse, and he's busting the Younger brothers, Cole, Jim, and Bob out of prison just to help. The whole gang is in arms and ready to ride up here. Raines too. Blunt has the whole prison on alert. Doubled the guard mount, I heard. Even on the Sabbath now. But I guess you knew that. Word to the wise: best lay low for a few days."

Grandpa laughed. "Oh, then I'll take yer advice and call the whole thang off."

"Honestly, Mr. Cantrell, I'm not here about the rumors. I really did come for a reason. I'm sorry for interrupting, but I've got something else you need to hear," Upham said. He hung his head. "It's about your case."

"Got a whole new charge against me? Do ya? Consorting with known outlaws? Well, I don't want to hear it. I'm spending time with my grandson. Now skat."

"You really should hear this," Upham replied. He wasn't giving up easily.

Grandpa didn't either.

"Do you know what it's like to be charged with murder, Upham?" Grandpa asked, gritting his teeth and throwing his jaw out at the marshal. "I think you do…"

"Yes, I actually do," Upham said.

"Yer dern right you do. You was tried for that very crime jes two years b'fore bringing me in. 'Member that? August, 1875? Fer crimes you yerself committed in '68. Right there in Woodruff County, Arkansas. Jes like me."

"Yes." The Marshal hung his head. "But I was acquitted on both counts. Self-defense, and that's the truth."

"We ain't altogether different, you and me. You remember that awful feeling, don't ya? Deep in yer gut?" Grandpa asked, pushing the marshal farther than he could comfortably tolerate. Sweat poured out heavier. "And you probably remember sitting right where I am."

"They didn't arrest me," the Marshal answered. "But I know what you're saying."

"Awright, lawman. 'Spose you tell my grandson and me exactly how them two murders in which you were merely defending yerself came to be. Give us the particulars. We'll hold court right here in this cell and see if yer innocent. And if not, we'll swap places."

The Marshal held out his hands like he didn't know exactly what to say. "You want to know what happened back in '68? With the two men I killed?"

"Yes. I want to hear it from yer own flappers," Grandpa said. He didn't offer the man a seat like he did Frank James. The marshal just stood there bobbing his head off the brick ceiling and wiping his forehead and leaky eye, and coughing into a handkerchief. I think Grandpa wanted it that way.

"It wasn't much, really. I happened upon two fellows out on the Hickory Plains Road. Klansmen, I assumed. Because they were half-lynching another fellow, and beating him with their rifle butts, kicking him and that sort of thing. And generally making the poor man mighty uncomfortable, if not killing him in the process. Is this what you wanted to hear?"

Grandpa waved him on. "What was they wearing?"

"The two bad guys? You know, spook hats and bed linens. One had the typical hood with eye holes burned in. The other, a flour sack under a set of goat horns."

"And the third one... What was he wearing?"

Upham looked confused. "I don't understand what this has to do—"

"What was the third man wearing?" Grandpa yelled.

"The man they were beating and fixing to hang?"

Grandpa snapped. "Yes."

"Just regular duds. Nothing special. He wasn't a federal, if that's what you're asking. Just a citizen." Upham wiped his brow. "I didn't get a good look at him, but he was just a citizen."

"One more question," Grandpa said. "In all the whole time you tracked me, did you ever see me wearin' that garb? Even once?"

The marshal thought for a while. "Guess not."

"No flour sack and cow horns?"

"I can't recall. But I guess not."

"Hmm. Awright, keep talking, lawman. What happened next?"

The marshal seemed confused but continued the story. "Naturally, I rode hard to save the man. The one being hanged, that is. But those two fellows fired shots at me. I was hit here in the hand, and once again in the back when I spun around." The marshal produced a large red scar on the back of his hand. When he flipped the hand over, the same red scar appeared on the other side. "See? Shot straight through, and broke these two bones." Upham acted like that was the end of the story. He was wounded, and that was that.

"Go on," Grandpa said.

"Naturally, I fired back," the marshal said, annoyed. "And I killed the two Klansmen. Satisfied? It was self-defense, and the jury saw it exactly that way."

"Keep going."

Upham shook his head. "What else do you want to hear? My objective was, of course, to save the man they were terrorizing. But in the confusion, he got away. I never learned his identity. But I sure could have used him. Without a witness, it was all I could do to convince the jury of my innocence. Those wounds were the only evidence I had—"

"So you had two dead bodies and no alibi?"

"Correct."

"Tain't good ta be without evidence, is it? Puts you in a bad spot, don' it? And yet you wuz just doin' justice out on that old country road. But nobody believed you."

"I guess. But in the end, I was acquitted. And that's the truth."

"Do you even know what justice is?"

"Of course. I'm a U.S. Marshal."

"But you took the lives of two men, nonetheless. Reckon that was justice?"

"Yes, I suppose," Upham said uneasily. "They were killing that man."

"And how's that different than what I did? Which was also justice for men like Eli Raines. And for dozens of others."

Upham didn't answer.

"So you never knew the man they half-hung that day?"

"No, sir, I did not."

Grandpa pulled back his black and white striped prison shirt. Under his collar was a faint red scar around his neck.

The Marshal pulled back. "You—"

"You act surprised, lawman. Woodruff County weren't that populated back in '68. And you cut a pretty big swath down there. I think your little militia killed or arrested every Klansman in the state of Arkansas. But I wasn't one of them. I want you to know that. And I'm not yer enemy."

"But you were the man those two fellows were going to hang?"

"I was," Grandpa said. "And yer dern lucky I was there."

"Seemed the other way around to me," Upham said. "You were lucky I was there."

"No, them two was fixin' to ambush and hang you out on that road. Did you know that? They thought I was with you and commenced to working me over first. You see, I'm not one of them."

Upham shook his head.

"So in a way, Marshal, I saved yer life."

"Then you'll be happy to hear what I came to say," Upham said. "Like I said, I came for a reason."

Marshal Upham wiped his forehead and coughed again. "I'm dropping this case and leaving for Little Rock tomorrow."

Grandpa jerked up.

"You heard me right. I've contracted consumption – tuberculosis of the lungs – and I'm headed back to Little Rock to spend my last days with my family. We may go back to Dudley, Massachusetts where I'm originally from. I'm not sure. But I'll probably leave law enforcement. My reappointment is coming up in June and I'll likely lose that on account of this illness."

"What about the trial?" Grandpa asked.

"I don't know about that. But I'm leaving the case. Pennypacker may drop it altogether."

"Have you told him?"

"He knows."

"You said some awful things about me," Grandpa said, sighing and shaking his head.

"I know. And I apologize. This has been a long and hard process. Please forgive me."

Grandpa nodded.

"How old are you?" I asked. "You don't look old enough to die of consumption." I felt bad for the man. I'd seen plenty of old folks die of it, and it was pretty ugly. I didn't want to see anybody die that way again. Even though he didn't care how Grandpa died.

Upham cleared his throat and thought a while. "How old? About the same age as your granddaddy: forty-eight. Old enough, I guess."

Death was on everyone's mind.

"I gave my life to Jesus, Daniel," Grandpa finally said, using the marshal's first name. Upham looked at him a little strange, maybe because Grandpa quit attacking him. Or maybe just curious about the name of Jesus. "All my sins is washed," Grandpa said.

"Hmm," the marshal thought for a while. "I've got sins..." His forehead wrinkled up and his lip twitched. Then he coughed hard. Maybe it was just the disease. I handed him another white linen handkerchief J.T. had given me. But he didn't use it.

"You want to be saved?" Grandpa asked.

"It ain't going to change things for you, Hiram. You must know that. But I will talk to Judge Pennypacker. Maybe he'll–"

"I'm talking about saved from eternal damnation. About the lake of fire and the worm that never dies. Not this case."

"I know. I know," Upham said, his head still bobbing off the ceiling.

"Take a seat."

Upham sat a while. "I believe I would like to be saved, Hiram," he finally said, also using Grandpa's first name. It was the first time I had heard the marshal talk to Grandpa that way. He even reached over and laid his hand on Grandpa's knee. And that made the marshal tear up.

They both sat quietly, old enemies, now at peace.

Upham finally nodded and smiled. "Yes, I believe I would, Hiram, if you know how."

Chapter Twenty-Five

"MR. JEREMIAH CLARK?" A SERGEANT yelled, busting through the rooming house door with a detachment of armed soldiers in tow. His men soon filled the small dining room. "You Jeremiah Clark?"

"Is there something wrong with my grandpa? Hiram Cantrell?"

"Please stand up. I also need Olin Cantrell and John Martin to come with me." The sergeant turned to Uncle Olin and Cousin Buford. "Are you those men?"

Buford was busy counting threads in a new white lace table cloth, and had already reported the number to be 56,821. For the tenth time this week. His eyelids flickered like maple leaves and it drove me to exasperation. I wanted to whack him with a wooden spoon. But you couldn't stop Buford when he was on a mission. And fabric was now his passion. Every kind of fabric, wool, jean-cloth, cotton, linen, even burlap.

Thread counting. Grrr.

"He's a halfwit," Uncle Olin said, shaking his head at Cousin Buford and then turning to the sergeant. "I'm Olin Cantrell, Hiram Cantrell's son. What's this about?"

"Where's John Martin?" the sergeant asked, looking around and ignoring Uncle Olin's question. "I got orders to bring him in too."

"Out in the privy, soldier boy. Why don't you fetch 'im out?" Uncle Olin laughed. "He's workin' at his morning occupation, as far as

I kin tell. But he may need a little Yankee help."

"We'll wait."

It wasn't two minutes before J.T. came through the door himself.

"I need each of you men to turn around and clasp your hands together."

J.T. looked at me, and I looked at him. "Do we really need to do this, J.T.? Did we do something?" He didn't know any more than me.

I did what the sergeant said, and he squeezed a set of cold manacles around my wrists. The big iron bolts cut into my skin. After an attempt at polite argument, J.T. did the same. He didn't want to, but quarreling didn't seem to help because one soldier pulled a Colt revolver and demanded J.T's surrender.

But when they came to Uncle Olin, it was a different matter.

"You ain't gittin' them bracelets on me in a hundred years, bluebelly." Uncle Olin slid an eighteen-inch Bowie knife out from his right boot and a revolver from his left. With both hands he fended off the Yankees. "I'll cut your blue heart out. I ain't got no compunction again' it. This little pig sticker has already killt three abolitionists down in Lawrence and another in St. Louis." He waved the knife around. "Another few won't make no difference to it."

He flicked the sword. "Come on, bluebellies. Git ya some a this!"

The soldiers tried to surround Uncle Olin, but he ducked under the table and came out the other side swiping and slashing. The sergeant got it across the arm.

Buford fell to the floor screaming and flopping around. He wasn't cut; he just did that from time to time and nobody knew why.

"Shut that idiot up!" the sergeant hollered. "Or I'll take him in too."

After a few minutes the sergeant had bandaged his arm and decided Uncle Olin could come along under bayonet guard without the handcuffs.

Uncle Olin consented to that, mostly because we were going anyway and there might be some entertainment in it, especially if it might involve another knife fight with Yankee bluebellies.

The detachment marched us across town and up toward the

military prison.

Uncle Olin turned around more than once, facing his enemies. "You ain't puttin' me in no abolitionist prison. I won't be reconstructed." He pulled the knife again and said he'd carve up the first man that put a monkey paw on him. The soldiers said he was not going to prison but Uncle Olin didn't believe that. He just kept looking up that hill and threatening the guards with another Centralia massacre if they didn't tell him where they were taking us. But they didn't.

After fifteen minutes of marching we turned the corner and headed up the white steps to the commandant's office.

"General Blunt is hot to get at you men," the sergeant said, reaching the top landing and turning around to face us. "He's about to throw his desk out the window so you best be watchful of your language. Especially you, Cantrell. You pull that Arkansas toothpick in there, and he'll have you in the prison dungeon in solitary confinement. I swear; he's in no mood."

Uncle Olin just cleared his nose on the man's boots.

The sergeant shoved us through the door. We landed in front of the warden, General Asa Blunt. And he did not look happy.

All his stuffed birds peered down at us.

"Got a little situation," the general said, hot in the face, scanning each of us with an unhappy scowl. "Just wondering what you boys know about the James gang and their whereabouts."

We all shrugged. I hadn't seen Frank James in over a month, ever since he visited Grandpa under the assumed name Alexander which I found out was really his first name, but he never used it. And he didn't say where he was going when he left. But I figured he was headed back into Missoura to fetch up that gang he promised Grandpa. Hard men, he had said. Known men. But then Grandpa didn't seem to want them so I wasn't sure if Mr. James rounded them up or not.

"Why isn't this man in cuffs?" the general demanded, nodding at Uncle Olin.

"He's well-guarded. We figured he's best handled at the point of a bayonet." The sergeant coddled his bloody arm but faced the general without complaint. He didn't mention the knife fight.

"Any notions on the whereabouts of Frank and Jesse James?" the general asked again. "I'm going to need to hear everything the three of you know about those desperados. We know they've been in here. And we know they visited Hiram Cantrell. So where are they? Are they ghosts? Can they walk right through solid walls and out again?" He waved his hands around like wisps of steam.

The general paced around us ten times, breathing out accusations about Grandpa's notorious friends. He demanded to know every southern outlaw that could stage a prison break, and a list of every person who had ever visited Grandpa in the last six months.

Uncle Olin just pestered him with what he considered smart and perplexing questions. Not enough to get thrown into the dungeon, wherever that was, but getting on the general's nerves nonetheless. But the general kept asking about the James gang, and outlaws, and plans for prison breaks. He wanted answers to the same questions he had already asked a dozen different ways.

I noticed movement out the window behind Blunt, who paced back and forth in front of it. A troop of men came across the prison lawn and headed for the same white stairs we just came up.

J.T. asked, "Can you tell us what this is about?"

"It seems we've got a missing man," he finally admitted, still steaming at the ears. "Hiram Cantrell missed role call this morning and has not been seen since Taps last night. He was in his bunk at lights-out, and not seen since. Now he don't just vanish through brick walls like the James gang, does he?"

The general stamped his boot on the wooden floor. "There will be no more escapes from the United States Military Prison. I will not stand for it." He glared at us again and skulked around, just to show he was serious.

"Can you take these off?" J.T. finally asked, nodding back at his wrists. "They're no longer necessary. You've got ten men with fixed bayonets." J.T. raised his eyebrows at the dutiful corporals and privates lining the room, each with polished muskets and gleaming bayonets, sharp as razors. "And as far as I know, none of us knows about any escape attempt."

The general accepted the request as an invitation to upbraid us further. Although he did remove the manacles first. "Do I need to get the dogs out? Search the woods? Dredge the river? I will if I have to, and it will be on your account. Now confess, if you know something."

He still hadn't seen the men coming up the stairs.

"Alright, I'm calling in Judge Pennypacker." The general waved an orderly over, wrote out an order and sent the man out the door with it. "He'll be up in ten minutes. Maybe he knows something about the James gang, or that rebel Raines. We never should have let Raines free once we had him. I've got a newly vacated cell just right for that—"

"General Blunt?" Lucas, the first sergeant said, coming through the door with his detail behind him. "You needed me, sir?"

"Yes, I need you to let loose the hounds and get a barge out on that river. It seems Hiram Cantrell is missing. You and your men—"

"He's in his cell. We just got back from town. Remember?"

"Remember what?"

The first sergeant tried to cover his mouth and whisper. "Tailoring a new suit. For the... ah... you know... the—"

"Oh, yes. Oh, oh, oh. Yes." The general covered his eyes and shook his head. "I am sorry; you are dismissed, sergeant."

The general turned to us with a red face. "It seems our disaster has been averted. You men may all go."

"What's the suit for?" I asked. "You said my Grandpa got a new suit?"

"Oh, don't worry about that. It's just—" The general waved us off and turned around to face the window again. His shoulders fell.

But just as we started for the door, he swung back around. "But while you're here. Why don't the three of you stay for Judge Pennypacker? We have a few details to go over." The general pulled up three chairs and dismissed the soldiers.

He never apologized.

And Judge Pennypacker never showed up.

But the next morning Judge Pennypacker did show up and we were all called back again. This time without the chains.

"When we met last—" Commandant Blunt began.

"You mean when you arrested us last," Uncle Olin blurted out.

And because Blunt didn't even look at him, Uncle Olin pulled his Bowie knife and started carving his initials on the antique wooden chair he was seated in.

The scratching filled the room.

General Blunt leaped over to stay the knife. "Yes, when I mistakenly detained the three of you, I told you I had something to go over." He looked down at Uncle Olin. "I apologize for that. You are good men and I showed poor judgment." Uncle Olin returned the sword to his boot but tapped on it and smirked like a child.

"There have been some developments in Hiram Cantrell's case," Judge Pennypacker said. He paused to consider his words. I knew what he was going to say, so I smiled. D.P. Upham was gone. Finally, this whole thing was over. It had gone on too long as it was, and there was nothing of consequence to go to court with anyways. The first sergeant would fetch Grandpa from his cell and we'd all ride home together. J.T. could stay with us as a hired man because Mother took a partiality to him, and she might like to watch him run cattle and stack hay. Because for some reason she liked to just sit there and look at him. Everything would be back to the way it was. What a great day!

I was so happy.

Judge Pennypacker continued. "Marshal Upham has resigned from this case. He is heading back to Little Rock to be with his family. Tragically, he has contracted tuberculosis and only has a few years to live."

J.T. gasped. But me and Uncle Olin smiled. Maybe for different reasons.

"Can Grandpa come home now?" I asked. "Is he coming up now?"

"Ah, no," the commandant said. "We've decided to take this case to trial even though the chief witness is missing. And even though he's dropped his case. We believe there is enough evidence for a…"

"A conviction?" J.T. interjected. "Why don't you just give this old man his last days in peace? Hasn't the south paid enough for reconstruction? It's over. Even President Hays says it's over. They're no longer waving the bloody shirt up north. And I say we walk out and leave these people be, for Heaven's sake."

"But you're a New York man?" Blunt asked, confused.

"Yes, I am. But it's high time these folks got their lives back. We've had bayonet rule down there for fifteen years. That's a whole generation of children who know nothing but war." J.T. stood up and threw out his hands. "Don't you think that's enough?"

"It is, J.T," the judge said. He stood up too to face him. "I agree with you all the way to Corpus Christy." Then he turned to me. "Missouri has been beaten nine ways to Sunday. First with the Emigrant Aid Society bringing in abolitionists to defeat them at the ballot box. And then the bloody war with Kansas. And the War Between the States. And finally, the second Civil War for reconstruction. In all, it's been over twenty years of war – almost half this man's life. I agree with you, J.T; it's time for a little peace."

"Then let my pa go and we'll be on our way," Uncle Olin said. He started to get real sour which meant he'd probably go for his sword again.

"No," the warden said. "We can't do that. He's going to trial."

"Problem is, it's a matter of law," the judge said, stepping in. "Ordinarily..." His words trailed off. "It's just that the man has committed crimes."

General Blunt jumped back in. "If that man went free this prison would be shut down in a week. Every prisoner in here would be clamoring for his freedom too. And honestly, we'd have no right to hold them. Not after freeing a man like Hiram Cantrell. Ninety percent of these men have never touched the depths of his–"

"What the commandant is trying to say," the judge said, "is that the penal system has to be fair for all. If one guilty man is set free, everyone would. It has to be equitable for every person. I hope that makes sense."

J.T. nodded, but didn't look happy.

The judge continued. "So I'm recommending that Olin and Jeremiah spend a week of respite with Hiram – out of this prison, in Leavenworth for a week. Under armed guard of course. And then Olin and Jeremiah can head back to Missouri before the trial begins."

"No!" I protested. "I ain't going back without Grandpa."

"This is going to be rough," the judge said, looking me in the eye. "You don't want to be here for this. Believe me; it will ruin you. I understand your mother is poorly. It would be best for you and your uncle to help her. I'm sure she needs you just as bad as Hiram."

"I'm not leaving Grandpa." I bowed up my neck and glared at the floor. Let them try to make me. I'd pull out Uncle Olin's boot pistols and hold them off.

J.T. laid a hand on my shoulder. "The judge may be right, Jeremiah. This could get ugly. Plus, I'll be here with Hiram, and we can focus on a strategy together. I'll bring in my father's lawyer from New York."

The warden raised a hand. "Civilian defense attorneys may not participate in the—"

"I know, but he can advise, Asa. Do research, file papers, and fine-tune the defense argument outside the courtroom. Hiram will have a vigorous defense. Especially with the man I'm thinking of. And if Upham really is leaving, this case could get awfully thin. That's a good thing for Hiram."

Judge Pennypacker raised his eyebrows my way. "That sounds like a good defense to me."

I scowled and drew ragged and hot breath.

What sounded like a good defense to me was Eli Raines, Jesse James, and their gang of Missoura bushwhackers.

Chapter Twenty-Six

May, 1879
Two years after the arrest

A PASSEL OF GHOSTS had moved into our old house. Broken windows whistled, weeds sprouted up through the parlor floor, and Ma's kitchen roof had fallen in and sagged almost down to the stovetop. Somebody had torn up all the painted floor cloth so that all the rotten boards showed. Several were tossed around the rooms. Vermin screeched and scampered out of my way. Trash and newspapers lay about, and somebody had lit a campfire in my old room. Or was it still my old room? Or even our home for that matter?

I decided to check the barn.

Even as I walked through the barn, sheds, and outbuildings, I did not believe that the property still belonged to us. Something was different. Maybe I was a trespasser on somebody else's place – like all the burned-out farms I had tramped and plundered in my youth. It was like the property had passed hands and I was no longer welcome.

There were no chickens to feed, no goats or calves to tend, no heifer pens to muck, and no hay to stack while Uncle Olin smoked pipes in stifling hay mows, babbling out the latest gossip, and how a proper hanging should be conducted. The old bloody chopping block hadn't been used in months. Our corn crib had slid into a sinkhole next to the creek. Some bad winter storm had ripped a big limb off the maple tree, but the bloody patch where we butchered was still there. I kicked the thick brown patch on my way through. The new steps Mrs. Branson had installed were still in place but they led right up into another sinkhole where the porch had been. Somebody had dragged off the rusty old corn grinder that sat in the middle of the dooryard for the last hundred years, and had thrown a dead mule down the well. It stunk like the sewer in Randalls Flats. The weeds in the dooryard where noisy kids had once played were up to my chest.

Nothing registered.

I started wondering if I might be shot by some old-timer coming out from behind the barn with a double-barreled shotgun. "Git off my land you thieving Jayhawker," I imagined him saying, and then emptying both barrels into my back when I wasn't looking. That possibility was actually worth watching for, but I didn't see anyone in this whole desolate place. Ma and the twins had obviously moved out a long time ago. All that was left was weeds. And ghosts.

The thought occurred to me to fix up the place. Grandpa would be awful mad if he came back and saw it in this condition, and I wasn't exactly sure when he was due back. They wouldn't tell me. Could be any day. But it was already getting dark and it had been a long trip down from Fort Leavenworth. Time to bunk down for the night. Black Jack and Rosebud were almost as tired as me, so I decided to camp before riding into Randalls Flats and looking for Uncle Olin and Ma.

I tore a few boards off the old barn and banked a fire. I wondered if the barn could spare them, seeing as how I could see straight through to the other side. And I worried that Grandpa would whoop me if he saw me do a thing like that.

But Grandpa was still up in Leavenworth, until they let him free.

No roosters crowed the next morning. No calves bawled for breakfast, and no cats crawled over me, licking my face until I threw them up against the wall. It was just like any other morning on the trail. Except that I had camped next to this old barn I didn't recognize. And an old house next to a sinkhole.

It just wasn't home.

After a last look I boiled coffee and hitched up Rosebud and Black Jack for the trip into town. They plodded into Randalls Flats like they knew the way. But it wasn't the Randalls Flats I remembered neither.

Twice as many negro and white women boiled laundries in their dooryards, yelling threats at scores of offspring in bare feet and unraveling jean-cloth. Dogs barked, chickens flew, pigs routed, and snakes fled. New barn-wood shacks hung to the river's edge, perfectly ready to slide in with the slightest encouragement. A few mules and draft horses dragged timber down the muddy road leading into the whole conjibulation. At the end of it, a hastily thrown up sawmill buzzed out new lumber obvious headed for some other place than this. Compared to the ramshackle nature of it all, Uncle Olin's old shack stood like a mansion on the hill. Judging from a hot flow of sparks from his crooked stovepipe chimney, I knew he'd be in there.

But instead I found Mother in bed, and the twins half-naked, feeding sticks into a blazing fire.

"Jeremiah," Mother said weakly, but smiling. "You're home! Oh, son." She coughed and pulled a threadbare coverlet up to her chin. "Come over and give me some sugar." She seemed to have no more weight than one of the twins.

"Jeremiah! Jeremiah!" the twins screamed, leaving their burning sticks to spill out onto the wooden floor.

I nudged the firebrands back into the hearth and hugged the three of them at once. "Where's Uncle Olin? He left Fort Leavenworth the day before me."

"We haven't seen hide nor hair of him," Mother replied, still coughing and holding her chest. "But I'm so happy you're back. It'll do me good to see you." She stroked my hair and smiled. "Will your grandfather be along by and by? Or is he outside tending the mules? Jeremiah, he's an old man. Almost fifty by now," Ma scolded. "You oughtn't to make him tend those nasty old–"

"He's still in Leavenworth, Ma."

"Oh. Well, I expect he'll be along any time. Now that you're home."

"Expect so," I said, but didn't tell her about the trial. "Ma, what happened to the farm? It's like a ghost town now. All the weeds are–"

"Oh, I couldn't keep that up. Not in my condition." Mother did not stir from her place in bed. Not even to sit up. She just spoke weakly.

"Are you ailing, Ma?"

"Worse than ever, son. We had to let the farm go, Jeremiah. Them northern bankers wanted it real bad, and now that they got it, it sits fallow like all the others. Dirty shame what they done. Done it to most all the old homesteads. Guess you probably saw that on yer way in."

"I saw a lot of new folks in town."

"All driven off, like us. Half the folks on this road. 'Member the Anderson's and the Jorgensen's? Dutchies! Even Duthchies is run off their land. Now don't that beat all in Jackson County?" She paused to draw enough breath. "The day Dutchies is run off by Yankees, you know it's rainin' hog's blood."

"So, the farm... Great, great granddaddy's homestead? It's gone?" The whole idea seemed like a bad yarn Uncle Olin would try on me. How was that possible? To lose a whole farm in one year? And one we had owned for a hundred years. But I knew it was true, even before Mother uttered the words. Just tramping through the old place told me that much. It wasn't ours any longer, and I could feel it in my guts. You know things like that when they're true. They get into your guts and you know it, even before nobody tells you. My guts told me that last night.

But it made me understand that you really never own things. If a Yankee wants your possessions, he will find a way to get them. Even if you owned them for a hundred years.

"Yes, son. The farm is gone." Mother gazed up into the water-stained roof planks, her head quaking a little. "I was just too tired to... Pa up in that northern prison. And you and Olin gone... I just... just couldn't hold on." She sobbed and turned toward the wall. But it took all her strength so she stopped talking and just breathed.

After that, Mother slept until the middle of the next day. But I wanted to know more about what happened. So while Mother slept, I took the twins and bought some new clothes for them and a sandwich with the last of the traveling money J.T. gave me. They needed shoes too, but the mercantile wouldn't give them on credit on account of them not knowing me. I told them I was Uncle Olin's nephew but they said "No credit" until they knew I had steady work. I guess that was only fair. But they didn't know I had two of the finest draft mules in the county, and could plow ten acres a day. That made me a pretty rich fellow.

Mother woke at noon and got up the strength to eat a few dried hoecakes crushed up in a bowl of buttermilk. That brightened her eyes enough to tell the rest of the story.

"The South has been redeemed!" Mother said, wagging her head and rolling her eyes like it was a big joke. "And every family sinks deeper into the mire."

"What do you mean, redeemed?" I asked.

"The governments... All the republicans are chased out. No more radicals in office. No more abolitionists. They're all run off and folks got things just about where they want them – back to the way it was before the war. 'Cept northern carpetbaggers still swarmin' like flies. All the big plantations is bought up and left fallow. Wrecked families are drifting. Fighting for jobs with freed blacks. Working for a dollar a week. It's not enough to feed their babies. Kids starve. Or run off. Or sell themselves for food and a bed." She sobbed and wringed her hands. "It's all gone bad, son."

"What are we going to do?"

"I got a tenant agreement with them bankers," Ma said.

"What's that?"

"Sharecropping. They buy seed and we plant. Then we split the profits. But they own the land. We just work it. Most all these folks are doin' it. Them that don't, work in the sawmill, and that's only about a dozen men. Do you think you can do that, Jeremiah?"

I guessed I could, but the notion didn't sound much better than a mess of horse manure. But still, Rosebud and Black Jack were the best mules in Jackson County. Grandpa had seen to that. And he told me to work them hard and earn a living for Ma and the twins. "A mule will give his own heart up if you ask 'm to," Grandpa had said. "But you got ta give yourn first." I guess I could do that too.

But I didn't.

Didn't much feel like it, what with Grandpa gone, and not knowing when he'd be back, and somebody else owning our own land,

and us just working it like white slaves. So I took a few odd jobs at the sawmill to keep Ma and the twins in beans and cornbread, but mostly I just fell in with Uncle Olin's old friends.

"What's the point," they complained, all leaning back on a pile of planks. "As soon's you make a few greenbacks, 'em bankers jes come right in an take it. It's a danged sight easier jes to maintain the peace around here, right here at the sawmill. And Shar-croppin? That's a colored man's occupation. I ain't fightin' fer no job with the likes a them. I kin make more brewing sour mash and corn liquor, and sellin' mason jars of it to city folk. Ya see 'em out dar in the field with their mules an seed bags, plowin' an plantin' fourteen hours a day. They ain't no better off than b'fore the war. Land owners got 'em right back in the field like before. Seem jes like slaves ta me."

I guessed the boys were right. So I laid around with them a good bit.

And cooked sour mash. And sold mason jars of it.

But Mother didn't stand for one minute of that.

Every day was like another knife in the gut. Jobs thinned out. Miss Patricia didn't come around. And Ma upbraided me every time she got out of bed, but I told her I was a man now and could lay around with whoever I wanted to. Of course, the boys were always there, down at the sawmill every day and night. And they understood the whole conundrum, while Ma just couldn't cipher it out.

"If yer Olin's kin then yer good enough fer us," they said, leaning up against the mill wall. "Come on over and we'll talker 'er out. And pass a jug of Oh Be Joyful, will ya." A jug of that will make you forget dang near anything.

Why not, if grandpa wasn't coming back.

That's about the time J.T. wired us from Leavenworth City.

Riding for Randalls Flats. Stop.
Everything finished. Stop.
More news to follow. Stop.

What the heck did that mean? Sure, I figured he'd be here in four or five days but what was finished? And what news was to follow? That didn't make a lick of sense in my mind. That is until J.T. and two gentlemen rode in on a new buggy. The gentlemen jumped out and walked into the shed before I had time to see them. But J.T. saw me right off and came over.

"I'm glad to see you, Jeremiah!"

"Glad to see you too. Did any rebels catch you on the way in?"

J.T. laughed. "Not yet. Have you found work?"

"Some, I guess. But it ain't easy. I'm still thinking about going west. There ain't much here for me."

"How about Miss Patricia? She's here."

"Aw. I don't think she likes me no more. Everything changed."

I felt like crying.

J.T. sighed. "Maybe your Ma could talk to her."

"Maybe. So where's Grandpa?" I asked.

J.T. sighed.

"I'm not going to draw this out, Jeremiah," J.T. said. "Have a seat over there." He laid a hand over my shoulder and looked me in the eye.

"Your grandfather has been executed," he said, shaking his head. Then he looked away. "Hiram's trial didn't go well…"

I didn't even look up.

A few flies buzzed around my feet and some tent worms crawled along the dirt. Their little feelers twitched along a meaningless path to nowhere, twitching this way and that, but going no place in particular – just twitching along and stopping to chew on a leaf or twig. I knew this news was coming, and felt just like the worms: a creature to be trod upon by the likes of any man who felt the compunction, or just wanted our stuff and had the power to take it.

I lifted my foot and smashed the bugs into the dirt. Their mangled guts twisted up and wretched in a slow death struggle before ceasing all motion. Then I smashed them again, just for hate. Spiteful hate.

"Did you hear me?" J.T. said. But he knew I did, and laid a hand on my shoulder. "I did all I could for Hiram."

Suddenly, it didn't seem good enough just to crush the worms. I felt the need to rub out everything they had ever found useful in this miserable world. I figured I'd execute my own Order No. 11 on the worm population of Jackson County. My heel attacked the black dirt, dragging out a deep furrow where the worms had been. Rocks and dirt flew out and a cloud of dust filled the space between us. But I didn't care. I just leaned in and went at the trench again.

"Hey, hey. Stop that with your boots. Look at me," J.T said. He looked cross and put a boot down on top of mine. "Look at me, son."

I looked up but my chin quivered so I had to look away. "I knew this was going to happen."

"No, you didn't. When you left your grandfather still had a good chance of winning his case. That's why I stayed. Half of Upham's case dissolved the day he quit."

"Nah. Uncle Olin said them northerners wanted him real bad. For how he embarrassed them for what they done in Woodruff County. For how they stole them lands. Abandoned lands, psst."

"That's just not true. That's not how the law works," J.T. said.

"It's how it works for us. Rebel scum."

"Hiram had a fair trial, Jeremiah. I was there at every step. And I even brought in a lawyer. Do you want the details?"

"Details of what?" Ma said, strolling up with a smile, pulling her coat tightly around her. She looked like a dried corn stalk heading into winter. I'd only seen her outside Uncle Olin's shack once when she tried to fetch firewood. I didn't realize how bad off she was.

J.T. smiled and placed an arm around her. "Hey, oatcakes!" He tried to warm her up and she liked that. She leaned into him.

"Where's Uncle Olin?" I asked.

Ma snuggled into J.T's breast like a dear friend. I guessed she needed the warmth and he didn't mind giving it. "Him and Buford headed into town. Didn't you see them?" Ma asked.

"No."

"Well, they did. I guess you know where." She glared just long enough to let me know she wasn't happy with my new friends. But I was man now – fifteen years old – and she wasn't going to tell me what to do. But still, with J.T. wrapped around her so tightly backtalk was too much of a risk.

She smiled up at J.T. "Now... what details?"

J.T. slumped. "I was just telling Jeremiah..." He sighed and kicked rocks, still trying to hold her.

A minute passed, and then he faced her.

"Hiram was executed Monday of last week."

Mother pulled back and nearly fell over. A glassy covering formed over her eyes and soon spilled down her white skin. "I never got to say... Oh, Pa..." More tears, and then a slow drizzle from her nose. J.T. tried to wrap his arm around her again but she pushed back and shrieked. "No!" Then she couldn't even push him anymore because her knees dipped and swayed. That's when she fell over – whiter than new milk.

Mother got better in a few days just like she always did. But I guessed when you fall over and don't wake up for a whole day, it's best to have a doctor come in and take a look. J.T. sat by her side and paid the doctor bill. It cost him a ten-dollar gold piece so we were glad he was there. And when Mother woke up and saw J.T. by her side, she smiled and laid her hand on his.

"Hello, little oatcakes," he smiled. "You're awake!"

But Ma wouldn't sit still until J.T. told her everything that happened to Grandpa. I'm glad she did because I wanted to know too.

But this time Uncle Olin was there. He had a new set of teeth and new hair. His mustache and beard were gone, and it looked like somebody had cut his fingernails and scratched them clean. I looked around for carpetbags.

"Jes a big pack a lies," he said, sweeping his hand through the air like the whole thing was just another Yankee sham. "I never seen none o' them murders, an I never left Pa's side. Not from the time we whipped Nathaniel Lyon down on Wilson's Creek until we come back up here to Jackson County in '69. Jes more Yankee lies."

"I don't think so, Olin," J.T. said. But I think he tried to watch what he said around Ma. Ma had a streak of hate for Yankees too, and J.T. knew it. He didn't want to mess up his chances with her. "I watched

Judge Pennypacker pretty close," he said, cautiously. "That judge would not tolerate accusations without at least two sources of evidence. Hard evidence. Did you notice that, Olin? Nothing got by him."

"But thar weren't no fourteen murders like Upham said," Uncle Olin said.

"You're right, Olin. Just Hiram's best attempts at justice for men like Eli Raines. For all his documentation, Upham sure had flaws. He never figured that out. But I guess that happens when you're tracking fifty men."

"Who's Eli Raines?" Mother asked. "The colonel you rode into Arkansas to fetch?"

"That's right," J.T. said. "He wasn't even at the trial. Judge Pennypacker threw that one right out. Wouldn't even allow it in the trial. It just didn't merit any further time."

Uncle Olin tilted his head. "And you nearly swept it out the back porch. Until I made you tell the judge what really happened."

"True again, Olin. I suffered conflict over that one until we rode down and saw the cabin for myself. Sometimes that's all it takes to clear things up. I'm sorry about that."

Uncle Olin lifted his eyes. "Takes a thievin' rebel to keep you honest, I guess." They both smiled.

"Mary," J.T. said, facing Ma. He paused and rubbed his lips. "In the end, there were three clear cases against Hiram. And try as I may, I could not dispute them. I will tell you that we fought them hard. One in Little Rock, another down on the border of Missouri, and one in Forrest City."

"Never been to Forrest City," Uncle Olin said, shrugging.

"That was the principle reason Marshal Upham accused Hiram of riding with Nathan Bedford Forrest – the old war general turned Klan Wizard. It was just so hard to separate Hiram's... ah... justice, from Forrest. I just think Upham got the whole mess jumbled up in his thinking, and labeled Hiram a Klansman along with the rest. After all, he was fighting it every day. And that wears on you. You tend to lump everyone together and go after them all for the same reasons."

Ma nodded. "I can understand that." She also didn't want to say anything against J.T, probably because he was so nice to her. They looked nice together, and she was feeling better every hour she spent with him.

J.T. nodded. "I want you to know that through it all, Hiram looked only to his Savior. That's unusual for men in his situation. I've seen a lot working with Upham. And it's not always like that. Hiram was a redeemed man. A good man."

"What's Upham doing now?" Ma asked. "He quit the case, you said?"

"That's right, Mary. He contracted tuberculosis of the lungs and had to go back to Little Rock. I think he's headed back to Massachusetts where his family's from." J.T. squinted. "I'm a little sad for D.P. Upham. His whole career has ended and he's only forty-some-years-old. He could die from this. And Massachusetts is not the best place for consumption. He should head for Colorado Springs. The best Lunger climate is out there at the base of Pikes Peak. Or so I'm told." He sighed. "At any rate, Upham is gone. He never even attended the trial."

"Are you going back to him?" I asked. "To work for him again?"

"No. His career is over. And I'm done with this type of work too. I said goodbye long before the trial even started. He sends his regrets for this whole mess. I can tell you that after he met with Hiram he was a changed man. Something was different."

"I was there," I said. "He asked for Grandpa's forgiveness, and then he wanted to be saved from eternal damnation like Grandpa. Maybe that was it."

"Maybe. Anyway, he's gone and I think he's pretty distraught. It's been a long battle for him. Arkansas was willing to kill over Johnson's reconstruction debacle. That never would have happened under Lincoln. And Daniel P. Upham was the target of every ex-rebel's bad intentions. He tried, but I guess things didn't go like he thought they would. But that's all over now." J.T. waved his hand. "Enough of Daniel P. Upham. Back to Hiram…"

Ma spoke up. "Did you see Pa? You know, at the end?"

"I did. He repented of his deeds. In fact, long before he was even captured. But he repeated that at the very end. I spoke to him, and he wanted you to remember the love he had for you, his children. His 'beloved children' he said. And the love he had for Missouri."

Mother cried. And Uncle Olin, too.

"I can honestly say Hiram was one of the finest men I have ever met. He loved you and spoke often of you. Everything he did was for you and Missouri and the south, which he loved passionately until the end."

"Can you say why he did… those awful things? Was he mentally sick?" Mother asked.

"Definitely not. He just could not tolerate a government that had invaded its own people – more than once. And turned a good segment of its citizens into so-called criminals. I suppose, in some way, there were enough injustices to guide his way of thinking. I might have done the same, given his history. You know, this whole thing started for him in '56 with the Kansas war and John Brown. It had been a long, wearying journey for Hiram. So maybe he just couldn't let it go. You know… of the cruelties of war and such. And all the injustices done to him. I don't know. Who knows?"

"That's probably right," Ma said.

Uncle Olin raised his eyes. "Pa sure swallowed the dog."

"We all did," J.T. added with a turn. "But Hiram has a fine marble tombstone in the prison yard. I saw to that. It sits under a cottonwood tree like those next to your creek. I think he would have liked that. And he's buried with his Bible and that old three-bander he carried around. I'd guess those two items were a pretty good representation of the man he was. A fighter, and a believer."

J.T. sniffed and cleared his eye. "You can be both, I guess."

Uncle Olin wiped his face. "Yep. You can."

We spent the rest of the day laughing and weeping for Grandpa. We told just about every story we knew and then cried because he wasn't there to yell at us. Even Cousin Buford seemed to understand, but mostly he was just busy with a new bolt of broadcloth he had picked up in Leavenworth City. He was counting threads, so I got ready for a whole batch of new numbers. Threads per inch was his new passion. On every type of fabric. On every cut of cloth.

"We do have some good news," J.T. said, coming in the next morning with four packages of butchered beef. Mother cooked up the meat while we gathered around the cook stove.

"Olin and I are going into business. Together, that is." J.T. gestured to Uncle Olin and smiled. I still couldn't get over his new teeth and hair. "We're going back to New York to set up shop. Show them your new duds, Olin."

"Nah…"

"Go on. Wait until you see this!"

Uncle Olin lumbered into the back room. He came out five minutes later like a New England dandy. I suddenly realized he was one of the gentlemen I had seen on the buggy. New frock coat, white shirt, tie, creased cotton trousers and shiny shoes. The twins burst into amusement. His bowler hat covered what was left of his shorn hair, which had just been slicked down with a thick dose of rose oil pomade. The aroma filled the cabin. He grinned through his perfect new teeth, and then pulled them out for everyone's inspection. "See!" he said. "Mother of pearl." And then he stuck them back in and became a gentleman again.

I practically didn't recognize him. A completely new man.

Cousin Buford shouted too, "New shoes! Eight new shoes. Fifty-six eyelets, One hundred and twenty ounces of patent leather, four ounces of cotton cloth, one half ounce of tin, and one hundredth of an ounce of shoe polish. Plus thread. Oh, eight new shoes!" he crooned at the top of his lungs.

"Buford has new clothes, too," J.T. admitted, smiling. "We're all going to New York together. Except Jeremiah. He's been casting an eye west, it seems. Colorado gold fields, I think. But it turns out Buford is a genius in fabric and garments. So he's going with us."

Mother smiled at J.T. "Wasn't your father a garment maker? During the war?"

"That's right. And I plan to take over and expand his business. Young Buford here can take one look at any man or woman and calculate a perfect fit."

"But how does he cut the—"

"He doesn't use scissors," J.T. broke in. "He just sizes up the person and marks cloth. No formal measurements. Just eyesight, I guess. I've cut and assembled ten garments based solely on his markings, and they're perfect fits every time. Just look at Olin and me. And Hiram's last suit was done in just this manner. A beautiful sateen frock and trousers. We made it in six hours! That's a quarter of the time my father takes. Plus, we saved one tenth of a yard of fabric."

"How can you save fabric?" Ma asked. "People don't shrink."

"It's all in how he marks the fabric for cutting. No waste. Absolute genius!" J.T. beamed at Buford who had no idea of the praises being heaped upon him. He just walked out onto the porch to count threads again. For the eighth time.

"I swear, he just marks and we cut. Just that simple." J.T. shook his head. "He'll earn a good wage and have folks to look after him."

"And how does Olin fit into this new enterprise?" Ma asked, smiling.

"Marketing manager. Turns out Olin is a firecracker with people. Not like me with rocks in my mouth. Olin can talk a tiger into tip-toeing. In a corset." Ma laughed. "You can put him anywhere," J.T. continued with a flourish. "In any situation, and he'll have people laughing and following his stories like he was Moses with an accordion. It's amazing. It even happened to me."

"Yeah, after I whooped your Yankee hide four or five times," Uncle Olin said, laughing. "Wait'll you see what them New Yorker's think of this Missoura chicken thief. You may not want me then."

Everyone laughed.

"Well, so that's it," J.T. said. "All except one thing."

He bent down on one knee and faced Mother like he was begging something off her. She turned from white to red.

"Mrs. Mansfield Clark," he said. "Will you marry me? And go to New York?"

Mother didn't even answer. Her mouth just fell open and she covered it and swayed back and forth shyly. But then she laughed and shrieked like Patricia used to do. For two days, Mother even sounded like Patricia – like a schoolgirl in a pink dress. I couldn't figure her out.

Every time J.T. came around, she wagged her head, sang little songs, skipped like a child, and twirled on one foot for him. It was almost embarrassing.

That went on for a good week, with him proposing at the start of every new day.

Making her dance and skip.

And her saying, "Yes!" every time he asked. And swinging off him. And kissing.

And then she just died.

Never woke up.

For what reason, I could not say. But my heart felt like it might collapse. Worse than when J.T. told me about Grandpa.

Nobody spoke a word until the funeral the next day. Not even a word from Uncle Olin or Buford or J.T. I didn't even know if I could talk again. Or if I ever wanted to. Mother was asleep, and this time she wasn't getting better. The doctor said it was a tired heart. She had suffered so greatly that it was too much for her. I didn't even thank the doctor. He just left the funeral service without a word and without his fee.

But Patricia came up beside me. I turned, but had no words in me. First Grandpa, and now Ma. All I could do was cry. And that made me feel like a baby in front of her.

Patricia laid my head in her bosom. Everyone left the service before she said anything. But I knew she had something on her mind.

She lifted my chin. "Ma says we should get married tomorrow, and take those twins in."

That made my head spin in a whole different direction. Like the push-go-round in grammar school. But I liked the idea right off. It gave me hope. It seemed Old Mrs. Branson had a thing or two worth listening to.

Patricia wiped back the tears.

"Are you through with those ruffians down at the saw mill?" she asked. "Because I won't have a man like that."

The answer was yes.

I wanted just three things now, and I aimed to get them all: to buck up and be a man, to marry Patricia like her mother said, and to go west with everything Grandpa and J.T. had taught me.